PENGUIN BOOKS
**the hut
builder**

the hut builder

Laurence Fearnley

PENGUIN BOOKS

PENGUIN BOOKS
Published by the Penguin Group
Penguin Group (NZ), 67 Apollo Drive, Rosedale,
North Shore 0632, New Zealand (a division of Pearson New Zealand Ltd)
Penguin Group (USA) Inc., 375 Hudson Street,
New York, New York 10014, USA
Penguin Group (Canada), 90 Eglinton Avenue East, Suite 700, Toronto,
Ontario, M4P 2Y3, Canada (a division of Pearson Penguin Canada Inc.)
Penguin Books Ltd, 80 Strand, London, WC2R 0RL, England
Penguin Ireland, 25 St Stephen's Green,
Dublin 2, Ireland (a division of Penguin Books Ltd)
Penguin Group (Australia), 250 Camberwell Road, Camberwell,
Victoria 3124, Australia (a division of Pearson Australia Group Pty Ltd)
Penguin Books India Pvt Ltd, 11, Community Centre,
Panchsheel Park, New Delhi – 110 017, India
Penguin Books (South Africa) (Pty) Ltd, 24 Sturdee Avenue,
Rosebank, Johannesburg 2196, South Africa

Penguin Books Ltd, Registered Offices: 80 Strand, London, WC2R 0RL, England

First published by Penguin Group (NZ), 2010
1 3 5 7 9 10 8 6 4 2

Copyright © Laurence Fearnley, 2010

The right of Laurence Fearnley to be identified as the author of this work in terms of
section 96 of the Copyright Act 1994 is hereby asserted.

Designed by Anna Egan-Reid
Typeset by Pindar NZ
Printed in Australia by McPherson's Printing Group

ISBN 9 78 0 14320506 7
A catalogue record for this book is available
from the National Library of New Zealand.

www.penguin.co.nz

The assistance of Creative New Zealand towards the production of this book
is gratefully acknowledged by the Publisher.

for Dave and Jan,
and Sputnik (1993–2009)

Whenever the opportunity presented itself, my father would lift down the framed enlargement he kept on the shelf above the cutting block and show it to the customer who stood waiting to pay for her meat.

More often than not, I was able to predict what would come next. The conversation always took a familiar shape. A typical example:

'Do you see who that is?' my father asked, jabbing his finger at the glass.

The woman, not one of his regular customers, took a step forward and peered at the snap, examining the blurred black and white image of two men standing side by side on the summit of a mountain.

'Your son?' she responded uncertainly, despite having seen me only a few seconds earlier as I started to refill some of the meat trays in the window. 'Boden, isn't it?' she guessed, squinting at the picture.

It was not the response my father was looking for.

'No, not him,' he replied, brushing my likeness with the edge of his bloodstained hand. 'Not him,' he repeated, his voice barely containing his excitement. 'Next to him. The big fella.'

At that point the customer often took the photograph from my father's hand and surveyed the mountain scene more closely, turning it this way and that to catch the light.

Behind the figures, disappearing towards a bottom corner of the snap, was a long, undulating ridgeline, punctuated by small shadowy indentations – footprints in the snow. Taking up the remaining background was sky, featureless around the heads of the men, but lower down it was possible to detect a white carpet of cloud. The surface of this cloud was smooth but not flat; it was rippled like sand exposed at low tide.

It was difficult to recognise the figures because both men wore metal-framed snow goggles. The dark lenses obscured their eyes but reflected the partial silhouette of a third figure – the photographer. Pushed back onto the crown of the shorter man's head was a balaclava, while the other man, the 'big fella', wore a white cotton peaked cap with neck and ear flaps – the kind of headwear favoured by soldiers in the desert. Though the sky was clear, the cloth of both men's jackets was flapping, indicating that the weather was windy. Indeed, if the customer had had more time with the photograph, she may have noticed that the sharp outline of the ridge behind the men was softened by spindrift, pluming skyward. But my father made a grab for the picture and, his voice rising hopefully, asked, 'Now do you see who it is?'

The woman shrugged. She was still uncertain. Could he give her a clue? I remained carefully out of the woman's line of vision, hovering in the small workspace separating the front of the shop from the chiller out the back. I could see the woman but I was too embarrassed to intervene. On the one hand I wanted to disown my father, but I also didn't want to deny him this small pleasure.

I experienced this conflict whenever he began his performance. If it hadn't involved me it would have been bearable. But it required my presence in order for my father to complete the show. And for me the performance was false. I knew only too well that despite appearances to the contrary – my jubilant smile, my raised ice axe – behind the dark lenses my eyes expressed alarm. No one could see it in the photograph but I was scared. My feet were rooted to the spot, my hands inside my mittens were clammy and my pulse, I remember clearly, was racing.

8

Having reached the summit of the Middle Peak of Mount Cook all I could think was: how on earth am I going to get down?

'Tell you what,' said my father. 'Take one more look and if you still can't guess . . .' He didn't get the chance to finish because at that precise moment a look of faint recognition surfaced on the woman's face. She frowned, puzzled. An inner voice said, 'It looks like him – but no, it can't be. Can it?' She didn't want to appear foolish but eventually, taking charge of the moment – if only to put an end to the game – she mumbled, 'Hillary?'

'Yes!' roared my father, the skin on his face flushing, so proud was he of the photograph, and what it implied. 'Sir Edmund Hillary . . .' he chortled, stroking the great mountaineer's hat with his stubby thumb. 'That's my son Boden on top of Mount Cook and beside him, as you so rightly say, is the greatest living climber of our generation.' He paused, beamed at the woman who, from the look of joy on his face, might now have been his closest friend and ally. Neither of them was aware of me in the background, muttering, 'Middle Peak – it's just the Middle Peak.'

At this stage in the game my father glanced my way. It was my signal to reappear. I hesitated. For once, could I not pretend I hadn't noticed, or turn my back and retreat into the cold safety of the freezer? I took a step forward and it was as if a spotlight had been hung from the ceiling, its beam falling on me. Where, minutes before, I was my father's invisible assistant, I was now the star act: me with my fingers clinging to a tray of pure beef sausages.

'Here you are,' said my father as I re-entered the shop. I nodded and smiled at the woman, who said, 'Hullo.' I stood looking at my feet, wondering if my father would launch into the second act. Before I had time to hope that he might abandon the show he remarked, 'See those sausages?' He nodded towards the tray in my hands. 'I sent a tray of those sausages up to my boy on Cook and I heard back – via Boden here – that Hillary thought they were the best he had ever tasted.' He shook his head in disbelief. 'Imagine, sausages made by my very own hands winding up on Edmund Hillary's plate . . .' Though a cynic could have detected a hint of false modesty in my father's expression, he was, in truth, deeply moved. The fact that Hillary had enjoyed his sausages – and for that I can vouch – humbled my father as completely as if the Queen had placed an order for one of his black puddings.

If only my father had stopped then, but, ever the businessman, he suddenly winked at the woman across the counter and said conspiratorially, 'You should take some for your husband. Sir Ed's bangers!' He paused: at this point he had been know to add 'as eaten on Everest!', but to my great relief this time he didn't. He simply reached across to my tray and speared a string with his fork, lifting it up for the customer to see.

'Go on, then,' she said, 'cut me off four.'

Her eyes were keen and my father, aware of her scrutiny, made sure to select four of the plumpest from the string. 'Lovely,' he murmured as he wrapped them in paper. 'Ed's bangers. Fit for a knight.'

The woman handed over her money and permitted herself a faint smile. 'It must have been a wonderful day,' she said to me as she dropped the package into her basket.

I nodded. I wanted to say, 'Yes – it's one I'll never be allowed to forget,' but her remark brought that day back to me: the exhilaration and joy I had felt once safely off the mountain and back at our shelter. 'It was a wonderful day,' I replied. 'Remarkable.'

fairlie

My father's public face bore little resemblance to his private one. I discovered this at a very early age and, strangely, it was a lesson I learnt from a photograph. Years before he began showing customers the picture of me on top of Mount Cook, Hillary by my side, I was busy showing my school friends – and others, too – an image of my father perched on top of a camel, a vast expanse of desert spreading far behind him. I knew no one else who had seen a camel, let alone ridden one, and it was with great pride – and a large dose of superiority – that I explained to my friends that during the First World War he had served briefly with the Imperial Camel Corps.

Without the photographic proof in my hands I would never have believed that the healthy, suntanned soldier in the snap was the man I saw limping around the butcher's shop in front of our house. It was very hard for me as a young boy to reconcile the two images in my mind. It was even harder to persuade some of my classmates, who, having seen my father hobbling about town, suggested that the photograph was some posed theatrical portrait. Even as I relayed the story of my father's bravery, which I naturally embellished – having no idea if he had been a brave soldier or simply an adequate one, repeating the little I knew of his being wounded during an attack on Gaza – I also had my own secret doubts.

My father was a quiet man who, through sheer willpower, gave the impression of being outgoing and confident whenever necessity required it, in order to deal with a customer, a stranger, or even sometimes my mother. He never talked about his war experience, and by the time I reached school age he had been weighed down by so much tragedy that he gave the impression of permanently staggering beneath the load of one of the meat carcasses he lugged from his van to the freezer. He was lopsided with sorrow and yet no one but my mother and myself ever knew.

My father tried to carry the full load of grief but my mother was just as broken, if not more so. I was not to learn of it until I was a teenager, but my mother had suffered several miscarriages between the birth of my twin brothers in 1921 and my own appearance in the mid-thirties. No one used the term 'miscarriage' and, looking back, I cannot but feel pained – on my mother's behalf – by the few enigmatic references I did overhear: whispered terms such as 'problems', pregnancies that 'wouldn't stick', or babies that were 'lost'. All these phrases, which I do not believe were uttered maliciously so much as carelessly, must have suffocated my mother in a cloud of failure and guilt.

Never once did I hear such talk escape from my father's mouth. His words conveyed only respect and pride. According to him my mother, like her older brother Boden – the man I was named after but never met – was a 'toughie', a fighter. Unlike Boden, who died before I was born, my mother battled on and, lo, one day, victorious, another healthy child appeared – me.

Because I didn't know about the sad episodes in my mother's medical history, I was not able to appreciate her strength. For as long as I could remember – insofar as my own personal experience enabled me to see – my mother seemed frail, hollow. She spent a great deal of her time sitting at the kitchen table, working away on jigsaw puzzles – 1000-piece depictions of exotic locations and grand buildings, which she laid out on a large tea tray made for her by Dudley, my parents' neighbour and only friend.

Connie, my mother, had been disabled by the grief that burdened us all. In 1941, at the age of twenty, my twin brothers, Ralph and Edward, had been aboard the HMS *Neptune* when it struck a minefield off the coast of Tripoli and sank. The air that we had breathed so freely immediately thickened in our lungs. I remember this quite clearly: the pain in my chest that increased minute by minute, day by day, week by week, month by month until finally, in desperation to break free from my suffocating surroundings, I begged my parents to allow me to move across the street to live with Dudley and his family. Remarkable though it now seems, they let me go. I can only imagine how strange this living arrangement must have appeared to our other neighbours. In a small town like ours we must have been the subject of gossip. But, out of respect for my mother's fragile condition, no one raised the topic – publicly at least. And so, blissfully ignorant, I lived with Dudley, off and on, for nearly three years.

Though I was only six or seven, this period remains fresh in my memory. I see myself hovering uncertainly between two worlds. It was as if a wall had been erected down the middle of our street. On one side was my parents' house and on the other was the house belonging to 'Uncle' Dudley and 'Auntie' Hilda and their children, Ted, Geraldine and Frith. On my parents' side of the wall everything appeared drained of colour, as if life had been captured on black and white film and was projected back to me on a makeshift screen. Though still a member of the family, I was absent from the film itself – and yet my presence was still strangely felt. I was like an audience member who accidentally comes between the projector and the screen, stooping awkwardly in an attempt to squeeze imperceptibly between the rows and yet, despite their best efforts, creating a large black shadow on the screen.

On the side of the street where my 'adopted' family lived, the world was full colour. But, though warm and golden, the light seemed artificial, turned on for my benefit. Because of this I always felt a little confused. Where I expected shade there was none. No matter what time it was, whether early morning or late at night, it was as if I was stuck in a perpetual high noon of sunlight, with not so much as a shadow to keep me company.

I walked between these two worlds, crossing the invisible line, on one side of which I would be drained of everything except some faint remnant of will, while on the other I was bathed in light. As a result, I never knew where I belonged. Dazzled by the generosity and love lavished upon me by Dudley and his family, I would yearn for a quiet room, one in which I could lose myself in my thoughts and not everything was rendered visible. Then, retreating from time to time to my parents' house, I would feel weighed down, burdened by all that went unsaid and lurked in the dark corners and empty rooms.

I never spoke of my feelings – or the terrible way I felt torn by these extremes. Looking back, however, I think both my father and Dudley must have had some idea of what was going through my head. My father, tuned in to unhappiness – as he needed to be, living with my mother – saw what was present within me. Dudley, on the other hand, who was always smiling, always happy and taking pleasure in life, must have seen what was absent. In me, he recognised a child who needed attention, encouragement and affection, all of which he lavished upon me, occasionally to the detriment of his own children. And so it was that Dudley, a carpenter by trade, began to take me out with him on Saturdays whenever he had a small job to complete. Ted often came with us but, being that bit older than me, he sometimes had inter-club sports. These outings were magical, for a number of reasons. Silly though it now seems, I remember feeling incredibly proud of being singled out by Dudley. I always knew when he was planning to take me because he would notice me being particularly glum or quiet over breakfast and would reach across the table and place one of his huge, slab-like hands on my shoulder, giving me a gentle shake. In his booming voice he would ask if I could spare him an hour or two to hold his ladder. Once he had dealt with the protests of the younger girls – who wanted to come too – he would butter me a thick piece of bread and off we would go.

On cold mornings there was a chance our departure would be delayed by twenty or thirty minutes – causing me great anxiety. Dudley's truck –

old by any standards – rarely started on frosty mornings, and one or other of us would be sent off on the bike to fetch the mechanic, who would arrive unshaven and foul-tempered in his late-model tow-truck; his muttered profanities inaudible but clearly visible in the vapour that puffed from his mouth into the freezing air. I was terrified of this man – Ray – and retreated into the house while he fired words of contempt at Dudley's truck, the tangle of jumper leads and the day itself as he settled into the job of getting the old wreck started. The more Ray cursed, the funnier Dudley found it. When he was in a particularly playful mood he would mimic and tease him to the point where the poor mechanic would go purple in the face, throw the leads on the ground and threaten to back over Dudley's truck with his own, more powerful vehicle. Rather than attempt to placate Ray or make amends, Dudley would all but collapse with laughter while I prayed that Ray would not carry out his threat.

It used to puzzle me why Dudley never asked my father to help. I was sure the butcher's van would have been up to the task of getting the old truck up and running, but whenever I mentioned this to Dudley he would simply smile mysteriously and say that Ray liked to feel needed. Later I learnt the real reason why Dudley always sought out Ray when, as he admitted himself, it would have been far easier to ask my father. It transpired that Ray believed he owed his life to Dudley and, through gratitude or shame, felt compelled to repay that debt over and over again.

The story went that one evening, towards the end of June, Dudley had been returning from a job in the small settlement of Burkes Pass when, rounding a frost-covered bend, he had caught sight of tyre tracks veering off the road towards a patch of scrub. Though it was almost dark and bitterly cold, Dudley pulled over to investigate and, scrambling down the bank, happened across Ray's tow-truck, which lay rolled onto its driver's door, with Ray floundering around inside. Blind drunk, Ray was disorientated by the unexpected layout of his cab and could not find the passenger door, which was now located above him. 'It was like watching a bee trying to escape from a closed jar,' Dudley explained. 'And not just any bee – but the angriest bee you've ever seen. When I finally got the passenger door open,' he continued, 'the smell of alcohol almost blew me off my feet. Ray was so busy cursing and thrashing that I had to reach down and grab him by his hair and pull him out. Just as well he still had hair back then, though I dare say he was a good handful balder by the time I finished with him.'

Ray could remember nothing of what happened, but, returning to the crash site and seeing his wrecked truck and the thick layer of frost covering it, convinced himself he would have frozen to death had he spent the night in the cab. 'He sobered up pretty quickly when he saw his truck, I can tell you that much,' said Dudley. 'He doesn't drink now, of course.'

So although in many ways Ray resented helping Dudley, at the same time he felt compelled to do so. Some echo of gratitude and a sense of male pride obliged him to repay the man who had saved his life. On top of that, he needed to re-establish the power he had lost as a result of that accident; he needed to regain his footing as an equal.

It was after one especially drawn-out episode involving Ray and his truck that Dudley, Ted and I finally set out one morning for the hotel at Burkes Pass, where Dudley had a small job to complete. It was bitterly cold and, to make matters worse, my trousers and jersey were slightly wet. I had been pouring warm water over the windscreen of Dudley's cab when Ted's large dog had come bounding down the driveway, hit a large frozen puddle, skidded out of control and side-swiped me. I was knocked off my feet and splashed with water. Not wanting to change out of my damp clothes and hold up the group any longer I insisted that I was fine and quickly climbed into the cab, making myself as small as possible so as not to be caught out.

The dog, an old huntaway called Bruce, was made to sit on the flatdeck at the back which, I am ashamed to say, filled me with satisfaction. Whenever I looked back through the small window behind my head I could see him shivering in the cold. We were little better off. There was no heater in Dudley's truck and we had to drive with the windows open to help demist the windows. It was almost a full-time job wiping the windscreen with my cuffed sleeve, and every time one of us talked our faces would be momentarily obscured by the vapour that accompanied our words.

By the time we arrived at the hotel I was so cold I stood in the kitchen shivering helplessly in front of the stove while Ted helped Dudley fetch his tools. My feet were the worst. No longer merely damp, they felt frozen, and as they thawed my toes began to sting with such violence that tears rolled down my cheeks. Just as the pain was becoming unbearable, Dudley noticed my tortured expression and ruffled my hair, and whispering, 'Good lad', then did something I have never seen done since: he wiggled his ears. How he managed this I have no idea. Many times I tried to copy this miraculous feat but no matter how much I willed my ears to move I could never wiggle them as Dudley had done.

While Dudley worked, Ted and I played 'dogs' out the back of the hotel. To our delight we had discovered a large boulder with a long chain attached to it and for an hour or so we took it in turns being chained up and barking while the other one of us would scramble over the boulder, pretending to throw pebble 'biscuits'. It was a great game, made all the more enjoyable by the effect it had on Bruce, who ran around barking, chasing the stones and jumping up on whoever was chained to the rock, knocking them to the ground.

When eventually we tired of this game we wandered around to a small enclosure beside the hotel where two deer were housed. Though kept as pets the deer did not seem tame and, despite our tempting them with grass, neither animal came to investigate. Later we were given deer-nuts to try. We eased our fingers through the netting and were rewarded with the doe feeding from our palms. It nuzzled our outstretched hands, and I remember its breath damp and warm against my skin.

Convinced that this was the best day of my life, I was even more thrilled to discover that lunch had been prepared for us back in the kitchen: a huge plate of mashed potato, fried onion, liver and kidneys. The smell in the kitchen was intoxicating: the oily, sweet-smelling onion blended with the darker, grittier smell of the coal range and then on top of that, and very subtle by comparison, was the dry smell of the wood shavings scattered on the ground where Dudley had been working.

I am sure I would have fallen asleep following such a feast had not a call come through from a lady on a farm on the far side of Burkes Pass, asking if Dudley could call by to give a quote for a new kitchen bench. Knowing that Auntie Hilda was at her sister's, I couldn't figure out how the woman had managed to track Dudley down.

Dudley barely raised an eyebrow. 'Edna,' he said, smiling at the housekeeper.

'Expect so,' she replied. Ted told me that Edna worked at the telephone exchange and tended to know where everyone was at any one time.

'How does she know?' I asked to which Ted just laughed and gave me a look that implied I was too young – or too stupid – to understand.

I had never been beyond the small settlement of Burkes Pass before, so had no idea what to expect as we crossed over into the Mackenzie Basin. The sky was a cloudless pale blue and although the road from the hotel to the summit of the pass was mostly shaded so that I felt as if we were driving through a tunnel, at the top I suddenly found myself in front of a scene of such beauty that it took my breath away.

Stretching before me, as far as my eye could see, was a vast plain of snow-covered tussock and grass. Because of our slight elevation, this plain appeared to me in its entirety, a vast carpet at my feet that spread towards infinity – before being reined in by the most glorious, faraway, twinkling mountains I could imagine.

I couldn't believe how much space there was. Everywhere I looked, I saw uninterrupted views of land and sky. If I had set out walking I would be travelling well into the night and throughout the following day – and perhaps the day after that. I remember turning to Dudley and saying, 'You could walk for ever,' and he looked across at me and nodded and I could see – I could honestly see – that he felt the same way. Like me, he was transfixed.

He pulled the truck off the road and we all got out and just stood looking. I could feel the stubbly, frozen ground through the soles of my shoes and when I kicked my toe, snow – like fine powder – spun around my ankles, landing on my socks like fairy-dust. The light was so bright that I was dazzled, but I didn't want to shade my eyes with my hand as

20

Ted was. I wanted to be dazzled. I wanted to stand in the full glare of the snowfield.

I saw tiny pinpricks in the snow where drops of water had fallen from the tussock. I saw the way the snow was an intense blue in the patches where it was shaded by the larger bushes. I saw footprints made by rabbits and hares, a crazy zigzag of steps going nowhere in particular, and I saw a spider's web, caught on the upper twigs of a matagouri bush, glistening like the most precious jewels strung on a bracelet or a collar or something – I didn't know what because it was more beautiful than anything I had ever seen and I didn't have the words to describe it. I felt it, though. Even though my feet were wet and freezing and my hands had turned to ice, so that I clasped and unclasped my fingers until they hurt – despite all that I could feel the scene in front of me and all at once I let out an incredible whoop of joy and skipped into the air, laughing and laughing; there was so much joy inside me. I couldn't contain myself. For the first time in all my memory, I could not contain myself.

Ted hit me square on the back of my head with a huge snowball. An explosion of ice-cold drift went down inside my collar and I yelped with surprise. Bruce, who had been sniffing out rabbits, ran back at the sound, leaping across the tussock like a dolphin surfing the waves. The snow that sprayed off his paws caught the sun and it was as if he was running across a field of stars. And then Ted wrestled me to the ground and Bruce jumped on me, and I could hear Dudley laughing and laughing, and then his voice telling Ted to go easy because we'd get wet and cold but by that time it was too late. We were covered – dusted head to toe in snow.

I glanced up, and in the sky was a huge hawk. It was hovering just above me and I had the feeling it had its eye on me – it knew I was there and it was watching.

And then, deep in the back of my mind, words began to form. Not words for just speaking but something new, something special – words for creating something. The first two words were 'bright' and 'white' and then, instinctively at first but soon methodically, I made a list by going through the alphabet: 'fight', 'height', 'kite', 'light', 'might', 'moonlight', 'night', 'plight', 'right', 'sight', 'tight'. These words were like socks in my drawer that needed pairing off. Some, like 'moonlight' didn't belong, while others, like 'plight', were too fancy. But others made sense to me. The snow, I thought, was so bright and white. The sky was bright and light – but big and blue, too. And then the hawk: its terrible might and the way it hovered like a kite.

Even after we got back in the truck, our bottoms creating damp patches on the seat, I kept these words inside me, rearranging them, trying them on, throwing them out and then picking them up again for one last try. Though I didn't know what I was doing, I had a sense of something vital, important. I was on the verge of some great discovery but I didn't quite know what it was. It was the first time I felt an urge to match something outside of myself with something that was part of me. What was happening didn't seem to be taking place in my head but in my body, my flesh and muscle – the warm, pulpy meat of me.

'Snow – so white and bright
Sparkling in the sun like a million twinkling diamond-lights . . .'

Time after time I stalled. I couldn't make the words big enough to capture how I felt. Even though I was young I knew my words were *not quite right*; I couldn't make them say what I so desperately wanted them to say. They refused to help. Now, of course, I'm used to such frustration, but back then I felt let down.

With the image of what I had seen still burning within me, the words tumbling about like loose marbles in my mouth, I experienced a sense of failure. But it didn't really matter – for I had seen the glorious Mackenzie Basin and I had almost composed my first poem.

It was after six when we drove back to Fairlie. The cold blue glint of the Mackenzie had given way to the gloom of the homeward road and as we neared Kimbell a dense fog enveloped us, seeping through the windows and into the cab as well as obscuring the road ahead. I smelled Fairlie before I saw it. There was a dank, unhealthy odour of coal that made me think of damp newspaper mixed with gas. I could almost taste it, feel the minuscule particles of black dust settling on my skin, smuts filling my nose and burning my throat.

For the past hour I had been shivering and, despite my earlier joy, I now felt cold and tired and somehow cheated. Though I knew Auntie Hilda would have dinner waiting and maybe a hot bath, I felt out of sorts. Once, when Ted nodded off beside me, his head falling against my shoulder, I jerked my shoulder away even though I knew that would cause his head to clonk forward, onto his chest.

Entering the kitchen at last I found that my mood, rather than being lightened by the warm welcome from Auntie Hilda and the girls, darkened. I was annoyed by Geraldine and Frith's endless questions and even more so by Ted's account of the day. He described everything that

23

had happened – the game of 'dogs', the feeding of the deer, the meal in the kitchen, the sight of the Mackenzie – as if it were all equally good. He obviously hadn't paid proper attention. He should have known that there was a scale: some things were good (like the lunch), whereas others (like the sweep of snow-covered tussock) were better, more impressive than anything either of us had ever seen before. But Ted yakked on about the snow fight, and when I reminded him about the soaring hawk he brushed me aside, saying, 'Mummy's not bothered about that.'

It was only after dinner when I was standing at the sink washing dishes, that I was able to think clearly about it all. There was almost nothing I hated more than scouring the mashed potato saucepan – something to do with the way the residue of dishwater-soaked mash felt against my skin – but somehow I managed to focus my thoughts once more on the vastness of the sky and the plain, and a sense of calm came over me.

I worked slowly, carefully, taking so long that Auntie Hilda came to check on me. She had put the girls to bed and must have suddenly noticed my absence. Usually I raced through the dishes but tonight I had fallen into a kind of daydream, in which I was trying to reconstruct everything I had seen in as much detail as possible.

As Auntie Hilda began to dry the dishes I felt an urgent need to explain it all to her. She was a good listener – she often sat down with Ted and me of an evening to press us for details about our day. As I began to talk, however, I discovered that I still could not find the words I needed to recreate the scene of the Mackenzie and so I changed tack and, without thinking it through, began to tell her how I had been moved to make up a poem. I had intended to keep this to myself – I wasn't sure how it would go down with my host family. I had never seen either Dudley or Hilda sit down with a book, though they did read the odd newspaper. I was worried that if I mentioned my poem they would get it into their heads that I was trying to be different, when in fact I wasn't. But, encouraged by Hilda's surprised smile, I carried on and recited the first few lines of my verse, adding at the end that it wasn't a poem really – just an attempt to put what I had seen into words.

I remember the way Auntie Hilda smiled when I was finished.

Whenever one of the girls did something like say 'thank you' to a shop-keeper without being told to, Auntie Hilda would beam with pride and then, afterwards, when we were outside the shop, she would make a point of telling the girls how good they were, how pleased she was. After hearing my poem she smiled at me with her mouth, but her eyes looked startled and she glanced around the kitchen as if hoping Dudley might come in and rescue her. She managed to say, 'That's lovely, Boden. You should write it down before you forget,' but she didn't really look at me. Feeling awkward, I quickly offered to take the milk bottles down to the gate. It says something about our state of mind that I made the offer and that she nodded enthusiastically, for it was a Saturday and there would be no delivery until Monday. As I turned to go she called me back and hugged me. She told me once more that my poem was nice and that, truly, she hoped I would copy it into her special notebook so that she might enjoy it again and again.

I grabbed the bottles and went out into the garden, repeating my rhyme to myself, lest I should suddenly forget it. As I dawdled down the path towards the gate I was aware of a dark shape moving towards me from the other side of the road. After a moment's hesitation I recognised the outline of my mother who, like me, was walking towards the gate. For a terrible moment I had the impression I was facing a mirror. It was as if I was walking towards myself, although I could see quite clearly even in the darkness that my mother was in her dressing gown with her hair pinned back in rollers, her head covered with a scarf. She hadn't seen me and I knew I should call out, as it had been two days since I had last spoken to her. But I didn't. I crouched down by a large hydrangea next to the path.

My mother reached the letter box and raised the flap at the back, looking for letters. It was clear to me that she wasn't expecting any but, just as I would have done, she checked anyway. Then she crossed the verge and stepped out onto the road. She took four steps and then, near the middle of the road, she suddenly stopped. I could see her face quite clearly. She was looking at Uncle Dudley's house, her eyes fixed on the dull light visible through the closed curtains of the upstairs bedroom where Ted and I slept. She must have stood for thirty seconds, just looking, and I knew I should call out to her but I couldn't. I watched her standing in the middle of the road and I felt scared. She looked like a crazy woman in her gown and scarf. Slowly she turned around and began to walk back to her own house – my home. I could hear her slippers scuffing and I had that same eerie feeling that we were reflections of each other, this time each retreating to our own side of the mirror.

I stayed where I was for a minute longer and then, running as fast as I could, I placed our bottles at the gate and rushed back up the path and inside, slamming the door behind me. No one saw me, and a few minutes later I called out goodnight to my uncle and aunt and clambered into bed, pulling the covers up over my head. When Ted asked what was the matter I pretended to be asleep.

I remember very little of the next few days. I recall feeling feverish and the doctor being called in to see me. I can picture the anxious look on Dudley's face as he bent over me, and I remember someone placing a thermometer under my armpit and me shivering because I couldn't get warm. I recall, too, that I developed a cough and that my ribs hurt so badly it felt as if someone had pushed their hands into my chest and pulled my ribcage apart, as if I was a chicken carcass being broken in two to fit into the stock pan.

And finally, when it seemed that every member of the household had peered down at me, eyes full of concern, and then crept away so as not to disturb me, I looked up and saw my mother, sitting quietly beside my bed, her chin resting on her hand, her mouth obscured by her fingers. Her skin was so pale that, in my feverish state, I would have taken her for a ghost but for one thing. I heard her sob, 'Don't take him too. Just let me keep one.'

I knew I had betrayed my mother: I should never have left home or her. When I thought about the trip I had made with Dudley to the Mackenzie I felt dirty. I had no right to be out, laughing beneath the open sky, while my parents sat at home, the rooms empty around them.

I was still a young boy, around nine or ten, when I moved back across the street. The Second World War was over and for a while I allowed myself to believe that things would be different, that my mother had changed. I had heard her beg for my life and I thought she must be better; she would now be as normal as any other mother – maybe even happy, like Auntie Hilda.

In the spirit of this new beginning I began to take a greater interest in school. Up until this time I had always found lessons somewhat dull. Sitting at my desk watching as the teacher stabbed at columns of figures with his walking cane while we recited the times table, I would often find myself praying that old Mr McDonald would lose his balance and topple over. Anything to relieve the boredom. It was around this time that Mr McDonald did actually tumble over – sadly not during class but late one evening, while walking home from the RSA. For almost two weeks we were taught by a younger, near-sighted man brought in from Timaru, a Mr Patterson. To our amazement Mr Patterson – despite being all but blind – began each day with a poetry reading. Like many of my schoolmates I was initially wary. Mr McDonald had introduced us to the 'pleasures of poetry' on several occasions. Given that the only poet he admired was Donne, the pleasure was entirely his. He would stalk around the room, a book held limply in his hand, and suddenly strike a desk with his cane and demand of the poor child seated at it, 'Read on!' Had the student not been paying attention, an uneasy silence would follow, filled in by the sotto voce promptings of his or her neighbour, whispering, 'And now good morrow to our . . .' If any of the poems made sense on the page, all meaning was lost in the barely audible performance by the struggling ten-year-old.

Mr Patterson read the poems himself, meaning that half the class – the boys, mostly – paid no attention whatsoever and spent the ten minutes or so gazing into space or passing notes. A small group, myself included, hung on his every word. Some lines made an immediate impact and have stayed with me over the years: 'When Icicles hang by the wall, and Dick the Shepherd blows his nail . . .' or 'Tyger! Tyger! burning bright . . .' Other lines I forgot almost straight away but years later I might be reminded of one of those long-ago readings, by a line from John Clare, Browning or Yeats. Of all the poems, there was one that I loved purely for its sound. By Tennyson, it began, 'The splendour falls on castle walls . . .' Even now I sometimes find myself repeating it, for no reason at all: 'Blow, bugle, blow, set the wild echoes flying, And answer, echoes, answer, dying, dying, dying.'

When Mr McDonald returned I once plucked up courage and interrupted him mid-Donne to ask about 'The Bugle Song'. His response was brief and to the point. I was sent to sit with my face in the corner for the rest of the lesson and then kept back after school and made to write, one hundred times, 'I must not interrupt the teacher when he is reading verse.'

Just as school life began to dull once more, so did home life. My mother hadn't fixed herself. What's more, despite having begged for my life a short while before, she now appeared to barely notice me. She fell silent once more, lost in thought as she shuffled around the house, smiling distractedly whenever my father or I asked her a question.

During my stay with Dudley's family I had heard the war mentioned and I knew that my own family was not the only one in town affected by loss. Dudley himself had been sent home wounded from the Solomon Islands. Hilda's brother, a pilot, had gone missing over Holland, and her cousin had succumbed to malaria while serving in the Pacific. I couldn't understand what it was that made life so much worse for my mother than for anyone else. After all, she still had me.

I began to feel bitter. Whenever I saw Dudley or Ted in their garden I would turn away and return to my house where I would sit reading until the coast was clear. I began to brood, thinking about how Dudley's family had tricked me – made me think life could be joyful and loud when everyone knew it was really silent and dark. I realised that Ray had guessed the truth; that when he swore and raged at Dudley it was because Dudley was incapable of *seeing*, of taking anything seriously. Dudley had no understanding of the way things really worked. He had only to come across the road to my home for a view of real life. But the only time Dudley or Ted ever crossed the street was to ask me to go swimming in the river in summer, or lambing at a friend's farm in spring, or snowman building in winter. My parents always encouraged me to go but I couldn't. I knew that if I went out with Dudley I would inevitably have to come home again and then things would seem even worse. The contrast between the two families was too much for me.

So for a long time I kept to myself, tagging along with my father whenever he was called to a customer's house to kill a lamb, calf or pig. Though the majority of home-kill animals were brought into the small compound at the back of the shop, my father often made the rounds of the local district and spent an hour or more bent over a lamb or hogget, working with the precision of a surgeon as he sawed, cut and chopped. I would stand transfixed, trembling with a mixture of horror and fascination as each live animal was led into the killing area, slaughtered and then divided into legs, loins, ribs, shoulders, offal, bone, fat, blood and skin.

My father worked methodically; he had a pattern in his head from which he never deviated, but I could not make sense of the animal beneath his blade and I always marvelled when, finally stepping back from his work, he would gesture towards the meat and verbally reconstruct the animal for my benefit. Nothing was wasted, no cut with his knife misdirected, and I am certain to this day that had he wanted, he could have recreated any animal in its entirety – save for some blood that soaked the grass by his feet.

I admired my father's skill but that was not what made the biggest impression on me. Back in the shop my father hung the meat before butchering it, but this was not usually an option when he slaughtered an animal on site. More than the slaughter – which took only a matter of seconds – it was the smell of blood and the warm, pulpy feeling of the flesh that most stuck in my mind. On cool mornings I would look on, watching the steam rise from the stripped skin and the carcass, and the air around us would be penetrated by a musty, heavy scent that somehow combined the smells of grass, shit, fat – but most of all blood. I could almost taste the air. In my mind a reddish haze hung above our heads like smoke. I could see the blood stick to the hairs on my father's forearms, and when he passed me a cut of meat, to place on a tray, I would be surprised by its warmth. In retrospect, I can see that there was an element of comic-book horror at play. I expected the severed heart to beat.

The smell of blood was difficult to ignore. As we travelled home my mind would invariably wander back to the day when I had gone with Dudley to the hotel at Burkes Pass. I would remember the more pleasant, dry, dusty smell of the wood shavings that had filled the room where he worked and I would become so lost in thought that my father would eventually nudge me and ask if anything was wrong.

Back home I would follow my father into the laundry where we stood side by side, soaping our hands and arms, passing the cracked yellow cake between us as the water ran milky down the drain. Our hands red from scrubbing, we wiped them on an old ripped towel hanging from a hook by the door before stepping out into the yard and surveying the scene before us. We gazed at the Two Thumb Range, its bulk visible in the fading afternoon light. We glanced towards the rear of our section where my older twin brothers had once built a tree-house in the branches of a huge willow tree. A thick, knotted rope hung from a low branch of the tree and swayed gently from side to side as we watched.

On several occasions I had seen my mother pause while hanging out the washing and look down towards the willow, but I never saw her venture towards that corner of the garden. The wooden blocks that my brothers had hammered to the trunk of the tree for rungs had partially rotted over the years and sections of the floor of the tree-house had also rotted through. I was careful about where I placed my weight when I climbed up. I once told my mother that the inside walls of the tree-house were covered with sacking onto which my brothers had nailed maps and drawings they had done using black ink and paint. I explained that each picture carried two signatures; my brothers must have sat together, side by side, labouring over every image. I told my mother this because I found it intriguing. I would have liked to talk to her more about the twins – brothers I barely knew – but hearing my mother gasp I fell silent. Tears had sprung up in her eyes and she looked so grief-stricken I felt ashamed of myself.

My mother was a good cook. Given her all-encompassing sadness I was frequently surprised by the effort she went to in preparing our meals. At 4.30 every day she would rise from her chair, make her way to the kitchen and begin painstakingly to prepare our evening meal. The care and attention I had seen in my father's eyes as he butchered a beast was matched by my mother as she washed and peeled the potatoes, turning them in her hand as she checked for brown spots and eyes.

In summer she dug new potatoes from the garden and I recall the sound of the knife blade scraping over their skin as she stood quietly, lost in thought. I remember the squeakiness of the runner beans she boiled for us. With each mouthful I experienced first a crunch and then a squeak as the coarse-skinned strips rolled in my mouth. Back then I hated beans and was only able to swallow them if I smothered them in white sauce or gravy.

Of all my mother's meals the one that sticks most in my mind is tongue. My father was well known for his pickled meats, sausages and offal, and because he liked the taste of tongue more than anything else we ate it on a regular basis. My mother, it must be said, expressed no preferences at all with regard to food. Though she took great care over what she prepared, she seemed to get no pleasure from eating. I am certain that, had she lived alone, she could have eaten the same meal, day after day, without noticing. I always noticed when we had tongue. I found the taste and texture of the meat neither pleasant nor repugnant, but what did hold my attention was the way my mother thrust her carving fork into the large saucepan of boiling water and then slowly raised the tongue up – the curl of muscle pierced through the centre and dangling mid-air.

Dinner itself was a quiet affair. Because we lived in such close proximity to one another there was little need to discuss the events of the day, the only exception being after one of our home-kill excursions, when my father might comment on the condition of the animal he had slaughtered, the state of a flower bed, the girth of a pumpkin or marrow in someone's vegetable garden. Sometimes he would offer a small piece of gossip – the fact that so-and-so was in the family way once more, or that old Mr D had suffered a stroke, or was painting his house, or had heard from his son in Auckland.

My mother would smile as my father talked, and from time to time I tricked myself into believing that she enjoyed hearing these snippets. I anticipated the time when she would open her mouth and ask a question – but if she was curious she never expressed it. Like the food she ate, my father's chat was swallowed without comment.

In this environment I found it hard to ask questions myself. I had the impression that any attempt to draw out the evening meal was futile. If I did add to my father's tale in any way he would invariably nod and reply, 'That's quite right!' or 'I hadn't noticed' but the conversation went no further, quietly dying, until, unable to stand it any longer I would ask to leave the table. To my enormous relief I was invariably given permission to do so.

Once free, I would slip quietly through the back door, cross our back

32

lawn and then squeeze through the hedge separating our garden from an empty section on the neighbouring street. I would then wander along a well-trodden path – one that documented my previous escapes – before making my first stop at a farm gate. In autumn I would spend several minutes simply gazing at the paddock, my eyes sweeping its grazed surface for signs of mushrooms. If I was lucky and no one else had beaten me to it I could hope to collect upwards of ten perfectly formed specimens, which I either concealed under a bush until my return home or bundled in my jumper or jacket.

From the paddock I would follow a shingle track that joined the main Fairlie to Timaru road near McLean Park. There was very little traffic and somewhere in the back of my mind I saw myself as an urchin stepping out into the great unknown, a character I can clearly identify now, having read Dickens, but which had no precedent back then as my main source of reading material was an occasional *Beano* comic or the children's page in the local newspaper. In truth, there was nothing 'unknown' about my destination. I was walking towards the trees that lined Peace Avenue, leading into town.

At first I hadn't understood that these trees did not mark actual graves. For some reason I imagined that beneath each tree was a buried soldier. I was so convinced of this that I created grisly images in my head – pictures of men in uniform, decaying, the roots of the trees reaching tentacle-like, through and around their fully clothed bodies. Moreover, I did not realise that my twin brothers were not among them. I searched for a plaque with their names on, and, finding none, I selected two trees myself for the purpose. Later, having studied their tree-house drawings, I decided that one tree would be better than two. I chose a large oak, one that I estimated at the time to be at least one or two thousand years old. From the ground at the foot of the tree I collected acorns which I stuffed into my trouser pockets, one brother on either hip. These acorns took on a special significance and I collected them with the determination of a squirrel storing nuts for the lean winter months.

I would then wander the streets of Fairlie, doing nothing so much as taking in the life of the place, or setting myself small exercises such as cramming as many onomatopoeic words as I could into one sentence. In summer this seemed a cheery way to spend an hour or two but in winter the opposite was true.

Located in a basin, Fairlie was often smothered in mist or smog. The combination of thick, icy smog and frozen ground made outdoor activity unpleasant. Many times I would turn back home simply because I was so cold. On these frosty evenings I would feel my solitude so completely that even the sight of a lighted window or the faint sound of a radio broadcast would fail to comfort me. And yet I was seldom alone.

More often than not, at some point on my journey I would hear a sound – a snuffle or the noise of a body moving through the undergrowth – and I would turn to see Ted's dog, Bruce, trailing behind me. It was clear he was following me – no doubt he had picked up my scent while out roaming the neighbourhood. Despite knowing me he never came close, always keeping his distance, stopping whenever I stopped, disappearing into a garden and then reappearing several houses later, a dark shadow in the distance. I thought that maybe if I whistled or called his name he would come trotting up to me but I was too scared to test my theory for fear of being ignored. Being ignored by Bruce would, I think, have been enough to send me over the edge, so I contented myself with the belief that he had sought me out, that he wanted my company, that we were somehow connected in spirit.

For some reason, when we reached Sloan Street on the final leg of my journey I would usually hear a woman calling for her cat. I could imagine her standing on her back step, a food bowl in her hand, as she called, 'Here puss, puss, puss. Here puss . . .' She would strike the bowl with a spoon and the noise carried through the still night, often causing Bruce to bark. I never saw the woman – or the cat – but hearing her voice struck me as a good omen. I would fret or linger on the street on the nights when her voice was silent.

I have little idea what my parents made of my nightly desertions. I suppose they had grown used to my absence during the years I lived with Dudley's family and my nightly wanderings seemed little more than an extension of that. They might have regarded me as being 'different' or 'peculiar', but if they did they never let on. I don't think they ever asked where I went but they always accepted my offerings of mushrooms, or occasionally chestnuts, with appreciation. And my mother never failed to look up from her knitting or her jigsaw and say, 'You're back. Good.' I am sure she would have waited up for me no matter how late I was and I am equally certain that she would have sent my father out to look for me had I not been home by bedtime.

I must have been living back at home for a year or two when something remarkable happened. My father, who rarely gambled, won a tidy sum of money betting on a horse called Lucky in Love at the New Year races. In a burst of joy – almost recklessness – he announced that he intended to close his shop for three days and take us on holiday. We had never been away before and I was all for going to the sea – to Timaru – simply because I had never seen the ocean, except in photographs. I dearly wanted to experience it for myself. I'm not sure what I was expecting but Ted – my greatest source of information at that stage – had assured me that the sea was unlike any river or dam I had ever swum in. It was warm and sticky and tasted like sweat, he said. Once, on a recent visit to his grandparents in Timaru, there had been news of a shark sighting off the beach at Caroline Bay. The shark, Ted insisted, attacked a dinghy, nearly sending its occupants into the sea, to be ripped to shreds and devoured. One of the fishermen whacked the shark with his oar and they were able to escape. The dinghy was damaged beyond repair. Ted had seen it with his own eyes, tied up beside a boat shed. It had a huge chunk missing from its stern, a gigantic hole that clearly showed where the shark's teeth had struck.

My mother refused to holiday by the sea and my father, despite my protestations, did not force the issue. I was bitterly disappointed, and although nothing was said to confirm my suspicions, I could not help blaming my brothers for my mother's stance. For the first time in my life I felt angry with them. I had a sense of injustice. It wasn't my fault they had drowned. Their ship had gone down on the other side of the world, in a different sea to the one I wanted to visit. We were in no danger of

35

attack. There was no logical reason why we shouldn't go to Timaru.

For the rest of the summer the subject of the holiday was not raised again and I turned my mind to other matters, none of them particularly interesting or memorable. Then, as Easter approached, my father reintroduced the topic, and before my mother had time to gather her thoughts he made arrangements for us to spend three nights at the Hermitage Hotel, Mount Cook. I didn't ask but I suspect that this idea didn't simply pop into my father's head. Around this time Dudley was working off and on at the Hermitage, and I think he may have helped my father with the hotel bookings. He certainly spoke with enthusiasm about the place. He was particularly proud of the various building projects he had been involved in, and impressed upon my parents that everything at the hotel was 'top quality'.

On Good Friday morning we clambered into our van and set off. I had very mixed emotions with regard to our destination. Except in the most general terms I had never spoken to my parents about my experience in the Mackenzie Basin. It was not that I was consciously excluding them; it just hadn't occurred to me that they would be interested. I think I also felt uneasy, knowing that by far the happiest day of my life had taken place in the company of Dudley and not them.

That day had remained in my memory and had retained all the excitement and joy I felt at the time. Rather than fading over time, it had become enhanced. There was a chance that my recollection now bore little resemblance to the actual physical location. What had moved me to capture the place in words, in a poem, could quite easily be just a figment of my imagination. And what if I had shared my vision of the Mackenzie with my parents only to have them feel that I had deceived them? What if the plain was not as big as I remembered it, the sky not so blue, the grandness not so grand?

I had kept my memories and my poem to myself. Though I was desperate for my parents to see the Mackenzie Country through my eyes, to share my feelings for it, I didn't want to hear them say anything about that landscape that they didn't mean. They had to love it as I had done — or admit they didn't. I couldn't bear the thought of them lying in order to protect my emotions. The Mackenzie had meant everything to me and I needed to know my parents were being honest about it, no matter what.

My heart started thudding in my chest as we began the slow climb from the settlement at Burkes Pass. Even though my father's van was far more comfortable than Dudley's truck I began to shiver, and my father, fearing that I was going to be sick, pulled off to the side of the road and made me get out.

He urged me to take deep breaths and fill my lungs; my mother remained in the van, staring through the windscreen, quietly waiting for our journey to continue. I didn't feel in the slightest bit car-sick but I was glad of the break. The journey had seemed slow and oppressively quiet, sombre in comparison to my trip with Dudley and Ted. I was grateful, too, for the opportunity to prepare myself mentally for our first sight of the Mackenzie Basin. I needed to gather my thoughts and open myself to the possibility that it might not live up to my expectations.

Already I was aware of several ill omens. The hotel deer that I had fed were not in their pen as we drove past. Fearing that they had been butchered, I asked my father if he had 'encountered' them during the course of his work, and was greatly relieved when he showed no signs of understanding my train of thought. Even so, I was subdued, wondering where they had gone.

Adding further to my unease was the sight of a wild pig skin, head intact, hanging over a farm gate. The skin was large but tattered around its edges. It looked as if it had been pulled from the carcass in a hurry – there were holes visible through the bristles. For no reason I felt it was a bad sign. I think, now, it was the head, with its staring eyes, that gave me the jitters.

When it became clear that I was not going to vomit, my father suggested we get going again as we still had a lengthy journey ahead of us.

As I climbed back into the van my mother glanced towards me and smiled, asking if I felt any better. I replied that I was fine. She nodded and turned back to the view through the windscreen, murmuring, 'That's good. I was worried.'

Perhaps to lighten the mood, my father began to talk, listing all the

37

things we might be able to do once we reached our destination. 'Do you think they'll have dinner ready?' he asked. 'I've heard they have their own supply of fresh meat. They meet all their own needs.' He laughed heartily, then he was on to the next subject before I understood the pun. Though not wanting to appear rude, I did nothing to encourage my father's monologue. I wanted him to be quiet so that I could concentrate on my surroundings. I needed my own internal silence, a space big enough to contain my thoughts and impressions of the scenery once we cleared the summit of the pass. My father of course had no inkling of what was going through my mind. Having exhausted the topic of meat he began on vegetables. 'I wonder if they can grow carrots up there?' Carrots were one of the few vegetables my father had trouble growing himself. No matter how hard he tried, he could not raise a decent crop of carrots and that annoyed him more than almost anything else. 'I suppose they can,' he mused. 'They're not that hard to grow – given the right conditions.'

The van skidded in the deep ruts and my mother jerked forward, steadying herself on the dashboard. 'Bit rough,' said my father. 'Do you remember, Connie, the last time we came up this way, when the twins were . . .' His voice trailed off and he returned to the subject of vegetables but I was no longer listening because suddenly the whole of the Mackenzie opened up before us and my heart gave a lurch.

It was not as I remembered but it was none the less for that. On my first visit the entire area had been blanketed by snow – a gleaming, sparkling white plain, but now it was now golden. The nor'wester had risen and the tussock close to the road was agitated, swaying and billowing in the strong wind. Fanning out from a central core one second, only to snap shut the next, each tussock seemed alive – breathing, sucking in the air around it. Though tussocks predominated, I saw that many other plants were also present. I didn't know their names; apart from gorse, broom and matagouri I had little knowledge of plants.

My father continued to talk but few of his words entered my mind. I was too busy looking around to pay attention to his observations. The sky, which had been a limitless pale blue expanse on my previous visit, was now partially overcast. Sweeping the basin were huge swathes of shadow that cast the ground in tones of blue and grey through to a steely black as the clouds obscured the sun.

If I had thought about things in a logical manner I would not have been surprised by the change in the landscape, or the view before me. I had replayed my snow-blanketed view so often in my head that I had almost assumed the Mackenzie to be incapable of change. I imagined it would remain, just as I had left it. In many regards, *my* Mackenzie was more imaginary than real. And so, if I was disappointed, it was not with the view but with the feeling that I had been left behind – that it had changed without me there to watch it happen.

I think this was the first time in my life that I was conscious of the passing of time. It was also, I should add, the first time I experienced a sense of longing, an urge to recapture the past.

By now the wind was very strong, buffeting the van from side to side as we jolted along the road. Until this point we had not seen another vehicle but now, at the end of a long straight, we glimpsed a car on the shoulder of the road with several figures milling around it. We were still some distance away and it took several minutes before we reached the stationary vehicle. My father, assuming it had broken down – although no one had waved at us, eased our van to a standstill and climbed stiffly down from the driver's seat calling, 'Hullo, there!'

Seconds later he returned. The group, he explained, were simply enjoying the scenery, snapping images of Mount Cook for their albums. At the mention of Mount Cook I sat up. I hadn't even noticed the mountain. My gaze had been so firmly fixed on my immediate surroundings that I had paid little attention to the distant mountains that rose up against a background of clear blue sky, beneath an arch of cloud. I was not sure which mountain was Cook but before I could ask my father he continued, 'I told them to save their film. From this distance they'll be lucky if the mountain even shows up.'

We sat in our van, the engine turned off, feeling the full brunt of the wind. My father appeared in no hurry to drive away and I remember feeling self-conscious, wondering what we were waiting for and why my father appeared so intent on staying put. I tried to become invisible but I couldn't help stealing glances at the men and women who stood posing for the camera, leaning against the bonnet of their vehicle while one or other of them snapped away.

'Maybe I should offer to take their group portrait?' suggested my father, once more opening his door. 'It won't show much, but it might generate a fond memory – in case they're not back this way again.' He must have sensed my discomfort for he turned on me, saying, 'Don't be like that, lad. You're going to be sharing a hotel with them for the next three nights – and we want to make them feel welcome.'

My father disappeared beyond the back of the van and I could hear his voice behind us. 'Go on, now,' he directed. 'Ladies to the front, gents to the back.' There was a sound of laughter and then my father's voice once more: 'One, two, three: sausages!' This was typical of my father. While most photographers settled for 'cheese', he insisted that 'sausages' created a far more flattering, natural smile. According to him, it was impossible to utter the word without smiling. I could hear someone thank him (though I sensed he was simply being polite, indulging my father) and then the conversation shifted to the topic of road conditions and I could hear my father warning them it would get rough towards Simons Pass, with several fords, all of which required 'extreme care'. 'If it gets too much, you'll find good refreshments at Pukaki,' he called out by way of a parting gesture. 'The Pukaki Hotel is well worth a visit.'

During this exchange I had been trying to identify Mount Cook. I was almost certain I had chosen the correct peak but, scared I had it wrong, I took the opportunity of my father's return to ask him. He gestured towards a far-off spot in the distance. It could have been anything. 'See that big, flat cloud?' he offered when it became clear his jabbing finger was not going to do the trick. I nodded, uncertain which cloud he meant. 'If you follow that cloud to its right-hand end and then drop down to the mountains you'll see one that's spikier than all the others. I nodded, turning my head helplessly from my father to the mountains and then back to my father. He sighed, began again. 'You see that telegraph pole?' Again I nodded. My father leant down, lowering his head next to mine as he pointed out the pole. 'Look about an inch to the left. Go up – there's a shadow on the cloud above it – it's shaped like a chop.'

My head began to swim. I thought I had the mountain in sight but my father's directions were confusing me.

'I reckon the lad might need glasses. What do you think, Connie? I've always thought he might be short-sighted. You never know – perhaps it runs in the family.'

My mother frowned and said in a quiet voice, 'It's the highest mountain you can see. It's at eleven o'clock.'

But it was so small. Now that I was certain I had the correct mountain I couldn't believe how inconsequential it looked. From this distance it was less impressive than the mountains visible from our back door.

'Course it's the highest mountain,' my father chimed. 'That's why it's called Cloud-Piercer.'

That seemed to settle things. Content, my father started the engine, skidded a little in the soft shingle and we were back on the road, jolting towards Cloud-Piercer, which suddenly disappeared behind a low rise in the road ahead.

It was ninety-six miles from Fairlie to the Hermitage. We had a Motorists' Road Guide that pre-dated the war. On page 162 were two advertisements: one for Mount Cook, the other for the Hermitage. I noticed that Mount Cook wasn't referred to as 'Cloud-Piercer' but as 'Aorangi'. I knew the word must be Maori and I liked the way it sounded, but I had no idea what it meant. The advertisement claimed that the mountain scenery was equal to any found in Switzerland, and that the Hermitage was the 'Most Luxurious Mountain Hostel in Australasia'.

Even as a youngster I was vaguely suspicious of such claims. For many years I had heard my father tempting his lady customers with 'the tastiest tripe in the whole of South Canterbury', 'the tenderest beef' cut from 'the finest beasts in the world' and, his favourite, 'liver so full of iron you won't want to risk standing next to a magnet!'

The journey had been long and tiring and we were all subdued as we covered the final few miles separating us from our destination. The sky, which had cleared during the course of the afternoon, was now cloudless and the sun, hidden from view behind the mountains, nevertheless cast a soft light over the snow-capped peaks that towered over the valley.

Mount Cook itself was cast in a bright, almost salmon-pink light, and was far more vibrant than any of the mountains around it. From its summit a long plume of spindrift was clearly visible, trailing hundreds of feet into the sky. The moon, just visible above the mountains, was silvery against the dusk sky. There was a star, too – just one, but every bit as bright as the moon.

It was freezing outside. As we climbed down from the van my mother shivered and pulled her cardigan tightly across her chest, holding it against her body with one hand while she carried an old battered suitcase with the other. The bulk of our belongings was packed into one large case, which my father heaved out of the van, almost throwing himself off-balance as he took its full weight. I had my school case – a grubby blue thing I now swung enthusiastically by its brown plastic handle in an attempt to make the blood flow into my arms and chilled hands. I was wearing shorts so my thighs and knees took the full impact of the cold air. I bounced up and down as I swung my arms, causing my father to step backwards, out of harm's way. 'Steady on!' he called. 'You'll have us all knocked off our feet in a minute.' No sooner were the words out of his mouth than he slipped on a patch of ice and landed heavily on his bottom. 'What did I tell you?' he growled, looking up at me and extending his hand for me to help him to his feet. 'You be careful there, Connie,' he called after my mother who, in her Sunday best shoes, was skittering towards the front entrance of the hotel.

I trailed behind my parents, reluctant to turn away from the mountain now that only a thin strip of sunlight grazed its summit. I didn't want to miss the moment when the sunlight disappeared altogether so I half walked backwards, glancing constantly over my left shoulder. As I stumbled along I suddenly heard an eerie sound, a cry that was as sharp as the still air and yet somehow crazy, otherworldly. I stopped and looked in the direction from which it had come. Two birds, dark in colour but with under-wings that were an orange-red even in the fading light, swooped past us, coming to land on the roof of the hotel. As their claws made contact with the roof they clattered and slid towards the gutter and then, despite scrabbling for purchase, both birds skated off the roof entirely, flapping madly to avoid crashing to the ground. Giving the impression of being annoyed, they took to the sky again and disappeared around the back of the building, screeching angrily as they did so.

'Keas,' said my father.

I asked him to repeat the word, which was new to me, and then I tried it myself. 'Kea, kea, kea . . .' I suddenly understood that that was the sound of their call. It was onomatopoeic.

'Clowns of the sky,' added my father, hefting the suitcase before him.

Even now, many years since that first visit, I am unable to see the interior of the Hermitage with a clear, objective eye. I can describe it neither accurately nor truthfully but only as I first perceived it: the opulence of its interior so magnificent that I could have been entering its Russian namesake (had I known back then that somewhere else in the world another Hermitage existed). Though I was to return to the Hermitage as a young man, I cling stubbornly to the first, dominant impression created in my mind on that childhood holiday.

The hotel was ablaze with lights. In all the public areas, hanging from every ceiling, above every table, chair and desk were massive chandeliers. To my young eyes – accustomed only to dull bulbs hanging forlornly over kitchen tables or inserted into standard lamps, with their heavy, fringed hoods beside my parents' armchairs, which seemed to absorb rather than cast light – these chandeliers were miraculous. It was as if someone had taken a bucketful of diamonds, tossed them into the air and commanded them to 'Freeze!' These clusters hovered close to the ceiling, suspended high above me, and their light was like no other. I felt happier than I had for a very long time and I believe my good mood was the result of being bathed by such bright, pure light.

Decorating the walls of the reception area and dining room were original paintings. At home we had one pictorial calendar and several dull prints of cut stems of pink or yellow roses but the Hermitage had real artworks, of a kind I had never seen before. They were huge landscapes – winter snow scenes of Mount Cook, pictures of mountain streams cascading over boulders – and I felt they could have been real. Each painting put me in mind of a window that opened up onto a view of such beauty that I longed to step outside and discover for myself the landscape rendered visible. I couldn't, of course, but what I could do was stand very close to each painting and take in every brushstroke, the detail and colour that made up each individual work. When no one was looking I reached out my fingers and touched the surface of one particularly striking painting. The image of its moonlit, snow-covered track leading through a forest towards a small hut lodged in my mind; I closed my eyes and allowed my fingertips to guide me over the scene. The track itself was cool and smooth, whereas the trees either side were rough – the paint layered on so thickly that I imagined I was touching real bark, actual foliage. I had never been to an art gallery but I had no doubt that few galleries could compete with the richness of the hotel's collection.

Of all the fittings that impressed me, I was most taken by the large brass telescope that dominated the day-room, its lens focused on the Hooker Valley and Mount Cook itself. The view through the telescope exerted a kind of magnetic force on me by drawing the mountains closer than they actually were. Sefton, Cook and the others (which I did not know by name) not only towered above us but pressed against us, dominating the hotel, which seemed small and fragile as eggshell.

But better than all of these things – more stunning than the view, more splendid than the chandeliers, more exciting than the paintings or the telescope – was the effect all these things had on my mother. As we were called into the dining room I heard her gasp. Anticipating some new source of anguish I reluctantly turned to face her and saw that her expression was one of utter delight. Her eyes shone and her fingertips rested against her bottom lip as, with child-like wonder, she murmured, 'Is it real?' A feeling of bliss went through me as she placed her arm around my shoulder and pulled me close, squeezing me tight. I was filled with such joy that I wanted the moment to freeze, to last forever. At the same time I wanted to rush forward, to seize the moment and show her all the things that I had seen. I wanted to share my own joy and make her happy. Dizzy with confusion I pulled away from her and rushed around jabbering and pointing wildly. 'Look at this!' I said as I dodged past the furniture. 'Have you ever seen such bright lights, so many windows and tables?' It was several minutes before I noticed that my mother was paying me no attention. She was so engrossed in her own impressions that she hadn't joined me in exploring mine. I stood still, looking at her, waiting for her to acknowledge me. After a moment she edged towards a table and sat down with her back to me. She reached for a pressed napkin which she fingered idly as she gazed at some spot in the distance.

I have no recollection of the meal. Though I was aware that my parents carried on a conversation of sorts – my father commenting on the meat, I suppose, or on the activities he had planned for us over the following days – I felt tired, aware even then, that I had wasted an opportunity, that I should have nestled against my mother's warm body instead of diving away. I don't remember what I ate, but I do recall the way in which the food balled up in my mouth. No matter how hard or long I chewed, I experienced the discomfort of swallowing each morsel whole. Maybe I was simply worn out by the journey but I was glad when, towards 8.30, I was led down the corridor to our room and helped onto a fold-out cot that had been placed at the foot of my parents' bed. I opened the book I had borrowed from the shelves of the hotel library: C. A. Cotton's *Geomorphology of New Zealand*. I had picked it up because I liked the sound of the word, Geomorphology, and because it had diagrams and photographs on almost every page.

I fell asleep almost immediately, waking only once in the night, when from nearby I heard quiet laughter as several unfamiliar voices called out 'Goodnight' to one another. I listened and heard the soft click of doors closing and then the night fell quiet and I drifted back to sleep, not waking again until I felt my father's hand on my shoulder, shaking me gently. He urged me to get up, as morning had broken and we had no time to lose.

So much of that holiday was new to me, far *bigger* than anything I had experienced before. My impression of the grand scale owes much to the view through the hotel windows. Though I had stared through the glass the evening before, as the light was fading, and felt a sense of joy and elation, the scene that greeted me on that first morning at the Hermitage had an altogether different effect on my mood. Standing before the window, taking in the dark, sunless valleys, the distinct boundary between shadow and sunlight on the higher peaks, I was overcome by a desire to climb a mountain. Given that I had never before felt even the slightest inclination to scramble up a hillside, I was surprised by my craving. It was a gut reaction, instinctual. I didn't want to spend my day in the shadow looking up, I wanted to be up there – wherever *there* was. I wanted to explore the jagged ridgelines that towered above me; I wanted to be so high that I could see what was beyond what was now in front of me; I needed to see what was on the other side.

My hunger to climb was urgent. Every second spent inside the Hermitage seemed wasted. This was brought home to me when, as I sat with my parents, silently spooning porridge into my mouth, I glanced up

47

and saw two men walk past the front of the building. While my parents were dressed in clothes they only ever wore on Sundays or special occasions, these men wore thick woollen jumpers and knee-breeches, long socks and hobnailed boots. On their backs were canvas knapsacks and one of them carried a stout walking stick. I couldn't hear what they were saying but they were talking animatedly, laughing as they passed the window and disappeared down a path away from the hotel. I was about to turn back to my food when a woman ran past the window to catch them up. She was also dressed in trousers and boots and her hair, a cascade of golden curls, was kept off her face by a bright red hairband, which she adjusted as she trotted after her companions.

If my parents noticed the group they paid them no attention. My father was concentrating on his breakfast, selecting each morsel of food carefully and chewing slowly as if about to grade it according to its flavour and texture. Occasionally, mid-chew, he would nod his head appreciatively and make a jabbing motion towards his plate with his fork, his mouth half-full. 'Very tasty, not bad at all.' My mother, who, like me, had picked porridge from the menu, smiled whenever my father nodded vigorously and added, 'It's lovely, just lovely.'

I was pleased to see my parents so happy but I was beginning to feel apprehensive. They were both enjoying their meal so much I feared we might be stuck in the dining room for the whole day. My father would call for more and more food and my mother would go along with his plan.

I was desperate to get outside and became increasingly anxious, anticipating that events might turn against me, things might start to go wrong. My mother's mood could change. I desperately wanted her to stay relaxed for the entire holiday but I didn't believe she would. At any moment she might recall her previous holiday at the Hermitage – the time she had visited with the twins, my brothers – and retreat into herself once more. It was important that I nudge her outside before this happened. Being in the midst of such beauty would be enough to save her. I knew she had packed one of her jigsaw puzzles and I feared that if I wasn't quick enough she might simply settle down in front of 2000 fragments of the Tower of London and content herself with an occasional glimpse through the window.

Convinced that what I so badly wanted was about to be snatched away from me I blurted, 'Can we go exploring outside?' I had intended the tone of my voice to appear casual, jolly even, but it sounded desperate – as if I were already certain of defeat. To my immense relief my father replied, 'Of course, lad. That's what we're here for.' He patted me affectionately on the head. 'Just as soon as your mother's ready.' He winked at my mother and she looked from him to me, conscious that I was watching her, willing her to hurry. 'We could go to Governors Bush,' she suggested, smiling at me. 'It's not too strenuous,' she added, glancing at my father. 'Do you remember, Nathaniel, how much we enjoyed the nature walk the last time we were here?'

My father nodded but my heart sank a little. I thought it would be foolish to risk going anywhere she had been before, with my brothers. I wanted my mother to venture into new territory, somewhere that held no associations for her. Perhaps I was jealous, too. I didn't want my mother to spend the weekend thinking about the twins. I wanted her to be with me, emotionally as well as physically.

Within minutes of finishing breakfast we found ourselves stepping outside, breathing in the fresh morning air and looking about in gratitude and amazement. At least that's how it seemed to me. My parents, I suspect, were not so powerfully affected, for my father, after a few steps, hesitated and re-tied his boot laces, complaining that the uppers were pressing uncomfortably against his bunions. My mother fussed with a hat she had knitted for me the previous week. I had purposefully left it behind in our room, with its flecked lime green wool and its pompom. I was put out to discover that she had picked it up and had brought mittens too, and was pressing them upon me with alarming vigour. Though they were knitted in a subdued brown I believed I was far too old for mittens, particularly ones that were joined by a long length of binding that went behind my neck and prevented a mitten from being dropped should I remove it from my hand. I wasn't a baby any more, and I was about to protest when a new group of guests burst suddenly through the hotel entrance, greeting my father, whom they clearly recognised from the previous day's encounter on the road.

Unlike the glamorous group I had spotted earlier, these people appeared as drab as us. There were three men and two women and looking more closely, I noticed that the women were dressed in a masculine manner: boots, tweed trousers, checked shirts, the collars of which were visible above the necklines of coarse home-spun jumpers. Two of the men – although dressed in a similar fashion to the women – were strangely prim. One of the men, I noticed (perhaps because my eyes instantly searched out his hands, looking for gloves) had slender wrists and long, tapered fingers. Standing slightly apart from the rest of the group, he smiled briefly at me and then moved away, leaving his companions to exchange early-morning pleasantries with my parents.

After a few minutes' chat, during which time the topics of road conditions, weather and breakfast were all dealt with, we parted ways: they were bound for a place called Kea Point whereas, as my parents had already decided, we were off to Governors Bush.

I was impatient to get under way: although I would have liked to be striking out for some high peak I knew it was out of the question. My father's wartime leg injury prevented him from taking strenuous exercise, and his ability to tackle uneven or steeply sloping ground was severely compromised. He was able to cope with the daily demands of his trade but he never walked for recreation, preferring to potter around, gardening or working on his van (which took up an enormous amount of his time and energy). Due to wartime shortages the tyres had been patched and repaired so many times that my father had joked – somewhat half-heartedly – that they were almost as useless as his own legs: either could be expected to give up the ghost at any minute.

My mother, although healthy, had little interest in the outdoors. I never knew her to walk for pleasure. During the summer, when Dudley invited us for a picnic, she would invariably make some excuse to stay home while I – the lone representative of the family – would pack my towel and trunks and disappear for the day, grateful to be out in the fresh air after a week of breathing in the various odours associated with my father's trade.

I was surprised my mother opted even to walk through Governors Bush. I was delighted that she was prepared to join my father and me but I half suspected that it was only because, given the outdoor focus of our accommodation, she would have felt self-conscious, even a failure, had she remained inside on such a beautiful day. As if to confirm my suspicions I heard her sigh shortly after we got under way, and not ten minutes later she said, 'I forgot how much uphill there was.'

We made a strange group. My father, having done his dash with social intercourse, had nothing more to say. He limped ahead of us, hesitating every now and then as he negotiated the roots of the large beech trees we walked around. My mother, no more talkative, fell into silence. She was not about to complain about the walk but I had the distinct feeling that rather than enjoy it, she was driven by willpower to see it through – nothing more. Once more I had pulled the short straw, forced to spend my day in the company of tired, worn-down adults when I might have been far happier by myself. And I could not simply run on ahead – something told me that such a simple display of freedom would be disloyal, that it would hurt my parents terribly when they were here tackling a bush walk as a favour to me. I believe now, as I believed then, that they were genuine in their attempt to give me a happy start to our holiday. That they were unable to take real pleasure from it was not the point. The point was that they wanted to give me something and it would have been churlish of me, unforgivable, not to acknowledge their kindness by staying close by. So on we walked.

Looking back, I wonder if my aversion to the bush dates from that early experience. Governors Bush was a beautiful remnant of beech forest with all the features one looks for in a forest walk. A pleasant smell – musty, sweet, woody – rose from the ground as my feet tracked over fallen leaves, broken branches and mud. The earthy scent struck me forcibly, and made an agreeable contrast with the crisp, fresh mountain air. The light that morning was spectacular. Golden, it tunnelled through the canopy of branches, settling in pools by our feet or spotlighting patches of moss, which glowed an intense green. As we walked, small birds fluttered ahead of us, darting from branch to ground and back again, perching

51

close to where we passed, seemingly unafraid – curious, if anything. But despite these wonders I felt hemmed in, and it was only as we reached the highest point and I was able to take in the face of Mount Sebastopol that I truly relaxed and breathed easily.

Standing on that spur, surrounded by subalpine scrub, I raised my arms and spun around in a manner I was to see replicated many years later by Julie Andrews in *The Sound of Music*. It was an extravagant gesture and immediately after I felt embarrassed, grateful that no one had witnessed my strange performance.

With lunch beckoning, we retraced our footsteps and returned to the Hermitage in good time. As we drew closer to the hotel my father – who had remained thoughtful throughout the morning – suddenly adjusted his features and called out a hearty 'hullo' to an elderly couple who were sunning themselves in front of the building.

After lunch was disposed of my parents retired to our room for a quiet lie down and finally I was able to head off on my own. During lunch I had come to the conclusion that I would follow the direction taken by the man with the graceful hands. My instinct told me that his group had a greater appreciation of the mountainous landscape than my own family, so they would have chosen a more interesting route than the one we had taken that morning. So, dressed in the ridiculous hat and mittens that my mother insisted I wear in case the weather turned, I stepped out into a peerless afternoon and hurried away before my parents had second thoughts about my solitary expedition and called me back.

I walked for thirty minutes or so, following a path that crossed a boulder and scree fan before it descended slightly and levelled out on open scrub- and tussock-covered ground. Suddenly unsure of myself – and of the whereabouts of Kea Point – I aimed for an isolated low hill that rose abruptly from its flat surroundings. This hill, also covered in scrub, reminded me of a desert island protruding from an otherwise calm, featureless ocean. The hill was the perfect size for one person and I lost no time scrambling to its summit, where I raised a pole I made from a damaged sapling. Facing a mountain covered in rock, snow and ice – which I realised was Mount Sefton – I turned in a slow clockwise circle to take in the Hooker Valley, the Footstool, Mount Cook, Mount Wakefield, the Tasman River, the road leading back towards Pukaki, and finally Mount Sebastopol and the Hermitage itself. For the first time in my life I felt I was at the centre of the world. All these wondrous sights were there for my pleasure and would remain so for as long as I kept making my slow, methodical circle. And yet turning my back on any one of these views struck me as a crime. If I faced Wakefield, I missed out on seeing what was happening on Cook. Watching Cook denied me the pleasure of seeing the stationary clouds poised above Sebastopol. So, while being in this place gave me an intense pleasure, it also instilled in me a sense of regret. No matter how hard I tried, or how long I spent on my hill, I could not capture the whole scene. I had to make a choice, a conscious decision of where to look, what to focus on – and what to lose.

It was a sound that finally settled things for me. I had been looking at another scrub-covered hill, opposite mine and quite a bit larger, when there was a crash followed by a thunderous roar. Glancing up, I saw half the face of Sefton disappear behind a rising cloud of spindrift. The initial sound of the avalanche continued for several seconds, its echo vibrating across the space between us. I imagined I felt the ground around me move, so forceful was the noise and the billowing cloud rising from the lower slopes, obscuring the sky. I recalled tales I had read about battleships, stories of Drake's confrontation with the Spanish Armada, and in my mind I drew vivid comparisons between the volley of canon-fire and the avalanche, the might and destruction common to both. It was thrilling but, having missed the avalanche itself, and seeing only its aftermath, I settled down and waited, anticipating a second, even more powerful, event.

I sat for over an hour. Every now and then I would hear a crack and I would search out what looked like a small trickle of snow falling through some deep gully, but nothing matched the earlier event. Deciding to give the mountain a rest, a chance to recover from its burst of energy, I began to explore my hilltop, cursing myself for not bringing a pencil and paper on which to draw a proper map. Below my summit was a hollow. At some point, I thought, there must have been a pond, or perhaps – I secretly hoped – a meteorite had fallen from the sky, landing where I now stood. For the most part, however, the hill lacked exciting features. There were no caves, middens, waterfalls or wild animals as far as I could tell. It was exactly what it had appeared to be at first sight: a scrub-covered hillock. Yet, having fully explored my island, I believed that I knew it better than anyone else and I quickly came to see it as my special place: my hill, my fortress, my island, my kingdom.

Immediately I began to grow anxious, wondering how I could protect my domain from others. The knoll created in me such strong, protective feelings that I convinced myself that someone would try and take it away, or destroy it. I know it seems strange but the mound seemed to me to be alive, a living thing, like a massive animal – an elephant or a whale, and it depended upon me to safeguard its life. I could not bring myself to leave, and when, towards nightfall, I did eventually walk away, I found myself turning back time and time again, searching out the pole on its summit until the sapling was no longer visible and the knoll itself was little more than a shadowy form rising up from the ground.

I was almost back at the Hermitage, scrambling across the scree, when I realised that there was a group of people walking just ahead of me. Had I had more time I would have waited, allowing them to gain some distance, but, fearful that my mother would be worried about me, I hurried on, praying that they would allow me to overtake them without comment. I was not so lucky. Just as I was about to nip past I stumbled and fell. Immediately the last person in the group turned around and, to my embarrassment, offered me his hand. I was surprised by the softness of his skin. His hand was surprisingly small, much narrower than my own, and as he pulled me to my feet I had the sensation of crushing his fingers in my stronger grasp. It was the man I had noticed earlier, the gentleman I had half-heartedly set out to follow before being sidetracked by my hill.

I felt awkward in his presence. His eyes showed no signs of unfriend-liness but nevertheless scrutinised me, as if he were weighing me up for the table. A thin man, he stood with his weight over one hip – a stance I had never seen in any other man. The men of my acquaintance stood solidly, on two broad feet. His hair, which was combed to one side, fell across his face and as we stood facing each other he raised his slender hand and brushed his hair away. I expected his voice to be thin and reedy but it was low and quiet when, suddenly smiling, he asked if I was all right. I nodded.

His friends, I could see, had stopped and were waiting a short distance away. One of the party called out, asking what was going on and the man replied, saying we would only be a moment, and that they should go on ahead as it was getting cold. He turned back to me and, asking me once more if I would survive, made way for me, allowing me to walk ahead of him. Once more I had the feeling – although I couldn't be sure – that he was watching me, watching me walk.

As I hurried on he made conversation, asking me where I had been, if I had enjoyed myself. He told me his party had been out all day; he had sat gazing at the view while his friends sketched and painted. He asked me if I liked art, and when I was unable to answer he changed the subject, asking if I liked being in the mountains. Hearing me respond in the affirmative, he took a deep breath and said something wholly unexpected and remarkable: 'I live not in myself, but I become Portion of that around me; and to me High mountains are a feeling, but the hum of human cities torture.'

I was stopped in my tracks. Two thoughts entered my head simul-taneously: What on earth had he said and could he repeat it? I asked him to say it again slowly, and I drank up every word – until the bit about the cities. I repeated my request and if he was annoyed or surprised he didn't let on but simply spoke the words again slowly, allowing me to fumble through them as I locked them into my brain. It didn't occur to me – not even for a second – that he was not the original source of those words. I had no idea he was quoting Byron. Nor for a minute did I doubt that he was speaking from the heart – albeit a collective heart, one that in some awkward, bumbling way included my own.

And then we entered the Hermitage and my mother appeared before us. She had been watching for me and before I could stop her she was at my side, ushering me into the dining room, nagging me about my hat and gloves while the man – the possessor of words – slipped away.

The next afternoon, as soon as my parents went for a lie down, I escaped to 'my hill', Foliage Hill, to sit and watch for avalanches.

Once there, I must have lost track of time because before I knew it the sun had eased behind the mountains and shadows seeped across the valley floor. In the growing dusk I discovered a sense of peace, gazing skyward as one by one the stars appeared and hearing far away the distant rumble of ice-fall: blocks falling from the mountain whose face I now knew more completely than any other – Sefton.

Running, I was guided back to the Hermitage by the lights that glowed and dazzled from behind its glass panes and sat down beside my mother, who was frowning over a puzzle of the *Titanic*. My father suddenly spoke up, and informed me that dinner would be served in ten minutes and then went on to describe the pleasant hour he had spent in the company of 'the artists' – his description of the group who had followed us up from the Mackenzie. I had just missed them, he said. He went on to say that a new member had joined their group. His name was Darroch – and he was the artist responsible for the paintings hanging on the walls of the hotel. Mr Darroch – Duncan – lived behind the hotel and he spent his days doing odd jobs, guiding and painting. I would have liked to hear more about this artist but my father, sensing he had my undivided attention, leant forward and, in a conspiratorial voice, whispered, 'Do you recall the stocky woman – the one with the dark hair?' I nodded, although truth be told, I hadn't noticed the colour of the stocky woman's hair. 'Well,' continued my father, 'she let slip, over a glass of sherry, that she is a vegetarian.' I waited, wondering what on earth my father meant. 'I asked her why,' continued my father, 'and do you know what she said?' I shook my head. 'She said she didn't like the taste of flesh.'

My father raised his eyebrows and repeated, 'The taste of flesh!' He laughed, a strangely hollow, pained sound. Ridiculous though it was, I could see that my father found the woman's remark hurtful. It was a personal blow.

'I asked for her address and told her I'd send some of my best sausages her way but she said I wasn't to go to the trouble. There was no point wasting good food.'

I gave my father what I hoped was a sympathetic smile. I was becoming more and more curious about these 'artists'. Despite their plain – even prim – exterior, they were exotic. I scrabbled for something to compare them with and to my immense satisfaction I settled on an image of a kea: these people were the equivalent of the dull green bird's scarlet under-wings.

In bed that night my mind raced over all that had taken place since we left home. To calm myself, I began to compose a poem. As before, I started with a word and then tried to find an appropriate rhyme for it by trawling through the alphabet, one letter at a time. 'Kea,' I began and then discovered I could go no further.

I lay awake, the crisp hotel sheets brushing my chin, my mind darting back and forth from one letter to another, sure that I had missed the obvious. After what felt like a lifetime I finally settled on a first line:

'It must be queer to be a kea . . .'

I created spaces between the sounds, sliding the words like abacus beads along a piece of wire:

'It must be que-er to be-a kea . . .'

It was dismal but I could do no better. I knew what I wanted to capture: the birds, their call ringing through the clear air, contrasting with crashing of the huge snow-capped mountains – but I couldn't link it all together. When the words wouldn't come I fell asleep: from frustration or boredom, I'm not sure which overtook me first.

As far as I was concerned, the journey back to Fairlie passed unnoticed. I was only vaguely aware of the Mackenzie Basin, of the intense turquoise blue-green of Lake Tekapo. I ate the mutton sandwiches prepared for us by the Hermitage staff in a manner I associated with my mother: absently, barely aware of the flavour of the meat.

Our arrival home was greeted by dense, clammy smog that cloaked the town. The clear, crisp days of Mount Cook seemed far behind us and the holiday was soon forgotten as I returned to school, my father to work and my mother to her chair at the kitchen table.

From time to time, while out roaming at night, I would recall vague images of Mount Sefton and Cook, or hear again the words spoken to me by 'the bard'. Whenever this happened I would stop dead in my tracks, aware of an intense longing to recapture and preserve that holiday in all its exquisite, painful detail. On the other hand, I wanted to ban all such images and words for ever.

My days fell into a tired routine. Now at high school I continued to plug away at my lessons and homework while the other boys in my class turned their attention towards football and cricket, sports that held not the slightest attraction for me. With a few other boys I was rounded up one day by a teacher seeking 'volunteers' for the school production of *Macbeth*. We drew straws, I recall, to decide who would play Macbeth opposite Lady Macbeth, a role performed with gusto by Mary Belcher. Mary, I remember all too clearly, was a scrawny girl with disproportionately large breasts and prominent nipples – the latter, noticeable through her cotton shift, were impossible to ignore and thoroughly disconcerting for any teenage boy trying to remember lines.

I was immensely relieved when the part of Macbeth went to an older boy named Athol. To his credit, he dealt swiftly and thoroughly with the teasing that followed. I happened to pass him one day as he was standing beneath the framed portrait of a former pupil, athlete Jack Lovelock, laying into a boy who had dared to call him a sissy for dressing up in tights and prancing about on stage. I played the porter, my stage-fright such that I forgot to breathe and could barely get through my lines without fainting.

Saturdays were spent helping my father. Gradually I acquired some of the skills he demonstrated to me – though I was far from being an expert, or even competent, for that matter.

I took little satisfaction from my work. Rather than becoming inured to the smell of freshly butchered meat, still-warm blood collected for black puddings, or gelatinous bones boiling in a pot, I became increasingly sensitive to the sights and smells of a butcher's trade. Often I would be forced to cover my mouth with a handkerchief and dash for the door, where I would stand shaking, gulping for air like a fish cast from its bowl.

It was clear to me that I was not cut out for my father's trade, but the thought that I should be anything but a butcher rarely entered his thoughts. He spoke often of my taking over the business and lost no time in introducing me to new customers as his successor, a 'butcher in the making' or, worse, 'the future butcher of Fairlie'. He said little about my sudden outbursts, my growing inability to control my responses to certain aspects of the trade, saying that it was just a matter of time before I settled into the job.

Only once did he ever express his true feelings.

He had received an order for a pig's head and, being otherwise occupied with pickling, asked me to tackle the job of preparing its brains, ears, cheeks and tongue for the customer. At the time I thought he was testing me but, looking back, I think he was simply too busy to do the job himself.

There were two butcher's blocks in my father's shop: one towards the back of the shop and a larger circular block next to the counter. This drum-like block was the one I selected for my task. For some reason I thought the head looked neater and was better suited to this block than the other, less public one. Up until that point I had only ever handled half-heads and my first surprise came when I lifted the head: it was all of fifteen to twenty pounds in weight. Feeling a little apprehensive about how to approach the skull, I hesitated just as I was about to land my first blow, the result being that my cleaver pierced the animal's thick skin and bounced off its skull, jarring my arm in the process. My father, who had witnessed my inept display, came across the room and showed me where to aim the blade. 'You need to split it cleanly,' he said, 'not just chip away at it. Come on, lad, put some elbow into it.' I was about to give it another go when he broke my concentration, adding, 'Just behind the ears. It will pop apart if you do it right and the brains will be clear to see. Make sure you don't go too hard at it – you don't want to mash the brains.'

As he spoke, my ears began to make an odd buzzing sound, which grew in volume as I repositioned the head on the block and raised my cleaver. I was on the verge of striking when suddenly I noticed the pig's lifeless, glassy eyes. The buzzing in my ears increased and I just managed to bring the blade down hard. There was a crack and to my horror the pig's eyelids fluttered and blinked as the animal's brain became visible.

I felt my head go woozy, and before I could stop myself my knees buckled and I slumped to the floor, knocking the block as I fell, sending the head toppling down after me. I don't believe I quite fainted but as I lay on my back I was aware of a ringing noise in my ears and I saw bright flashes of light, exploding like bubbles.

My father stood over me, a look of shock and disbelief on his face as he bent stiffly to retrieve the head from the floor. He held it, gently cradling the split skull in his huge hands as he said, in a voice filled with wonder, 'Well, that's a first.'

He was genuinely amazed – as astonished by what had happened as I was shocked. 'Goodness me, lad,' he said, giving me his hand. 'You didn't half give me a fright.'

I couldn't speak. My head felt light – hollow somehow – and even though I was back on my feet I was as wobbly as a newborn lamb.

Eventually my father put the head down and said, eyes wide, 'I don't think we'd better mention this to your mother. Let's not worry her. What do you say?'

I left school in the early fifties, at the age of sixteen. It wasn't that I was struggling academically but my father was struggling physically with the demands of his trade. His leg often caused him great pain and, although he rarely mentioned it, his face had a tendency to show it whenever he had heavy lifting to do.

I was not forced to leave school. My father wanted me to follow in his footsteps but he took care not to bully me exactly. For several years my parents had been asking me about school, and my favourite subjects and, in recent months they had questioned me about my future. What were my plans? I could not answer – I had little idea what I could do with my life. I had hoped that by the time I reached the age of eighteen I would know – but at this stage I really didn't. Part of the problem was that I had excelled at none of the serious subjects – chemistry, physics, mathematics and the like – which might have led me towards a career in engineering or medicine. English and history were my chosen subjects but they only led to teaching and journalism, neither of which held any attraction. I could not see a way of putting either subject to good use.

My form teacher, who was also my English teacher, offered me no clues. He was due to retire at the end of the year and was far more interested in his own plans than in the future of any of his students. When I asked what I should do he responded that I was a good all-rounder and that I would no doubt succeed in whatever career I entered. I prompted him for more information as to what that career might be but he brushed me off with the surprising statement, 'Just follow your heart.' My knowledge and experience of the world was so limited that I had little idea of my options. Of course, had I known, I might have been paralysed by indecision – or guilt. So in the end I concluded that being a butcher was as good a choice as any and, seeing the look of joy and relief on my father's face when I told him, I felt I had done the right thing.

I quickly learnt to manage my revulsion at certain aspects of the job. My father and I came up with a compromise: he took charge of offal and I did all the heavy work – the lifting of carcasses and such like. Everything else, we shared. The system suited us both and, much to our surprise, my mother started to join us in the shop, making Cornish pasties which we sold on Fridays.

During this period my father appeared more content than I had ever seen him before. For years he had been watching my mother, anticipating her mood shifts, but now he visibly relaxed and dropped his guard. He frequently glanced around the shop and remarked that he was a lucky man. He had always dreamed of running a family business and at last that dream had come true. My mother let his words pass without comment, never once reminding him that we three were the *remains* of a family, nothing more.

The more reinvigorated my father became, the more reserved I was. Boys I had known since childhood began to leave Fairlie. I would sometimes catch sight of them standing on the station platform, chatting and smoking as they waited for the train. If they saw me they would call out good-naturedly, 'Be sure to look me up if you're ever in Christchurch!' Some, I knew, planned to travel overseas, working their passage on one of the passenger ships leaving from Auckland. Others, boys older than me, were heading to university. Even Ted, who was two or three years my senior, was leaving town. He had found work with the Canterbury Steam Shipping Company.

And then, just when it seemed that no one else could leave – for they had already gone – stories began to trickle in, news and gossip passed on to my father from various customers about how well each boy was doing. 'I've had a letter from Duncan,' said one woman. 'He's in Canada now but he's not sure for how much longer. He's thinking of moving on to Alaska.'

'Alaska!' my father cried. 'Who would have thought one of our boys would end up in Alaska!'

If I was in the shop he'd turn to me and say, 'Don't you go getting any ideas. I need you here with me.'

The customer would smile in my direction. She might say something along the lines of: 'You're lucky to have him, Nathaniel. There's nothing more important than family.' And my father would nod and say, 'You're right, there.' A knot would tighten in my stomach and I'd have to step outside, just for a moment, until the customer left.

After dinner I would take once more to the streets, wandering to the outskirts of town where I would stand and gaze across the countryside, watching the lambs graze and leap about in vivid green paddocks. Rather than taking comfort in the scene I would brood. My eyes would single out one lamb, registering its bleating search for its mother and then watching its long tail waggle as it yanked at the ewe's teat. I wouldn't know whether to envy it or feel sorry for it. In the end it was all the same – it was only a lamb.

After one such outing, I returned home to find my mother looking pale, her face strained with worry. 'It's your Grandma Nola,' said my father. 'She's in hospital.' I looked from my father to my mother, who was staring at her hands, unable to meet my eye, even though I could tell she was listening. 'Your mother,' continued my father, 'may have to go to up to Auckland.' I think my mouth must have fallen open because he quickly added, 'I know it's almost Christmas but we'll be all right, Boden. In any event, it would only be for a short while – we'll manage.'

As the evening progressed I slowly gleaned more information from my father. My grandmother had had a stroke. A neighbour had found her. She'd become concerned when she'd noticed Nola's uncollected milk at the gate. The neighbour knew something must be wrong so she had called my mother's sister, Gwen, and then she'd called my mother with news of Nola's admission to hospital. It was touch and go, she said. The doctors were doing all they could, but, really, one had to prepare for the worst. She would phone again when there was more news.

And so we sat in the kitchen, all three of us, waiting for the phone to ring. We couldn't bring ourselves to move in case we missed the call. I was used to quiet, even sombre evenings in our house – nights when we did little, talked infrequently and seemed merely to fill in the hours before bedtime, but this evening was unlike even those tired-out nights. My mother brought out a puzzle and sat hunched, staring at the jigsaw as if she found some strange meaning or consolation in its fractured image. My father, more conscious than ever of my mother's subdued mood, attempted to make conversation. Including me in his mission, he would suddenly smile, laugh quietly, nod his head and then say to me, 'Tell your mother what Mrs So-and-so said today.' At my helpless expression, he would continue, 'You know, tell your mother about the possum . . .' Why he couldn't tell her himself was beyond me, but nevertheless I found myself repeating a story about a possum that had caused a power cut in Winscombe after climbing onto the wires and being electrocuted. As I finished the story my father broke in, 'I bet that wouldn't happen in Alaska!' to which my mother's head jerked up and she stared at him blankly. My father, floundering, then passed on the news about Duncan, about his wanderings from Canada to Alaska, and then he looked at me once more and said: 'I told Boden not to go getting any ideas. We need him here, don't we, love?' My mother tried to smile but at that moment the phone rang and it was as if time – or our hearts – lurched and we sat looking at one another until my father leapt stiffly to his feet, snagging the tablecloth with his belt or his watch as he did so, sending the jigsaw puzzle tumbling to the ground, pieces scattering everywhere.

My mother and I froze on our seats, waiting for news. It seems strange now that he didn't pass the phone to my mother but I suppose the strangest thing was that she didn't stand up to take the call in the first place. We watched my father's face, saw him nod, heard him mutter, 'She's a fighter, all right,' and 'Doesn't sound too good.' Then he said my mother could be there in a day or two, for Christmas; he would arrange it. His final words, before he rang off, were, 'Chin up.'

He stood behind my mother, his hands on her shoulders as he conveyed the news to us. 'Nola's not so good,' he began. 'She's in no pain,' he hastened to add, 'but she's in a serious condition. Gwen doesn't think she'll . . .' His voice broke. Fearing that he might cry, I scrambled down from my chair and busied myself searching for jigsaw pieces, staying on the floor until long after my father blew his nose and suggested a strong cup of tea.

My mother left the next morning. We went with her as far as the station, waiting until the train left before we turned our backs on the last carriage and drove slowly home. My father remained deep in thought throughout the day. I quickly understood that he was imagining my mother's progress, mile by mile, hour by hour. 'She'll be in Timaru, now,' he remarked early on, and then later, 'She'll be aboard the ferry . . .' He fell silent and I knew why. My mother had no heart for the sea and we knew that the overnight voyage from Lyttelton to Wellington would fill her with fear. We had listened to the weather forecast and early the next morning my father tuned into the marine forecast, waking me with the news that the crossing would be calm, that my mother should sleep well. I doubted she would, but I could hear the relief in his voice. He had been worried, cursing himself for not accompanying her, for not seeing her right as he kept promising.

The following day I heard my father mutter various place names, tracing the route between Wellington and Auckland. Familiar towns like Palmerston North followed by names I had never heard before: Mangaweka, Ngaruawahia – words that sounded exotic to me and which my father pronounced slowly with one finger planted firmly on the atlas. 'She won't call until she has news of your Grandma Nola,' he said. 'She'll phone once she's settled in and rested.' And so we waited in a state of suspense, working as usual, cutting meat, wrapping parcels of mince and sausages in paper, making small-talk with customers while all the time our thoughts were elsewhere, with my mother who we hoped – though we did not know – had made it safely to her destination.

And then the unimaginable happened. Early the following morning my father woke me, shaking me roughly and urging me to wake up, wake up. Disorientated, I remembered it was Christmas Day and I thought that a call must have come through from my mother at last, but there was something about my father's startled expression that scared me. He barely waited until my feet touched the ground before he pushed me towards the kitchen. To my surprise, the radio was on. And as I listened, I realised why my father was so upset. There had been a railway disaster. At a place called Tangiwai.

Time stopped. I can remember standing in the kitchen, my eyes scanning the Christmas cards my mother had arranged on the mantle above the coal range. I fixed on a picture of a red-breasted robin, its spindly feet curled around a sprig of snow-dusted holly, and I shivered, I couldn't stop myself. For months I had seen myself as an adult, a man in employment and yet, faced with the uncertainty of my mother's whereabouts, I became once more a child in need of comfort. I tricked myself into hoping that as long as I didn't ask my father for details about

Tangiwai, or about the possibility of my mother being on that particular train, everything would be all right. If I didn't ask we would be able – somehow – to pass beyond that awful moment and Christmas Day would return, hymns would replace the news bulletins, messages of goodwill would be broadcast, children might pass our front window, wobbling on brand-new bicycles . . . the sun would shine brightly and we would go to Dudley's for dinner, just as we had arranged. I opened my mouth to speak but my father hushed me, saying, 'Hundreds are feared lost. The bridge collapsed. The country will never recover . . .' He didn't mention my mother. Perhaps he couldn't bring himself to face the fact that she might be one of those lost.

'Mother will be all right, though?' I asked. 'I mean, she's already in Auckland, isn't she? You did say "Auckland" yesterday, didn't you?' I heard you say "Auckland".' In my mind I tried to account for the hours she had been away. Although I had heard my father pronouncing one place name after another, I hadn't followed the journey paved by his words. I hadn't paid close enough attention and now I was confused. If she had caught the overnight train she had originally booked, we should have heard from her by now. She could have called last night. But then my father had said something about her not ringing until she was settled in. She would only telephone before then if something had gone wrong – if she'd missed the train or ferry. Surely, in that case, no news was good news? She would phone on Christmas Day. Today, in other words. But my heart sank. There were perhaps hundreds of people out there waiting for word of their loved ones.

And how could no news be good news?

Sensing my growing apprehension, my father instructed me to go to the phone while he hunted out my aunt's number. 'I don't know why I didn't think of this earlier,' he said, his voice wavering with emotion as he passed me the number. As I lifted the receiver I heard a voice snap, 'Line's busy!' I replaced the phone on the hook, looking at my father for further instruction. 'The line's in use,' I said, although my actions had already made the problem clear. 'Who is it?' asked my father. I shrugged, 'Mrs Liddle, I think.' He frowned. 'She'll be talking to her daughter.

Could be hours.' We hovered in the kitchen for several more minutes, shuffling around but not speaking, and then my father marched over to the phone, lifted the receiver and, in a voice I had never heard before, barked, 'Mrs Liddle? This is Nathaniel Black. We have an emergency – can you please clear the line.' I could just make out the sound of a muffled voice at the other end but I was not sure if she was protesting against my father's interruption or simply prying for details of the emergency. It seemed to me that she gave up her place on the party line reluctantly but within seconds my father had Edith, the operator, on the phone. Once more, I could only hear half the conversation but I gathered that it was not going to be easy to put the toll call through. Demand was heavy and the operator had had trouble all morning but she would try her best and she would call us back when she got through.

My father looked grim but managed a smile. 'I know Edith, she'll do her best.' And then we sat down at the table, not speaking, but listening as more news slowly filtered through.

Although both my brothers had been lost in the war, the events of this day struck me far more forcibly than the news of their deaths. The magnitude of the disaster, the fact that it had taken place on Christmas Eve and the images in my mind's eye of the train crashing off the bridge and into a black, torrential river unnerved me. I imagined my mother's complete and utter terror in the seconds between sensing something was wrong and being flung around the carriage. I hoped that she had died instantly – I couldn't bear the thought of her drowning. She was so scared of water.

I listened carefully to each bulletin. The radio announcer's controlled and measured voice was at odds with the confused scene he described. When I glanced up I saw that tears had formed in my father's eyes, and he made no move to wipe them away. And, even though I thought I was strong, I realised that crying was the right thing to do – and so we sat there, my father and me, and we wept, but we did it privately, our gaze fixed on the table top, not on each other.

After what seemed like an eternity my father spoke. At first I couldn't make out what he was saying, his voice was so quiet and hoarse. He told me about my mother – about the day they met and how he had had to work hard to win her over. She was so beautiful, he said, she could have had her pick of all the boys. She had chosen him and then he'd had to start the wooing all over again, this time working on her mother, Nola, and her father, Edward. He spoke of my mother's joy when the twins were born. Connie had wanted a large family – six or eight children, at least. She loved children. She was a magnet when it came to children – they all loved her. And then he told me about the other business – how she had tried for years and years to add to the family. He told me things I had not heard before, and I am certain he would not have said them had he not been so scared – or certain – of losing my mother that day. He talked about the pregnancies that did not make it beyond the first few months, of the weeks of recuperation that followed each miscarriage, and of my mother's strength. She never gave up. He said he would have thrown in the towel but not her – she never gave up hope.

And one day, he said, everything changed. Without the twins knowing a thing about it, my mother had persuaded my father to 'explore other, less heart-breaking options' as he put it. They were all at home one morning, eating breakfast, when a telegram arrived. The news it contained struck them like a thunderbolt, despite all their preparation. A baby was available, the telegram stated. It was one day old and it was a boy. My father looked at me, his eyes fixed on mine.

'It was you.'

We went to Dudley's for Christmas dinner, as we had planned.

My mother was not among the dead. She had been safe in Auckland at the time of the crash.

We were invited into Dudley's front room and we sat quietly, sipping from glasses of warm lemonade or beer, trying desperately hard not to ruin Christmas Day for the younger members of the family – or Hilda, who had gone to so much trouble roasting the turkey.

From time to time my father would shake his head and it was all he could do not to repeat, 'Connie could have been on that train.' On the few occasions when the words did slip out he looked ashamed. We had a fair idea how many people had lost their lives.

After dinner Hilda passed me a present. I wasn't expecting one and I felt awkward because I had not even bought her a card – though I could see that my mother had, on the family's behalf. Back then my mother bought her cards in packs of ten, all with the same image: a winter street scene, with children outside throwing snowballs. The children in the images wore mittens similar to the pair I had worn at Mount Cook. That was the only thing we had in common, those children and me.

As I unwrapped the present my hands began trembling. I couldn't stop them from shaking and the parcel slipped through my fingers and fell to the floor. Through the torn wrapper I could see a cloth-bound book. When I bent to retrieve it I felt tired, as if the act of lifting the small volume required more strength than I could muster. I had the impression that a hand had reached up through the floor and grabbed hold of me, dragging me back down.

The book had a blue cover and navy-blue lettering. It was a book of English verse. The dust jacket was missing. When I opened it I saw Hilda's name written in black ink. Her writing was small, neat – and there was a date: 1932. I wondered how she had come across the book: had it been a gift or had she bought it herself? I had never seen Hilda with a book in her hand. At any other time I might have asked her – if only to make conversation – but all I said was, 'Thank you, Hilda.' She smiled and I turned to Dudley and thanked him too.

Then I opened the book at random and stared at the page.

My father never again raised the subject of my adoption. Everything that could have been said, had been as we sat waiting that Christmas morning for news of my mother. I'm not sure if my mother ever learned of that conversation. I imagine she probably did.

My father could tell me very little. I was born in Christchurch – not, as I had always assumed, Fairlie. My real mother was a schoolgirl. She did not hold me when I was born. I was not hers. During the first moments of my life I belonged to no one. Hearing that, I shared the sharp pain of my mother's humiliation.

My father told me everything he knew. It wasn't much.

In the days that followed I spent long periods by myself, walking the back paddocks and streets, remaining outside until long after nightfall. The evenings were often warm and I seldom had the streets to myself. As I passed neighbouring houses I would be greeted by people I knew. They would call out to me and ask if I had had news from my mother. How was she getting on in Auckland? Was my grandmother any better? Some would add, 'I expect you're missing her!' and others would say, 'I bet you and Nathaniel are getting up to all sorts of tricks!' It made no difference to me what they said. I just smiled and promised to pass on their regards, their best wishes, next time I spoke to Connie.

It was only when news got around that my grandmother had died and that my mother was staying on to help sort her belongings and sell the house that the neighbours' behaviour changed. From then on my father and I would dine on bacon and egg pies brought around to the house by his regular customers. He invited each visitor to come in but they declined, preferring to linger on the doorstep, exchanging a few words about the weather, my grandmother's advanced years and so on before adding, 'At least it won't be long now before Connie's back.' They might turn to me and add, 'You'll be glad when your mother gets home, won't you?'

Until that summer I had never noticed how often the word 'mother' entered our conversations.

I took to carrying a small mirror around in my pocket. Whenever I was alone, when I was sure no one was looking, I would get it out and stare at my reflection. I noticed that I was no longer the spitting image of my father. Where once I had his eyes, his nose, even his smile, I could no longer take such things for granted. My ginger hair, which up until that point had never held my attention, took on a new meaning. I didn't know anyone else with ginger hair.

I found a photograph taken of me at my christening. I still have it. I am dressed in a long gown and propped on my mother's knee, my tiny fist clamped around her finger. She is smiling for the camera and I am staring pop-eyed at something. I imagine my father was waving something to catch my attention. I am neither smiling nor crying.

There is another photograph, taken on the same day, of my twin brothers and me. They are dressed in their Sunday best and their hair is sleek with pomade, side parted and neatly combed. They were teenagers when I was born and yet this age difference had never struck me as out of the ordinary before. They were always strangers as far as I was concerned. What, I wondered, had they made of me?

Some thoughts attacked my head with a violence I found unbearable, while others crept up behind me slowly – and were no less painful for that.

I remember the day I was helping Dudley repair the wire on his hen-house when it dawned on me that he must have known all along. He had lived across the road from my parents for more than twenty-five years; he knew my father from school. There had been no outward sign that my mother was expecting another child – and yet one day, out of the blue, I had appeared. Why hadn't Dudley told me?

My heart thudded in my chest as I passed Dudley a roll of chicken wire. A lump tightened in the back of my throat and I realised I had to ask him. I wanted to hear him tell me the truth. Even though it was a hot day my hands felt cold and when I opened my mouth to speak I had the sensation that my tongue had frozen to the roof of my mouth. I cleared my throat but then I lost my nerve and asked which of all the hens was his best layer. He answered without looking at me and I remember wishing the rooster – which had been crowing all morning – would just be quiet for a minute. Even Bruce had stopped barking, tired out from the effort of matching the bird, bark for crow. The dog was now slumped in the shadow of the wheelbarrow, too exhausted to so much as raise his head at the sound of each hammer blow against the frame of the cage.

'I've always kept hens,' said Dudley. 'You may well laugh but they're good company.' He laughed himself and then he turned to face me and the smile slipped from his face.

'What is it?' he said. 'Are you feeling poorly?'

My heart balled up in the back of my throat. The back of my neck prickled and I wiped my hands down the front of my trousers. My fingers were still cold.

'Nathaniel and Connie aren't my real parents.'

I swallowed and my heart wedged in my sternum, a hard cricket-ball lump.

For a fraction of a second Dudley's eyes opened wide with surprise. And then they narrowed and he stood very still, his hammer dangling loosely from his hand as he surveyed a spot on the ground by his feet. He was so still, so quiet, that the emptiness around him caught me off

73

guard and, with tears beginning to pool in my eyes, I was forced to repeat myself. As I reached the word 'real' he stopped me. I couldn't read his expression: his eyes appeared full of compassion and yet his mouth was tight; he was biting his lip. I had the terrible sensation that anything could happen – but I had no idea what would.

'That's not how I see it,' he replied slowly.

He shook his head, and when he looked at me again I saw an expression of dismay on his face.

'You mustn't think that,' he murmured.

He reached into his pocket and brought out a large crumpled handkerchief which he passed to me. He watched as I dabbed the corner of my eyes, and when I went to give it back he said, 'Keep it,' and turned back to his work.

I decided not to think about who I was any more.

My mother returned from Auckland: a paler, quieter version of her former self. My father and I met her at the station and my father was so pleased to see her that he hugged her and apologised for not going with her. 'You've been through such an ordeal,' he said. Later, as we drove towards home, he said, 'We thought we'd lost you.'

The house had been cleaned in preparation for my mother's return. My father had spent the previous evening starching and ironing the sheets for their bed and then, so as not to crumple them, he had slept the night under a blanket on the couch. He wanted everything to be 'just right'. I had done my best to help but whenever I finished a task my father had come along and redone it. Even plumping the cushions became a matter of contention. I placed all four cushions along the length of the couch – their corners pointing skywards so they looked liked diamonds – but my father had other ideas, rearranging them two at either end of the couch. Not satisfied, he moved them again and then he caught my eye and said, 'What does it matter?' and left the room to attend to dinner. He was nervous. He couldn't stop fidgeting.

In the end I had retreated to the back doorstep, and sat flicking through the book of poetry Hilda had given me, thinking about the second-hand motorbike I had seen for sale at Ray's yard. I had managed to save almost two-thirds of the asking price and Ray had given me his word that he would let me know if anyone else showed any interest. Deep down I doubted that anyone would. I believed the bike was probably overpriced but I was too timid to say anything to Ray. I had been scared of him since childhood, when I had been forced to fetch him to help start Dudley's truck, and I confess I was still intimidated – even though he was both frailer and shorter than me. He hadn't mellowed. His tongue could still lash out and he had little time for boys who knew nothing about engines.

Home at last, my mother looked around, said how lovely everything was, then sat down at the table and removed her hat and gloves. My father fussed in the kitchen making a cup of tea. In a quiet voice she asked how I was, and, hearing my reply – that I was good – she reached into her handbag and brought out a pale blue square envelope made from thick cartridge paper. She placed it on the table. I could see that it had my name on it – in her handwriting. For a full minute I stared at the envelope, reading each word separately: Boden Nathaniel Black. It was my name and yet I felt no connection to it. Perhaps that's why I felt no curiosity about the envelope's contents.

My mother sipped her tea and then, glancing at the envelope – as if she, too, had only just noticed it, said, 'Your Aunt Gwen and I have sold your grandmother's house.' She hesitated, as if she had lost her train of thought, and began again. 'All the grandchildren . . .' Her voice trailed away and once more she appeared lost. 'It's a little gift – a share. You've all got equal amounts.' She slid the envelope across the table and I reached out and drew it towards me. I didn't open it immediately. I didn't want to appear too overly eager, or worse – greedy. But something else held me back. I didn't feel entitled to it. I was deterred by the name.

I might have left the envelope untouched had not my father said, 'Go on, Boden. Have a look.'

From my pocket I took out my penknife, slipping it carefully into the envelope and cutting it open. I could see the folded notes inside and my immediate thought was that now I would be able to buy the old Matchless. But I didn't take the notes out. I looked at them and thanked my mother. Despite my father urging me to count the money, I left the envelope on the table and excused myself, ducking through the back door, where I hovered, listening and heard my father ask how much it was. My mother responded, 'Eighty pounds.'

When I returned for dinner I spotted the envelope propped up on the mantelpiece and, days later, when I still hadn't moved it, I discovered it on top of my chest of drawers, tucked away behind my binoculars. Only then, in the privacy of my room, did I allow myself to finger the notes, counting them once before returning them somewhat guiltily to their place.

Dudley accompanied me to Ray's when the time came to purchase the motorbike. I believe he had picked up on my nerves. Looking back, I can see that buying that bike was a defining moment in my life. More than being old enough to be served in a bar, old enough to be conscripted or to vote, it was that first, violent kickback as I started the engine, followed by a wobbly drive down the main street, that symbolised my manhood.

As soon as I had some experience and confidence with the bike I decided to make an overnight journey. It would be the first time I had travelled anywhere by myself and I was both excited and apprehensive. Knowing that my mother would be concerned, I decided to go to Christchurch. I had never biked further than Geraldine, but I thought the roads separating Fairlie from the city would be safer than those leading inland. I pointed this out to my mother, stressing that I would be travelling for the most part on a sealed surface. I also promised not to ride at night. After some hesitation she reluctantly agreed.

It was spring, and although the peaks around Fairlie were still laden with snow, there were signs of new growth on the trees and in the paddocks as I sped by. I had prepared for the cold but I found it hard to keep warm. Passing through Geraldine I bought a newspaper, which I stuffed down the front of my jacket for extra insulation. Despite my discomfort I was happy as I skirted around the mountains towards Mayfield before heading out to the coast. I stopped from time to time, simply to take in the view of the foothills and to breathe deeply.

It was only when I reached the main highway that a sense of urgency overtook me. I recall crossing the Rakaia bridge – Dudley had told me it was the longest in the southern hemisphere – and glancing down at the dirty grey floodwaters swirling below and feeling horrified by the river's power and immensity. It had a threatening quality, related in no small part to the number of large branches tumbling by. The water moved with such speed that I felt dizzy and had to concentrate with all my might on reaching the bridge's end. Safe on the other side, I pulled over and collected my thoughts before continuing. The road was now straight and smooth, the paddocks falling behind me as I passed through Dunsandel and caught my first glimpse of the Port Hills before eventually reaching Burnham, followed by the outskirts of Christchurch – and the endless suburbs leading into the city centre. It was only as I circumnavigated Hagley Park that it dawned on me that I had no idea what I would do now that I had reached my destination.

I left my bike near the old university college and made my way down Worcester Street towards the Cathedral. Standing at the edge of the Square, watching all the goings-on of the big city, I found myself searching the faces of the women passing by. The oldest and youngest women made little impression on me but I was drawn to those whom I estimated were fifteen to twenty years older than myself. I was barely conscious of what I was doing.

Once, I spotted a woman with my ginger hair colouring and I stood watching as she walked towards me. As she drew closer I noticed that her eyes were bright blue, like mine. She must have noticed me staring because she frowned and looked hard in my direction, then hurried past, glancing back over her shoulder as she walked away. My gaze lingered on the retreating figure, watching the way she walked, her erect head and very straight back. I kept my eyes on her until she became lost in the crowd and I could see her no more. I had no idea who she was, and I never saw her again. To my surprise, I suddenly felt very much alone and I wished I was at home.

I must have made a rather forlorn sight because, every now and then, a stranger would meet my gaze and smile sympathetically. Yet the faces of all these people were quickly forgotten. By the time I reached Cashel Street I felt terribly conspicuous and was relieved to duck into Ballantynes department store, where I was able to check my reflection in the men's cloakroom mirror before sitting down to a cup of tea in the tearooms. I noticed as I sipped from my cup that I was the only male in the establishment, and while this did not appear to arouse any feelings of hostility or suspicion on my fellow diners' faces, I chose not to linger over a third cup but hastened outside and headed for Whitcombe and Tombs.

Inside the bookshop I stood for a moment, gaining my bearings. I browsed happily for several minutes before a woman's voice interrupted my reading with the question, 'May I help you?' I felt caught out and to disguise my guilt I said I would like to buy the book – if that was all right? My reply amused the young shop assistant but, being careful not to offend, she took the volume from me and glanced at its cover, giving me a slightly puzzled look as she read its title aloud: 'A Book Of New Zealand Verse.' Her voice was soft and yet confident somehow, as if talking to strangers was something she took for granted as part of her profession. She looked at me again and asked, 'Is it a gift?' She smiled and I had the sensation she was teasing me, though I couldn't understand why. 'It's for me,' I said, immediately regretting my remark. None of my friends would be caught dead reading poetry and for an instant I worried that my admission might colour the girl's impression of me. I thought she might find me slightly effeminate.

'Do you read much poetry?' she said, casually flicking through the book. In different circumstances I might have admitted that I liked poetry but had never encountered New Zealand poetry before. I had read various British poets – could even recite some of their work by heart – but I could not name a single New Zealand poet. I was surprised to discover that a book of New Zealand verse even existed. With these thoughts in the back of my mind I shifted uneasily, but before I had time to respond to her question she all but demanded, 'Curnow or Glover? What do you think?' Given that I had never heard of either of them I was about to shake my head in a non-committal sort of way when I noticed that the book in my hands had the name 'Allen Curnow' on its cover.

Taking this to be a good sign I replied, 'Curnow' in a voice I hoped she would find both convincing and authoritative. She scrunched up her nose. I wasn't sure what to make of her. She was not much older than me, two or three years at the most, and yet she struck me as so much more precocious than any other girl I had met. 'You don't strike me as the poetry type,' she suddenly said. As the words left her mouth she blushed a deep crimson and, for the first time since arriving in Christchurch, I felt I had the upper hand. Maintaining a dignified silence, I followed her to the counter.

As I paid for the book she smiled at me and told me in a less bossy tone than before that she sometimes attended a poetry study group. Perhaps I looked confused because she added, 'We have readings and discussions, that sort of thing. You should come along . . .' Her voice trailed away and her cheeks reddened again. 'I mean,' she stammered, 'everyone's welcome.' She quickly mumbled the details of the date and venue and then added, 'My father goes with me. It's not like I just . . .' She lowered her gaze and I felt sorry for causing her such discomfort. In an attempt to make amends I thanked her for all her help and for the invitation and said, as casually as I could, that I might see her one day. Even as I uttered the words I knew I wouldn't. I had already forgotten the name of the venue and I didn't dare ask her to repeat it. I wonder, now, if she detected the false tone in my voice because when she met my gaze her expression had hardened. She more or less shrugged and walked away to serve another customer without waiting for me to gather my bag and leave.

I returned to Cashel Street, walking slowly in the direction of the Bridge of Remembrance, my thoughts drifting, focused one minute on what subject New Zealand poets might write about and the next on try-ing to recapture the face of the shop-girl I had spoken to. I passed several shops before coming to a standstill in front of a sporting goods store. I stood for several minutes gazing at the window display: a somewhat contrived camping scene complete with tent, sleeping bag, a billy and a campfire consisting of sticks arranged around a crumpled sheet of red cellophane. Leaves had been scattered around the ground for added effect and towards the corner was a pair of boots, laces undone, with one boot lying on its side as if it were about to be dragged away by a rat or some other creature. The only thing missing from the scene was a man and, aware that I had nowhere to sleep that night, I half contemplated offering my services. Having been reminded of my lack of accommodation I felt a little apprehensive, wondering where on earth I would go once darkness fell.

As I stood gazing at the window my eye was caught by several notices on a board beside the shop's entrance. They were mostly handwritten and offering various goods for sale, but one printed leaflet stood out from the rest. It was an announcement of a slide lecture taking place that night at the Overseas League. 'Mrs. D. Urquhart, member of the first all-woman party to climb Mount Cook, will address the audience and speak about her recent capers and successes. Refreshments served. All welcome.' I re-read the notice several times before turning back to the street and continuing down the road, pausing once I was on the bridge to look over the side for trout or eels.

I spent the rest of the afternoon wandering around the Botanic Gardens, admiring the daffodil display and then visiting the museum, where I spent an entire hour gazing at the skeleton of a giant blue whale. As evening fell and the light faded, the city appeared to grow in size and I was aware of the smell of car and truck fumes as well as the constant sound of trams and buses hurtling by, their interiors lit up and crammed to overflowing with passengers. I watched people gather in front of brightly lit cinemas but felt no inclination to join them. Seeing so many people, all talking happily to one another, merely heightened my sense of isolation. I knew no one.

It was in this anxious state of mind that I found myself outside the entrance to the Overseas League. I am sure that deep down, somewhere in my subconscious, I had planned to attend the event but nevertheless I was surprised to find myself joining the thin stream of people entering the rooms. I chose a chair to one side of the hall, hoping to go unnoticed.

As more and more people filtered in I had the impression that everyone knew everyone else. Small clusters formed; lean men in tweed jackets talked and laughed or called out as new arrivals sidled in. From where I

80

sat I could hear two men with refined British accents making plans for a trip into the hills. Each time they spoke, wafts of smoke from a pipe would envelop me and the smell made me feel as if I had been caught in a gentlemen's club.

Eventually, after several announcements and a formal introduction, the evening's programme got under way. A woman took to the stage and, in very modest tones, began to describe her party's ascent of Mount Cook. I had only seen the mountain from a distance but I was amazed that a group of three women would undertake such a challenge without back-up from professional guides or at least one strong man. My own mother, I knew, would no more climb a mountain than she would swim to Australia and yet, standing before me in a plain brown twinset was a woman who had achieved this impossible feat. My own trip to Christchurch paled by comparison and I felt a little sheepish for thinking of my journey as an adventure.

My head swimming with details of the woman's climb, I suddenly became aware of a face in the audience — the face of a man who smiled at me and raised his hand in a slight wave before turning back to face the stage. It took me a moment to recognise him, but it was my school-mate from Fairlie, Athol, whom I knew from our production of *Macbeth*. He was never a close friend but I was happy to see him there. He had always been a rather domineering boy — not a bully but somewhat opinionated and, I'm afraid to say, arrogant.

Question time followed the lecture. One of the men with the British accent asked Mrs Urquhart — Doreen — if she had plans to attempt any other major peaks. Mount Everest, perhaps? Once the laughter died down another man in the audience spoke up, saying that very little was known about the effects of high altitude on a lady's body but that the general opinion was that it could be quite detrimental to a woman's health, particularly — he coughed — her reproductive health. A discussion followed, becoming quite heated as some people appeared to take offence at the speaker's remark. Mrs Urquhart did not enter into the discussion. It seemed that, having given her lecture, she was no longer expected to contribute. Still, I enjoyed her talk immensely. I was impressed by

81

her manner and I made sure to tell her so when I spoke to her briefly at the refreshments table, where she stood holding a plate of biscuits for everyone to help themselves.

'Goodness me, I didn't expect to see you here.' At the sound of Athol's voice I started. Gone was the roughness that I remembered so well and in its place was a confident, if not pompous, vaguely British accent. To the best of my knowledge Athol had only ever lived in Fairlie and, more recently, Christchurch – where he was a student at the university college. Given that his parents had both grown up in Canterbury I couldn't make sense of his newly clipped tones. In truth, I felt embarrassed for him.

'So tell me,' he continued, 'what brings you here?' Before I could reply he led me towards a group of men not many years older than myself, saying, 'This is Boden – from Fairlie.' Introductions made, Athol turned his attention to the group and entered their conversation, swapping tales of recent climbing and tramping trips, while I stood awkwardly to one side. From time to time one of the group would glance my way and I would nod or smile, but I had little or no idea where any of the places they mentioned were. At one point, during a lull in the conversation, I brought the subject back to Mrs Urquhart's talk and commented on her wonderful adventure. To my surprise, my remark appeared to fall on deaf ears and an uncomfortable silence followed. Disconcerted, and wishing to make amends, I asked if any of my new acquaintances had climbed Mount Cook, and, if so, what was it like? If anything the silence deepened and one or two of the men wandered away to refill their cups from the huge teapot on the trestle table.

Somewhat abruptly, I thought, Athol changed the topic completely, announcing, 'Oh, by the way, it's all on for the work party this summer.' I gathered that plans were under way to construct an alpine hut high above a glacier on the flank of Mount Cook. Most of the building supplies were to be air-dropped, and men were needed to prepare the site and build the shelter. Athol, it seemed, was on the building committee and he was keen to enlist volunteers for the jaunt.

As they talked, I began to form a visual picture of the location. I imagined the summit of Mount Cook towering high above a pristine snow slope. A broad glacier, such as those I had seen during my brief holiday to the Hermitage, flowed gently down, its dazzling blue-white surface broken at regular intervals by large, deep blue crevasses. I imagined a small rocky outcrop, a patch of tussock or snowgrass and a small, perfect shelter standing proud, holding its own against so much nature.

Deep down, I felt envious. My own solo trip to Christchurch – my grand adventure – was nothing to what these men were planning. I felt diminished in their presence and, perhaps to compensate, I thought about extending my trip – driving through the night and doing a quick tour of the North Island before returning home to take up my butcher's apron once more. I gradually became aware that several of the men were looking at me and I realised they were waiting for me to respond to some question I had not heard. Noticing my sheepish expression one of the group, Douglas, said, 'I'm not what you'd call a handyman myself.' I had the feeling this was meant to be a clue, but, completely lost, I looked at Athol who added, 'Oh, Boden here is very handy with a hammer. He spent his youth running around training our local carpenter, passing him nails, filling his thermos and suchlike. There's nothing Boden doesn't know about a bit of four-by-two.'

I was reminded of why I had never warmed to Athol. He was older than me so I'd never had that much to do with him but I had bumped into him from time to time, mostly with Ted, and each time I had been put off by his overbearing nature. 'He's as strong as they come,' continued Athol, oblivious to my annoyance. It was as if he were describing a prime cattle beast; for one awkward moment I feared he might prod me in the ribs to prove his point. 'We could get him to carry all the heavy stuff. He'd be good at that.' The others laughed uncomfortably and, not wishing to make a scene, I joined in. I noticed that Douglas smiled at me and rolled his eyes slightly towards the ceiling. That one small gesture made all the difference. I pushed my uncharitable thoughts about Athol to the back of my mind. He was all right in his own way. 'I'll put your name down then, shall I?' asked Athol. I started. I hadn't seen this coming and was unable to do much more than stammer, 'I'll have to check with my father.'

'Oh, just tell him you're going to be away for a fortnight – three weeks at the most. It's over summer anyway. He can talk to me if he needs to know more.'

I was put out by Athol's manner, but at the same time I was secretly thrilled to have been asked. I wasn't even a mountaineer and yet it suddenly seemed possible that I might do something exciting, something I could not have foreseen. Despite myself I must have beamed because Athol's expression suddenly softened. In a quieter voice, he said, 'I'll take care of everything, get you some gear. Don't let us down.' And, just like that, it was settled.

It didn't occur to me until after I had said goodnight to the group and wandered back to my bike that I should have asked if I could spend the night on the couch at Athol's lodgings. I was momentarily annoyed with myself but managed to see the bright side. After all, sleeping beneath the stars would be good practice and I needed to toughen up before the summer.

I had a sensation of the world opening up with the promise of a grand adventure as I rode the length of Colombo Street and up through the suburb of Cashmere to the Summit Road, which ran the length of the Port Hills overlooking the city. I pulled off the road and dragged my bag from my bike, walking a short way towards a low rise. I located a rocky outcrop that I hoped would provide shelter from the breeze and the dew.

From my resting place I looked down on the city and allowed my eyes to wander over its countless lighted streets, following trails towards the outer suburbs and then the complete blackness beyond. To my right, a huge orange moon rose above the ocean, hanging in the still air. It was larger than any moon I had seen before and I wished there had been some way to capture the image so I could show it to my parents who, like me, had most likely only ever witnessed an inland, milk-silver moon.

My mind was racing through the events of the day. I recalled the way the girl who sold me the book of verse had blushed, the magnificent blue whale skeleton, my meeting with Athol. I found it impossible to settle down so I reached for my torch and took out my new book. For a moment or two I simply stared at its bright yellow cover, enjoying a slight buzz of excitement as I took in its unadorned title, reading aloud the words 'A Book of New Zealand Verse' simply for the pleasure of their sound. Then I flicked through its brand-new pages, taking in its smell and the furriness of its paper before looking at, rather than reading, its lengthy introduction. I recalled the shop assistant's question, 'Curnow or Glover?' and, deciding to try my hand at answering her, I turned to Curnow's work, scanning one or two poems impatiently before flicking through the pages to those of the other man, Denis Glover. Despite having been taught the fundamentals of poetry appreciation by various teachers, I felt ambivalent towards both poets' work. On my first reading I was far more aware of what was absent from their poems than what was in them. In place of the colossal monument to Shelley's Ozymandias was Curnow's run-down homestead, located not in an antique land but beneath a row of blue gums. The might of Tennyson's majestic eagle, surveying all that was below, had its New Zealand counterpart in a flock of Glover's magpies. Of course I was comparing poems from one century against those of another, but even so I was taken aback by the ordinariness of what I read. I turned to 'Sings Harry', but each time I came to the chorus I couldn't help but visualise a rather simple man from my own town, who used to wander the streets with an old flea-bitten dog in tow, cursing all the cars on the road, which he believed to have been sent by Satan. It wasn't a fair comparison and I decided that once it was daylight I would spend more time reading, studying both Curnow and Glover's work, so that I could at least say I had given them a fair go.

Before putting the book down I flicked through its pages once more, starting from the back and working my way forward. A title caught my eye. I propped my torch between my knees, and slowly scanned the page. The poem was written by a woman, Ursula Bethell. Even more surprising was the title of the poem: 'By Burkes Pass'. That anyone had thought to write a poem about a place I knew so well astounded me. Despite having just read about homesteads and magpies I felt a special kind of pride to discover that my neck of the woods was thought worthy of a published poem. I had read about all sorts of exotic locations – London, Italy, Xanadu – but I can honestly say that none of those places brought me as much pleasure as the words 'By Burkes Pass'.

It was as if Ursula Bethell's poem had been written either for me or about me . . . or by someone who was like me. That was it: it was written by someone who *could have been me*. In my eagerness to consume the poem I could barely follow the words. I wanted them to describe that magnificent view I had first spotted all those years before when, in Dudley's company, I had seen the Mackenzie Basin for the first time. I wanted this poem to say all those things that I was incapable of saying: I hoped that this woman, Ursula Bethell, would put into words my innermost thoughts and feelings.

I read the first line, followed by the entire first and second stanza, and then I put my torch down and simply stared at the night-shadowed form of the book as I tried to reconcile my image of the Mackenzie Basin with hers. I couldn't do it. Fragments, the occasional phrase I recognised, but on those first few readings I found it impossible to grasp the intent or the tone of the work. I felt a surge of panic rise up from a place deep within me. How could I not see what the writer was getting at when the place she was writing about was so familiar, such a part of me? It was as if I had been given a doctor's note describing the intricacies of some disease within my own body but which I could not fully grasp because of the words used.

I re-read each stanza, concentrating on every word and phrase individually. Why had she written '. . . the corn-stacks aureate'? What did 'aureate' even mean? I re-read the line and tried to look at it as if from a distance, as if looking up at the sky and trying to make sense of all the stars. Why had the poet used 'aureate' and not a more common word? There ought to be a reason why someone had chosen such a word. Perhaps the answer lay in the poem itself. I picked out more and more words – words that seemed not to belong to my Burkes Pass. I read, 'Soft mien assumes of kindly ministrant' and 'Suspend her folding arras'? Why those words? I went back to the first line and read it through. The poem's narrative made sense to me but the tone put me in mind of a sermon. It struck me as religious. 'Nature, earth's angel, man's antagonist . . .' What's more, I couldn't agree with its sentiment. What reason did the poet have for presenting nature that way? And not just any old nature but in a specific location, Burkes Pass – the place that had filled me with joy and made me feel almost giddy with pleasure. Surely the poet had missed the point?

I looked up from my book and took in my close surroundings. I could see no further than the faint glow of my torch's beam. All around me were rocks and tussocks. My back resting against a boulder, I was aware of the dusty, mossy smell of its lichen which mingled in the night air with a fresher, grassy smell, that of the new spring growth popping up between the clumps of tussock. Not far away, but out of sight, I could make out the sound of an animal grazing. It moved quietly but I could hear the tearing sound as its teeth pulled on the grass. It was a peaceful sound and I found it comforting.

The ground beneath me was cold and hard and when I put my hand down, I was aware of dew forming on the blades of grass. I knew then that I might be in for an uncomfortable night, but I was happy. This outcrop was a source of richness and I had none of the poet's sense of being dominated by the land. I couldn't agree with her.

In one final effort I turned back to the poem and read it through again, start to finish. Really, I just wanted to prove to myself that she had got it all wrong. But, gradually, little by little, I was drawn into the work. Words that had filled me with annoyance now aroused my curiosity. I noticed a pattern, a rhythm I had overlooked before. There was a rhyme but it was subtle, unlike my own attempts at writing poetry. As I read, I asked questions: Why did she say that, why did she use that word? Slowly I picked over the words, sounding them out in my head, hearing them on my lips and then seeing them on the page, wondering why the poem looked the way it did, why the words were arranged that way and not like the words on the earlier pages. Before long I felt myself drawn to the writer's craft rather than the poem itself. I felt myself enter into the poem. I relaxed and it opened up before me.

And I knew, at that exact moment, that I wanted to be a poet too.

the hut builder

More tired than I had ever felt in all my life, I rested my weight on my ice-axe and stared in disbelief at the sight before me – the entrance to a cave dug into the snow.

I had left the Hermitage late the previous afternoon in the company of two others, Douglas and a man I had not met before, Len, following a route up the Hooker Valley for three hours before stopping for the night at a small tramping hut perched on the edge of the moraine. Now, after a full day of being roped together, slowly negotiating our way over glaciers, we had reached our destination: a location on the western buttress of Mount Cook, where we were to erect the new hut.

Our camp – or rather cave – which Athol and several other members of the building party had created before my arrival, was in a steep snow bank a short distance from the building site. The location was glorious. Perched on a rocky platform at 8000 feet, the new hut would be surrounded by towering peaks, the names of some – Nazomi, Dampier – I had only just learnt, while others – Cook, Footstool, Hicks, Sefton – had entered into my consciousness a decade earlier. Yet it was not the view of the mountains that held my attention at that moment but the snow cave, which had been built to accommodate our building team over the following days and weeks.

Tentatively I entered the cave and found myself in a short tunnel, a kind of vestibule built to hold supplies and equipment. Beyond this icy cloakroom the cave opened out in a living area large enough to sleep eight men on a platform cut into one wall of the shelter. Against the opposite wall, separated from the sleeping platform by a narrow space, was a broad shelf on top of which stoves and kitchen equipment had been neatly arranged and stacked. If I hadn't been so dazed by the fact that I was standing underground, in an ice shelter, I might have described the scene before me as homely.

As I stood, glancing about for signs of structural weakness in our dwelling, I noticed that the cave was not as cold as I had expected. Though steam was rising off my sweat-soaked parka, the air temperature was above freezing – certainly warmer than my father's coolstore, my closest point of reference. If the temperature took me by surprise, so did the quiet within the cave. Sheltered from the breeze that had been our constant companion throughout the day, the domed cave interior both absorbed and distorted sound. I am not certain if the others found it so – or whether it was just that I was new to this – but the voices of my companions struck me as other-worldly, an impression I could not shake off for several days.

It was summer, February 1955; the days were long. Inside the cave it was easy to feel disconnected from my surroundings – cut off from the outside world, removed from both sunlight and weather. Time itself seemed all but redundant in this new setting.

My general unease at being inside the cave reached its height on my second or third day in camp. A storm blew up, forcing us all to remain inside. This was a disappointing interruption to our work, which had been progressing smoothly. Athol and some others had finished off work begun the previous season to create a level building site for the new eight-bunk hut. Retaining walls had been erected and the site was ready for the foundations. Athol had arranged for an air-drop of building supplies: mostly pre-cut timber and iron as well as bundles of wire, wire-netting, malthoid and nails. There would also be kapok mattresses, pots, pans, several Primuses, fuel and food.

However, a combination of strong winds and low cloud meant that the aeroplane, a Bristol Freighter, could not fly. We were also prevented from working on the site by the blizzard-like conditions.

All eight of us were confined to the cave, where we lay in our sleeping bags, reading and dozing, drinking tea and occasionally summoning up the energy to sustain a few minutes' idle conversation about the weather or our favourite food. Not having experienced a mountain storm before, I was perturbed when the entrance to our cave began to fill in with spindrift, trapping us inside. I was not claustrophobic by nature but I was apprehensive as I imagined being buried alive: a slow death by suffocation. I wondered if my body would ever be recovered or if it would remain buried under tons of snow, entombed and frozen like those of Captain Scott and his team of heroic explorers.

No one else in the group appeared the slightest bit bothered. After a few jokes about the drawbacks of an outside toilet, no one showed any interest in getting out of their sleeping bag to tackle the snow-blocked tunnel.

Then Wim, a Belgian, and Maurice, a hospital porter, took it upon themselves to propose a game of bridge. Their suggestion was eagerly accepted by Athol and his Christchurch acquaintance Hugh, a toolmaker. They huddled together at one end of the platform, leaving me, Douglas, Len, a printer, and the older man, Walter, at the other.

While my closest companions read, I couldn't help but hear the animated conversation taking place among the bridge players. For some reason their joviality only added to my misery. I began to recall stories about canaries down mineshafts and was gripped by a rising sense of panic, imagining that if we weren't to suffocate through lack of oxygen we would fall prey to poisonous fumes from our poorly primed stoves. When after another hour or so Douglas glanced up from his book and suggested yet another brew, I could not contain myself. I snapped that we had only just finished the last cup! I could tell that Douglas was bemused by my tone of voice – I did sound somewhat shrill. I mumbled that we couldn't very well keep on drinking when there was nowhere to empty our bladders. This last remark provoked a bit of reaction and for one giddy instant I thought someone might suggest clearing the entrance. But no. After a short discussion an empty water bucket was christened 'The Pee Pot'. Problem solved, the Primus was once more lit for a fresh pot of tea.

At one point the kerosene suddenly flared, filling the air with black smoke. Wim gave a low chuckle and began to reminisce about a night he had spent in a back-country hut with three deer-cullers. 'They were all so frightfully uncouth,' he began, his remarkable English delivered through a thick accent. 'I could not abide their foul ways.' Smiling to himself – either from the memory of the trip or from the pleasure of selecting words from his eccentric repertoire – he described how one by one, his companions lying on the top bunks had become drowsy, and it had been left to him to jump up from his bottom bunk and drag them outside. 'Those unfortunate, disgusting creatures were dying from toxic fumes,' he chortled, 'but I rescued them.' He looked around, to make sure we were listening, before concluding darkly, 'Imagine how different things might have been had I been asleep.' He roared with laughter and slapped down a card on the cleared space in front of him, wiping the tears from his eyes as he muttered, 'Life is a fragile beast.'

Hearing his story I abandoned all hope of getting out alive.

The only person not to take part in the increasingly bizarre conversations of the past half-hour was the older bushman, Walter. In fact, I had not heard him utter more than one or two words the entire time we had been trapped in the cave, and I wondered if he was even listening to the banter. It was quite likely he had fallen asleep – through lack of activity or plain boredom.

I could not place Walter. He appeared to have no connection to the other members of the group so I had assumed that his inclusion in the working party was because of his experience as a builder. I guessed him to be in his late forties or fifties – a good ten to fifteen years older than Maurice or Wim, the next oldest in the group. Walter lived on the West Coast, somewhere in the vicinity of Franz Josef from what I could gather. I had gleaned by eavesdropping that he had set out from home alone, crossing over the Southern Alps at the Copland Pass before dropping down the Hooker Valley to the Hermitage. He then travelled back up the glacier, reaching our camp four and a half days after first leaving home. His pack contained not only his clothing and sleeping gear but also his tool belt and favourite hammer. 'I attempted to lift his pack,' I had heard Wim remark earlier, 'but it was completely impossible. Only a god with supernatural strength could lift such a weight. It is beyond the strength of mere mortals.'

I hadn't really paid much attention to Wim's comment, assuming he was exaggerating. Walter was smallish – no more than five foot eight – and wiry. By comparison Wim was all of six foot three and as strong as an ox. Wim's insistence that Walter was 'the strongest man to have walked this earth' was outlandish. There was another thing about Walter's appearance. Unlike the rest of us, he kept the top button of his shirt securely fastened in the manner of a schoolboy. He looked not so much prissy as 'done up'. He didn't roll up his shirt sleeves when he worked and I never saw him without his jersey, the collar of his shirt clearly visible above its crew neck. While the rest of us removed most of our clothing before climbing into our sleeping bags, Walter merely took off his trousers and loosened his top shirt button. When asked about this, he had responded that he felt the cold, then added, 'I mean I don't like cold drafts against my skin.'

In my short time on site I had discovered that he was also fastidiously clean. I had caught sight of him crouched down behind a low rocky knoll scrubbing at his naked body with snow. He was shy to the point of being furtive and when he glanced up and saw me he grabbed his longjohns with such haste that he lost his balance and stumbled to his knees. I had not been spying on him but I felt ashamed of myself for having witnessed his awkward display. The next day I caught sight of him again, a good way off from camp – presumably on his way to some more remote spot where he could scrub himself down in peace.

I think Walter's fastidiousness created some kind of barrier between him and the other members of the team. He was not unfriendly but he rarely took part in general conversation. Any remarks he did make were

95

limited to matters relating to the hut. In the evenings he kept to himself, reading when he wasn't working. He was shy, but, it was more than that. He was awkward. He struck me as a solitary man.

However, his skill as a hut builder was unquestionable. He had worked on several shelters in the Mount Cook area over the past few years, helping to rebuild the Malte Brun hut, among others. And he was an experienced bushman and mountaineer – he had taken part in the high-altitude mountain rescue of a woman called Ruth Adams in 1948. I'd heard about it from Athol and the others. Apparently the La Perouse rescue was famous – the injured woman had been carried on a stretcher over the mountain and down the Cook River to the West Coast, a feat that could only have been achieved with the relentless hard work and co-operation of a team of strong men. Walter had been one of the first to meet the group as they began their descent to the coast and he had stayed with the party, cutting a track through the thick undergrowth as they made their way slowly – over many days – to safety. The rescue sounded remarkable, the stuff of legend, but I couldn't readily accept that Walter's part had been all that substantial. He didn't strike me as capable of such an undertaking. I was inclined to believe that the great Edmund Hillary, who was also involved in the rescue, had played a far more significant role than the small, buttoned-up man in our group.

Because Walter seemed so introverted I decided not to trouble him with chat. Nevertheless, I hoped that once he got to know me better he might come out of his shell. I was curious about him and wanted to hear his version of the La Perouse rescue. It was possible I had underestimated him. Perhaps he had led an adventurous life after all. Yet, despite my curiosity, I decided to leave him alone.

Athol – who had taken on the role of leader – had different ideas. Without consulting either of us he decided to pair Walter up with me. He wanted the bushman to take me on as his apprentice, a builder's mate. Walter himself made no response to Athol's instruction but I was pretty worried about the arrangement. My lack of skill in combination with Walter's reluctance to talk – let alone offer instruction – filled me with concern.

Still, at that moment, my apprehension over being stuck with Walter was nothing compared with my fear of being trapped in a snow cave. No longer scared of appearing foolish, I decided to dig myself out.

I was glad to be doing something to set us free and it was only as I shovelled snow from the blocked entrance that I realised I had nowhere to put it. The best option, I decided, was to change tack and burrow my way out, creating a smaller tunnel through which to crawl, Winnie the Pooh style. I gathered from the remarks behind me that this was an acceptable plan and so, on hands and knees, I started work. Snow settled on my back as I wriggled into my narrow tunnel, its drifts easing through the gaps in my clothes, seeping down my neck. It was an uncomfortable feeling, made the more so because the physical exertion of digging was also causing me to sweat. I was breathless, hot and chilled simultaneously – a state that put me in mind of a dose of the flu more than anything else.

My discomfort increased the more I worked. My back ached. At one stage I stopped to admire my tunnel and it struck me that I had made almost no progress at all. To my annoyance I heard some of the others take bets on how long it would take me. Determined to make one last-ditch effort I went at my tunnel with renewed vigour, and after another twenty minutes or so of back-breaking work I felt a faint breath of air against my face before clambering out into the coldest blast of air I have ever felt in my life.

The wind almost knocked me off balance. Had I not been crouching, holding on to the shovel for support, I might well have been blown down the hillside, tumbling head over heels, never to be seen again. I retreated into the cave entrance, noticing as I did that spindrift was already beginning to fill the area I had cleared. I crouched, gulping in the fresh air which was painfully cold against my lungs, and took in my surroundings.

It was dark but there was a full moon, the light from which all but flashed as clouds cleared and swept across its beam. Where the moonlight hit the face of the mountain the snow glittered, then just as quickly dimmed as another cloud passed overhead. As my eyes grew accustomed to the dark I had the impression that the mountainside was bathed in a supernatural light. I could see quite clearly the rock buttresses beyond our camp, and the level rock platform we had constructed – even though it was more than a hundred yards away. Everything seemed alive. Shadows from the clouds swept the surface of the snowfield, each shadow warping and stretching according to the ground it covered. To my eyes, it appeared as if giant slug-like creatures were passing in front of me. Then the wind would drop briefly or the moon would vanish and the whole scene would transform, becoming murkier, the cloud shadows no more than faint stains. Just as an absence of light and movement settled over this scene, the breeze would pick up once more and the shadows would distort, racing now to catch those ahead of them.

As I watched I kept imagining that I could see something – some object moving in the distance. I couldn't work out what it was. It seemed to be running towards our camp, but then it would stop as if it had changed its mind and run away. It disappeared and I tried to relocate it, pondering over what it could be. It couldn't be a man. No one would be out in such a storm – and besides, where could he have come from? Yet, as the thing came once more into sight I was convinced that it was human. I was about to call out to it when it disappeared altogether. I waited several minutes, anticipating its reappearance, but after watching for a time I gave up and reluctantly admitted to myself that it was no more than an apparition, a shadow rendered human by the other-worldly light. I turned my attention back to the cloud shadows and the sky, which continued their impressive display long after I felt my feet become numb with cold.

I did not want to return to the cave; I felt intoxicated by my surroundings. Taking advantage of a lull in the wind, I walked out a few yards, gasping as the full force of the wind caught me. Visibility was quite good but I didn't go far as I didn't want to be caught out should the clouds roll in more thickly, extinguishing the light I now enjoyed.

I felt alone as I clambered over a rocky knoll not far from the cave. Using my shovel for support I stood in the lee of the highest boulder, nevertheless feeling the wind buffet me as I watched whirls of spindrift whipping around my boots, minute particles twinkling as they caught the light from the moon. Occasionally, drifts would rise up around me and I would feel the cold sprinkle of snow against my face, chilling it until my jaw ached. My ears began to fill with snow and I pulled my parka hood tighter around my head but still it flapped and vibrated with each wind gust, so loud it reminded me of a jackhammer. That was not the only sound: I was also aware of a constant roar reverberating around me. As the wind funnelled down the slopes it gained momentum, drawing up snow, sweeping past rocks and boulders until its force manifested as a primal scream. The thought still causes the hair on the back of my neck to prickle whenever I think back to that night. It was hard to believe that the inside of our cave had been so removed from such a cascade of sound.

The sky suddenly cleared completely and I saw looming above me the great pyramid shape of Mount Sefton, its summit ridge as clear as if it had been broad daylight. I could see a gauze-like curtain of snowdrift rising up from its sky-line several thousand feet above. So great was the force of the wind, its power and frenzy, that I felt vulnerable, utterly inconsequential. It was a sobering and at the same time liberating moment. Liberating because I felt no desire to compete with my surroundings. In the face of such strength I was aware of being human. I was no match for the storm, but I could weather it.

I raised my eyes towards the upper ridgeline of Mount Sefton once more and for one brief instant I thought of my mother — my mothers. I pictured them, as clearly as if we were posing for a photograph, one either side of me — and me, taller by a head, a fully grown man standing between them.

Mist filled the valley below, lapping against the moraine walls, the rocky outcrops and the smooth, newly dusted snow slopes below us. Above us were high peaks, snow capped and glistening beneath a clear blue sky. The washed-pink summits of several mountains indicated that the sun had risen and yet, still cast in deep shade, we shivered and stomped our feet as we gathered together, waiting for the aeroplane. Two air-drops had been scheduled for that morning, with the second following hard on the heels of the first, weather permitting.

The atmosphere was one of excitement. Since the storm had abated, we had lived in a state of constant anticipation, impatient for the air-drop of building materials to take place. Some members of our group – those who were obliged to return to civilisation and their occupations over the next few days – were more anxious than the rest. Hugh and Maurice, who had worked so hard preparing the hut site and making it safe from falling rocks, had to leave in a day or two and clearly wanted to make a start on the hut proper before it was time to pack their bags. I could see the look of concentration on their faces. Like me, they were listening for the first faint drone of the Bristol Freighter's engines.

As usual Walter stood a little way off, his attention focused on the mountain, La Perouse. His detachment was noted by Douglas, who remarked – rather cruelly, I thought – that Walter was the most solitary, diffident human being he had ever met. 'Not only does he lack charm, but he's devoid of even the most rudimentary social skills,' he continued, knocking his pipe against his trouser leg as he spoke. 'I wonder if he's married . . . somehow I doubt it.' As he packed his pipe with tobacco he glanced at us, as if seeking agreement. I was shocked by Douglas's tone. Although he was reticent, Walter had done nothing to deserve such an attack, and the fact remained that he was by far the hardest worker of all of us. As soon as the storm had passed he returned to the rocky ledge on which our building platform was being prepared. He worked steadily, lugging rocks to the site and finishing off the retaining wall we had started. He didn't join us when we stopped for a break – but that was no reason to criticise him. In fact Walter was little different from many of the farm workers I had encountered on my rounds with my father. My father had often joked that the animals we were about to butcher seemed to have a lot more to say for themselves than the men who farmed them. I had grown up in a house of silence and was used to being around people who kept to themselves. I couldn't help wonder if part of the problem with Douglas was that he was British and had spent his childhood in a large city – London – so he was more comfortable in social situations than we were. It was quite possible he had not rubbed shoulders with a man like Walter before.

I have to admit I found Douglas snobbish and condescending. He came from a wealthy family – his father was a surgeon and his mother the daughter of a diplomat, a Lord somebody-or-other – and he was studying Classics at university. I felt uneasy in his company. He seemed to resent the fact that no one had wanted him – rather than Athol – to be the group leader. Actually no one had asked Athol either: he had appointed himself. But Douglas nevertheless harboured a grudge and was given to small cruelties, the occasional snide comment and less than generous action.

He once caught me scribbling down the lines of a poem and quipped that there couldn't be too many 'sonnet-writing sausage-makers' where I came from. I laughed with him at the time – it was on our first day together – but I saw later that there was an ugliness lurking behind his comment. By contrast, whenever I heard Wim refer to me as 'The Poet' I knew I was in for little more than some friendly ribbing, no different from the silly banter directed towards Hugh, 'The Card Shark' or Maurice, 'The Tea Lady'. Of all the members of our group, the only men Wim had not nicknamed were Douglas and Walter.

We had been standing around waiting for the aeroplane for more than half an hour when we finally heard its engines. The sound was distant, muffled by the mountains, but within moments the machine appeared above us, circling overhead like a hawk scanning for prey. I was taken aback by its size. I had known Bristol Freighters were large, but seeing the bulk of its gleaming silver body suspended above us I felt my heart begin to race. Surely it was too large for such an enclosed air space; I was certain it would not be able to manoeuvre safely and that before long we would be forced to witness a terrific collision between aeroplane and rock. My heart thumping, I heard Len express my own thoughts: 'Cripes, I hope these Air Force blokes know what they're doing. I don't see this going well.'

The plane completed circling the area and then, to my amazement, began to descend, coming in even lower over the glacier, passing close to the hut site and aiming for the target area we had identified with flags.

At an open door in its side a large drum suddenly appeared, stalling in the entranceway before toppling earthwards, a white parachute billowing above it as it drifted towards us. Then it hit the slope and rolled off down the hillside in the direction of a large crevasse. More drums followed, some landing with a muffled thud in the snow, others rolling a few yards before coming to a standstill. The Freighter passed above us and someone waved from the doorway. Then the plane made a sharp turn and appeared almost to scrape its wings against a rock buttress before returning, its engines roaring, as a fresh load of materials appeared at the open door.

I watched horrified as the plane hurtled towards us, its metal body gleaming in the sunlight. Everything seemed to be happening so quickly that I couldn't decide what to do. If I ran to recover a load, I risked being struck down by the next falling object. But if I made no attempt to recover the materials as they landed there was a chance they would roll away – already we had lost one load to a crevasse. Eventually I joined the others, doing the best I could to retrieve the loads as they dropped.

By the third or fourth fly-over I was calmer, appreciating the rhythm of what was happening. The parachute-attached bundles, floating this way and that, suddenly took on a gentler demeanour, more like snow-flakes than bombs falling about our heads. The aeroplane itself seemed somehow slower, more controlled. There was nothing cavalier about the way the pilot handled his craft. The accuracy with which he circled before swooping down to the target area was testament to a great skill but even so I was glad I was standing on solid ground looking up rather than inside the aircraft looking down.

As the plane lined up for another drop several lengths of four-by-two suddenly emerged oar-like from its doorway. Whoever was feeding them out was having trouble – the length of each piece in combination with the air pressure was preventing them from exiting cleanly and for one chilling moment it looked as if one might collide with the Bristol Freighter's tail. The men inside the machine must be cursing the day they were ever talked into taking part in such a nerve-wracking exercise.

My heart was in my mouth as I saw the aeroplane swing back towards us and come in once more. This time the lengths of timber spewed forth from the gleaming silver hulk. On the next circuit they were followed by sheets of bright orange iron, which twisted and spun as they fell to the ground. My eyes fixed on the aeroplane, I caught sight of an object resembling an axe handle appear, whizzing straight towards me. Had I not run for my life, I believe I might have been hit, for it was not attached to a parachute.

I was annoyed with myself. Angry that I had more or less panicked and taken flight when I would have been perfectly safe had I just stayed put. I walked across to the place where I had seen the object fall. A perfectly round hole a little larger in diameter than that of a golf ball greeted me. Peering into it, however, I could see no sign of any object. I was still gazing stupidly at the hole, transfixed by its perfect symmetry, when Athol came running up with a shovel and began to dig at the snow by my feet. 'I reckon that was a crowbar,' he said as he destroyed the hole I had been admiring. 'It must have gone straight in. God knows how deep it is.' From the tone of his voice and the way he kept stabbing at the snow with the shovel I could tell that he was on edge, probably more nervous than I was given that he felt responsible for everything.

In the hope of appearing helpful – while secretly wanting to get rid of him – I offered to dig out the crowbar. It was good to have a task to focus on and I set to work with far more enthusiasm than I had managed to muster for collecting up the building supplies, which continued to fall from the sky. After several minutes of digging the crowbar was still nowhere in view. It had free fallen but even so I was amazed at how deeply it had burrowed into the soft snow. Looking up, I noticed that the aeroplane had climbed high above us and, as I watched, it disappeared behind a bluff, silence descending over our surroundings immediately. For the first time all morning I began to relax but the tranquility was short-lived. Barely had the plane vanished than Athol's voice rang out, urging us to 'keep up the good work' and promising a hot cup of tea and a slice of fruit cake at the end of the morning.

Having set out to retrieve the crowbar I felt obliged to continue. From time to time the others men would take a break from their strenuous work and come and stand next to me, watching quietly as the snow flew off my shovel, marvelling that there was still no sign of the tool. On more than one occasion I was asked if I was digging in the right place. I had doubts myself. But, looking down into the pit I had created, I could still make out the outline of a perfectly formed hole disappearing further into the snow. Despite the absurdity of the task, it was quite good fun.

Perhaps because I was in a hole I failed to notice that the wind had sprung up and clouds were beginning to form around the mountain tops. It was only when the pile of snow I had cleared away began to blow back onto me that I realised its true force. I clambered out of my hole and caught sight of Len, Maurice and Wim struggling to secure some sheets of corrugated iron to the pile stacked beside the building site. As I watched, a sudden gust took hold of a sheet, catching Maurice on his hand, causing a nasty gash. And then all hell broke loose. A second untethered sheet of iron began to slide, sledge-like, down the slope, gently at first but gaining in speed as it travelled away from us. I was too far away to give chase but I saw Walter head after it. Wallowing through thigh-deep snow one minute and then regaining solid, though icy ground the next, he was almost upon the iron when all of a sudden he lost his footing on a patch of ice and slid fifty feet before disappearing over a small ledge and vanishing completely.

Everything happened so quickly that I couldn't make sense of it. My shovel in my hand, I watched dully as Wim and Len ran past me, calling to Athol and the others to fetch a rope and ice axe.

Although I am far from stupid, I am something of a slow thinker. My reaction time is always well off the pace. At school I envied the boys who were praised for their fast reactions or who were good at sports. Being flat-footed as well as indecisive, I was never one of them. If a rugby ball came flying my way I would be so unsettled that I would become rooted to the spot, watching it fall, barely able to move before it narrowly missed my head or outstretched hands. As a very young boy I was never invited by Ted to join in a game of Snap. I knew my slowness frustrated him. Despite flipping out his cards as slowly as possible on the few occasions when we did play, he would quickly snap up all the cards, leaving me with none. More recently I have been aware of identifying objects only after they have disappeared from view. A rabbit skittering across the road, a trout darting towards a deep black-watered hole – or a man vanishing over a ledge – become fragments of information that are slowly reconstructed, piece by piece, in my brain. And yet physically I am not slow. Once I have a destination in mind, I can move as fast as most people.

I must have arrived at the spot where Walter disappeared only a minute or so after my companions. I saw that it was not a ledge that Walter had fallen over but an *edge*. Originally obscured from view, a narrow crevasse now presented itself to me. It was only a few feet across, and with a good run it would have been possible to clear it completely. It was not particularly long either. Had Walter not been sliding out of control he might have been able to avoid it altogether. But luck was against him and he had dropped into the crevasse. How far down I could not see.

We all stood looking down into the hole where Walter had fallen. He had been lucky. Wim's sing-song admonishment, 'You want to be more careful where you put your feet!' followed by Len's grumbling, 'We'll have a hell of a job getting you out of there!' confirmed that no real harm had been done. Though the crevasse fell away sharply at first, it was essentially wedge-shaped, its walls coming together fifteen feet below the surface. I could see Walter quite clearly now, his face looking up out of the bluish gloom, his eyes dark and his expression like that of a dog chained to a kennel hoping to be let free. A wave of relief went through me. I realised that I had been scared; I had expected the worst.

In that brief moment of relief I found myself imagining my mother's strained response to this accident – to everything that had taken place over the past few days – and suddenly I began to giggle. It was nerves, a release of nervous tension, I'm sure of that now, but my response was greeted with a stony stare from Douglas and a remark to the effect that if I wasn't going to help could I please go and attend to Maurice's hand.

I didn't move, however. Maurice could take care of himself; Walter's predicament was far more worrying. I had no experience of rescuing a man from a crevasse so I had nothing to offer by way of expertise, but I felt compelled to stay so that I could assist if we were reduced to man-hauling him out from the icy well.

While I stood by, awaiting instruction, Athol and Wim got to work setting up a belay from which to anchor a rope lowered down to Walter. I was impressed by how quickly they worked and the skill with which they set up the equipment needed. The only other rescue I had participated in had happened many years before when I had helped my father drag a stranded cow from a boggy ditch. Then, as now, I spent more time poised, ready to lend a hand, than assisting in any true sense of the word. Back then I took pride in my moral support, whereas now I simply felt surplus to requirements, my major contribution being to stand clear and relay messages between Athol and Walter whenever the former was out of range.

It was a chilled, badly shaken man who lay gasping for breath at our feet less than half an hour after the rescue had begun. I had barely had time to take note of Walter's condition before Douglas started on at me, suggesting that now might be a good time to get a brew on. I was happy to help at last, but a little put out not to be involved in the more manly task of helping Walter back to camp. Foolish though it now seems, I felt overlooked.

By the time Walter appeared back in the cave his face was grey and he was shivering. He looked like a man on the verge of death but he appeared to rally once he was wrapped up in his sleeping bag, a mug of hot tea in his hands. As he mulled over what had happened, he was dismayed to notice that a hole had been torn in the elbow of his woollen jersey. More than the pain from his injuries, he was clearly upset by this. As he drank his tea he muttered to himself, rambling slightly, that he would have to search out his darning wool and get it mended.

His behaviour, his concern for his jumper, led the rest of us to believe that he had not only hurt his shoulder and ribs but had bumped his head too. It was decided that I would stay in the cave to watch over him in case he took a nasty turn, while the others – including Maurice, whose hand had been bandaged – went back to stacking materials.

I knew I wouldn't be let off entirely. As Athol made to leave the cave he suggested I take charge of dinner that night. 'Go to town,' he called, to which Wim added, 'A magnificent feast, cordon bleu.' I had no idea what he was talking about but I was happy to oblige with a hearty meal.

I was chopping onions when I heard Walter ask me to fetch his sewing kit. 'You'll find it towards the bottom of my pack,' he said, gesturing towards the gear in the entrance vestibule. 'If you could just fetch the kit – don't bring across the whole pack.' I wasn't sure whether his request for his sewing kit was a sign that he was improving or not. The way he was still fussing over his jumper struck me as odd. There was an uncomfortable moment, but to my relief Walter added, 'You never know

107

when you might need to do a spot of repair work.' This remark sounded quite sensible. I never carried wool and a darning needle but I did like to keep a pocket-knife and a length of string handy.

As I rummaged through his pack my hand came across several books, one of which was soft-backed and smaller than the others, perhaps a diary or a sketchbook. I hadn't seen Walter do any writing or drawing, however, so I decided I must be mistaken. Had I been alone, and unobserved, I might have been tempted to pull out his belongings and take a proper look. But, I continued to wriggle my hand deep into his half-empty pack, stopping when I eventually felt a tight roll of hessian like material, containing, from the feel of it, small objects like scissors and needles. Retrieving the roll I heard Walter say, 'Yes, that's it,' and he stretched out his hand, gesturing to me to hurry.

Looking back now, I can't help wondering how we would have looked to a casual observer. Two men in a snow cave, one bent over a needle and thread while the other chopped vegetables. Had our shelter been a warm, wood-lined cabin rather than an icy, subterranean dwelling we might have cut a somewhat domestic – if effeminate – image. As it was, I suspect we simply looked incongruous.

I stirred the contents of the billy watching Walter out of the corner of my eye. To my surprise he was a dab hand with the darning needle – I was taken by his skill and how quickly he worked. He had obviously done quite a bit of darning in his time – I could barely thread a needle and I was curious to find out where he had picked up his unusual skill. I was working out how best to broach the subject when he looked up and caught my eye, answering my unspoken question with, 'I taught myself . . .' He paused, lowered his eyes back to his work and added, quietly, 'It was a handy skill to have in prison . . .'

I picture myself now as a young man, barely twenty, a small-town lad hearing this confession and I imagine how my jaw must have dropped. Eager to hide my surprise I turned away and began stirring the pot with renewed vigour. Was it true? If it was, what on earth might he say or do next? When after several seconds it appeared he had nothing to add, I looked up and found him watching me. I mumbled something about my mother being a skilled knitter. This remark made Walter smile. 'That's something I never managed,' he said. I felt even more uneasy, wishing the others would hurry up and return.

Feeling somewhat desperate, I scraped the stew from the bottom of the billy where it had started to burn and began to hum very softly, a tune I made up on the spot. Then, thinking my humming might irritate Walter, I stopped and instead began reciting, even more quietly, a few lines of verse I remembered from my volume of New Zealand poetry. When even this did nothing to calm me I allowed my mind to wander and immediately recalled a conversation between my father and the local policeman from Tekapo. The constable, Derek, had come in to Fairlie on business, popping into my father's butchery on his way home to buy a few chops for dinner. As my father wrapped the meat he asked the policeman about work, mentioning in passing some story about escaped convicts that was in the news at the time. The constable didn't have much to say on that subject but he did mention that his occupation often required him to dress up in civvies and go down to meet the bus from Christchurch. 'It's surprising how many men we pick up,' he said. According to him, criminals often tried to 'disappear' into the countryside. He caught sight of me as he spoke and seemed to give me the once over, as if checking my face against some police file in the back of his mind. 'This your son?' he asked my father, thereby confirming my suspicion. He nodded when my father replied in the affirmative but nevertheless continued to weigh me up. 'Mount Cook,' he suddenly continued. 'That's another place. Men who like to keep a low profile – that's where you'll find them.' My father nodded eagerly. 'Who would have thought, eh? Who would have thought?' To my annoyance, he also turned to look at me and then, shaking his head in disbelief, added, 'Right in our back yard. Who would have thought?'

For the next few days my father repeated the policeman's story whenever he had the chance. In the evening, relaxing over the newspaper, he would suddenly draw my attention to some article or item from the court news, wondering aloud how long it would take before so-and-so, the wanted criminal, would find his way down to our neck of the woods.

Had not my mother also grown tired of my father's sudden interest in the criminal underclass, as he called these men, and asked him to desist from his nightly crime-watch, I believe he might have begun prowling the platform at the train station, scanning the faces of the disembarking passengers as if expecting the notorious sheep rustler James McKenzie and his dog Friday to emerge from the past.

It was unsettling that these events, which had taken place several months before, should establish themselves in my mind. I tried replacing the images of 'wanted men' with others of a more appealing nature: girls I knew from school and town. I latched on to the image of a teenage girl I had said hello to once when I saw her leaning against the wall next door to the grocer's, flicking through a magazine while her mother wondered aloud what had become of the girl's father, who had gone to the garage to get a tyre mended. The mother questioned me about the location of the garage and the girl smirked. Then, catching me glance at her, she raised her eyebrows in such a provocative manner that I had blushed to the roots of my hair. She sniggered and her mother sighed with exasperation. Having recalled this girl – whose identity I did not know – I found myself reddening once more as I struggled to stop myself picturing the two of us alone together in the snow cave . . .

Eventually, after what seemed like hours of internal struggle during which time I also summoned up the unfortunate image of Mary Belcher in her Lady Macbeth costume – a loose-fitting, sheer cotton nightgown – I remembered the books I had come across while searching in Walter's pack. Hoping I would be on safe ground, I asked him – as casually as I could – if he had a favourite author. At first he appeared not to hear my question, but after some time he looked up from his mending and said it was hard to know where to start, there were so many to choose from. This reply surprised me. Even though I had seen him reading, I had not pictured him as a book lover. Curious now, I mentioned the books in his bag. I enquired whether they were favourites, ones he carried with him always, or if just something he had picked up. He might have found some battered volumes lying about in one of the huts he had passed on his way up to our camp. I had noticed one or two myself, cheaply printed westerns and thrillers mostly, nothing that had tempted me.

Again, Walter gave the impression of not having heard my question. He inspected the hole he had been mending, easing the sleeve of his pullover inside out so as to see his handiwork from both sides. Seemingly satisfied, he pulled the strand of wool tight in his fingers, snapping it off, before turning his attention to a second, smaller hole. After a moment he looked up at me and squinted – perhaps adjusting his focus from his close-up work to my more distant figure. 'Take a look, if you're interested,' he said.

His tone was not brusque but it was hardly inviting. I was extremely inquisitive about his reading matter, but at the same time I was reluctant to be seen as pushy – or, worse, a nosy-parker. Exercising a great deal of restraint, I held off rushing to his pack and pulling out his books, and instead began to talk about some of the authors I had read at school. I mentioned my old English teacher, Mr McDonald, and his love of John Donne. Then I found myself talking about my life in more general terms.

Before that moment I had never thought of myself as a topic worthy of conversation. I had led an unremarkable life, growing up in a small town – hardly the stuff of legend. But little by little I warmed to my subject, recounting details of my childhood, my twin brothers' deaths and the effect on my family. I set down my story in a slightly jumbled chronology, beginning with my earliest memories of my mother's devastation and retreat into silence. I mentioned my years living with Dudley and his family, and that it was from Dudley that I had picked up the few building skills I possessed. I talked about my first trip to the Mackenzie Basin and my childish attempt to capture the experience in words. I even mentioned the family holiday at the Hermitage and my encounter with the artists – and the man who had recited from memory the words which I had recently learned were Byron's.

At the mention of Byron I hesitated, unsure of where to go next. I felt a pang of anxiety. Should I raise my family secret? My discovery of being adopted? Should I let on about my love of poetry and my decision to be a poet? Or should I keep that to myself and describe only my butcher's apprenticeship, that I was to follow in my father's footsteps and become a man whose entire life achievement could be summed up in the words painted above the shop window: Nathaniel Black and Son. Quality Butchers.

I had never before exposed my life to such close scrutiny and now, finding a silent audience in Walter, I relived the loneliness of my youth. I wanted to crawl into my warm sleeping bag and pull it tight around me. In this pathetic state I glanced at Walter and, to my surprise, realised he was watching me, waiting for me to continue. Amazingly, the last remnants of self-consciousness left me at that point. I had probably already said too much – there was no point withdrawing now. I trusted that whatever I said would go no further than the walls of our shelter and so, with a certain sense of resignation – even obligation – I continued my story, recounting my journey to Christchurch where I had discovered there already existed poets who wrote about the places I knew – Burkes Pass and the like. It was my hope, my intention, that one day I would devote myself to writing poems about . . . and here I cut myself short. I really had made a fool of myself now. I shut off the Primus and mumbled something about needing to check on the rest of the group and call them in for dinner. I scurried outside, leaving Walter to finish off his darning, no doubt quietly laughing to himself.

When I awoke the following morning I was still feeling foolish, and angry with Walter for allowing me to rabbit on about myself. My mood became even blacker when I discovered during breakfast that the rest of my team had apparently decided to leave our camp and travel down to the village at Mount Cook in order to arrange a new schedule for the remaining air-drop and to bring back the sheets of glass for the hut's windows. Maurice and Hugh were leaving our group to return to Christchurch but the rest of the men planned to return to our camp in two days' time, weather permitting.

I wasn't sure what offended me the most: the fact that Athol and the others had made all these plans without informing me or that they had decided among themselves that I should be the one to remain behind to keep an eye on Walter while he rested and recovered from his injuries. Of course, no one had any reason to guess the other cause of my ill-temper – which I blamed on Walter. Even so, my pride took a severe battering. They didn't need me to accompany them back to the village. I was a barely competent tramper, lacking mountain experience, and they had clearly decided I would be better suited to staying home in the kitchen while they – the real men – tackled the hard work.

My response was, I am sad to say, childish. I retreated into myself, listening without comment as Athol made a list of the materials that had been lost or damaged during the first air-drop, which he hoped could be re-supplied during the second. After several minutes Douglas glanced my way and mentioned, quite casually, the missing crowbar. I believe now that his remark was innocent, with no malice intended, but given my temper I took it as a personal insult. Muttering darkly that a replacement would not be necessary, I grabbed the shovel from near the cave entrance and stomped off across the snow towards the hole I had worked on the day before.

I was so absorbed in my digging I didn't notice Athol and Douglas standing over me, waiting to say goodbye. It wasn't until I heard Douglas call, 'Hullo, can you hear me down there?' that I looked up.

'Boden?' asked Athol, his voice full of self-importance. 'Can you think of anything you might need?' He coughed and then added, 'Anything *crucial*?' I caught Douglas's eye and thought he was looking particularly smug. Then I noticed a notebook and pencil in his hand; he was poised, like a secretary, ready to add to the list of essentials.

'Some more sheets of paper for your poems?'

I ignored Douglas's remark – though I really would have liked more paper – responding curtly, 'I'll have this crowbar out in a minute so you can scratch that off your list, Douglas.'

Douglas laughed. He probably meant no real offence, but I felt a sudden desire to wipe the smirks off my companions' faces. Recalling my conversation with Walter the previous day I hissed, 'Did you know Walter's a criminal?' I immediately regretted my remark but it was too late.

'What did you say?'

I retreated, mumbling, 'Nothing.'

The damage had been done.

'Wouldn't surprise me at all,' said Douglas, eyeing me suspiciously. 'I had a bad feeling about him . . .' His voice trailed away and for one brief moment I thought that was the end of the matter.

'He actually told you he was a criminal? He used those words?' said Athol. 'What did he do?'

I shrugged. I had no idea what Walter's circumstances were. He had admitted to being in jail – that was all I knew.

'It's probably nothing,' I said, hoping to end the discussion.

Douglas shook his head and turned to Athol. 'What do you think?' I saw Athol shake his head and then he gave me a stern look, which left me in no doubt that I would be held responsible if anything went wrong while they were away.

I might have tried to sort things out once and for all but at that moment Wim called across that everyone was waiting.

Once they had gone I felt sick at what I had done. There had been no need to tell them about Walter. Anyone who had witnessed him quietly darning the holes in his jersey, as I had, would have seen that he was not a dangerous man. I had betrayed his trust and I felt ashamed. I wandered away from my digging pit to sit by myself while I planned what to do next.

I was still sitting on my rock a good twenty minutes later when Walter appeared from the cave like some animal emerging from its burrow after a long winter's hibernation. He didn't see me at first. He must have assumed I was still down my hole, going after the lost crowbar. I watched as he took a few steps away from the cave entrance and then he hesitated, wrapping his arms around his body as if in pain. I began to get up, intending to offer to support him, but because I hadn't worked out what to tell him about my conversation with Douglas and Athol I hung back, waiting to see where he would go. Gingerly, he walked across to the area where our latrine was sited and disappeared from view, his body obscured by a large boulder. A few minutes later he reappeared and glanced my way. He stopped and to my surprise, he half raised his hand in greeting. Taking this as a form of encouragement I got down from my perch and went to meet him.

The contrast between us as we stood side by side could not have been more apparent. Walter was clean shaven but I had not shaved since arriving at camp and the lower portion of my face was covered in coarse ginger-blond stubble. I would not have known my beard was gingery coloured had not Wim drawn my attention to the fact one day over breakfast. Looking at me while he ate, he had tilted his head sideways and appraised me before remarking that the hair on my chin was the colour of a tiger's skin, whereas the hair on my head was paler, the colour – and here he had paused as he further contemplated my unwashed, scraggly mane – of a ginger tomcat.

'But there's almost no difference between those two reds,' mumbled Maurice, glancing up from his porridge and giving me the once over. There followed a lengthy debate over the various shades of ginger-red – from the orange-red of an orangutan to the paler colouring of a dingo.

Maurice had just got around to guinea pigs when Athol quite suddenly called a stop and raised the subject of windows. Slower than the others to make the mental leap from one topic to the other, I busied myself pouring a second cup of tea while Athol asked for ideas about how to carry the sheets of glass back up the valley to our camp. To my irritation, no one paid Athol any attention while another animal – an ocelot – was named. This started off another round of creatures whose skins, feathers or scales bore some slight resemblance to my hair or beard colour. In the midst of all this, Wim suddenly recollected a story from his childhood in Belgium, a tale concerning windows. I was glad the focus was off me at last.

The story, delivered in Wim's usual theatrical style, made me laugh. As a child of six or seven he had been playing with his best friend when he heard a rumour that the Germans were about to invade their village. Between the two of them, they decided the Nazis would probably want the school for their headquarters – it was one of the few buildings big enough to house troops. So that night they hatched a plan to break all the school windows. Knowing the glass could not be replaced – and that winter was approaching – they intended to make the Nazis as uncomfortable as possible. Wim's laughter as he continued hinted at a twist to his tale, but the others got it before I did. 'You can guess those Germans were not to be trusted – they went to the next town, one with a grand town hall. I was thrashed by the headmaster and made to sit all winter by the window, freezing to death . . .'

Wim then explained that as a result of sitting in a drafty classroom he had never been able grow a beard as an adult. This statement baffled me but I was never to become any the wiser, for the conversation changed tack and he didn't ever refer back to it.

With Wim and the others gone I became even more conscious of my own scraggly beard. My face itched and when I scratched my chin I was aware of uneven tufts protruding at all angles. The whiskers above my top lip also caused discomfort. They had a tendency to freeze onto my lips, causing a second's pain whenever I opened my mouth to speak.

From the slight redness of his skin I imagined that Walter had shaved in cold water. The impression he made, as he stood next to me surveying the hut site, was one of a man dressed and ready for church. His top button was securely fastened and a thin woollen tie was knotted at his chin and tucked away neatly into his skilfully repaired pullover. I was so taken by how he looked that I almost forgot to ask how he felt. When I did get around to inquiring after his health he frowned and said, 'I'll live,' but then changed the subject, suggesting that we take advantage of the calm weather and get cracking.

I don't believe we spoke more than fifty words the entire morning, and yet Walter seemed far more relaxed in my company than before. Once or twice he smiled as he worked, and every now and again he would catch me looking at him and raise his eyebrow in acknowledgement – as if some private joke had passed between us. Perhaps he also was pleased to be free of Athol's scrutiny and bossy instructions.

To my immense surprise – and relief – it seemed I had picked up more building skills from Dudley than I had allowed myself credit for. I felt quite at ease with what we were doing, and was pleased to notice that Walter seemed satisfied with our progress. After some hours I was all for beginning on the framework but he suggested we stop for a break and a bite to eat. I hadn't noticed until then but the day's work had taken its toll on him and he appeared to be in pain. His face was pale and he moved stiffly, panting with each step. He had done too much and I felt partly to blame. In my enthusiasm to contribute I had forgotten about Walter's physical condition and so, somewhat guiltily, I now followed him back

117

to the cave to make tea and reheat some of the previous night's stew. I decided to try and feed him up.

In the course of the morning the sky had begun to clear, and through the patches in the mist we could see the tops of several peaks, La Perouse and Nazomi among them. We were sitting outside the snow cave, eating and drinking quietly, when Walter cleared his throat and appeared to be about to speak. Catching my eye, however, he changed his mind and went back to eating, spooning the remaining mouthfuls of stew into his mouth before wiping his plate with a piece of bread, working methodically until the dish was as clean as if it had been washed in hot water. Then, leaning back, his eyes sheltered by his hand, he suddenly asked if I had ever come across the writing of a fellow named Harry Scott. The name meant nothing to me and I told him so, reluctantly fearing that my admission would mark the end of a conversation barely begun.

But Walter continued, telling me he had come across this Scott character during the war. I hadn't heard Walter talk about his involvement in the war, and was curious to hear more about the part he had played. Because he was such a circumspect character I decided the only way I could be confident of getting a straight answer was to ask him straight out where he had been stationed. There was an awkward silence and then he made a kind of gurgling noise, a pained laugh, and said one of the places he had been 'stationed' was Mount Eden jail. I started stirring my tea, even though it had no sugar in it.

Walter pretended not to notice and continued, saying he had come across Scott – who he said was not only a writer but an academic and a mountaineer too – while in detention, and that it was through him that he had been introduced to literature. Scott, it seemed, had been something of an informal librarian, recommending and handing out books to his fellow inmates. 'So he was in Mount Eden too?' I asked. Walter shook his head. 'No. I bumped into Harry before that. I really only spent a short time in his company – a few weeks, that was all. There was another fellow too. A theatre man from Dunedin – Rodney Kennedy. He used to direct us in plays and suchlike.' Walter broke off from his story and looked off into the distance, lost in thought. Then, clearing his throat, he murmured, 'I was sent up to the Manawatu. Whitanui. That's where I met them.' He exhaled, a long sigh, then stood up. 'It was Harry who gave me one of the books you felt in my pack. And yes, it is one of the few things I treasure.'

Up until this point I had tried to limit the number of questions I asked. I had the impression that my role was to listen, and I hadn't wanted to interrupt Walter, or voice any of the ideas whirring through my brain, for fear that he would shut down and retreat back into himself. It was difficult because I desperately wanted to know why he had been in jail, but I didn't want to force him into saying anything he wasn't prepared to offer.

I watched as he carried our plates back to our shelter, mulling over what he had said. Something didn't make sense. The more time I spent in Walter's company, the more certain I was that he was no criminal. He was quiet and reserved, but I had the feeling that, more than anything, he was sad. He reminded me a little of my mother. But I was puzzled also by the descriptions of his fellow inmates. I didn't know much but I was reasonably certain that theatre directors, academics and book lovers were not generally among the criminal class. I was also baffled by the name Whitanui. Mount Eden was often referred to in newspaper reports but I had not come across Whitanui. But then, I thought, how many prisons could I name? Maybe one or two – so that didn't prove anything.

It was late in the afternoon when we went back to the building site. We worked at a slower pace than we had previously, due in part to Walter's physical condition. He didn't complain but it was clear his chest and ribs were causing him pain. Every now and again he would stop working and lean with his head down, panting slightly. I was concerned about him. He didn't look well but whenever I suggested stopping for the day he would shake his head and say something like, 'Might as well give it a bit longer – while the wind is down.' As much as I was concerned for his well-being I was also impressed by his strength and resolve. I recalled the way I had doubted Wim when he had described Walter as the strongest man to walk the earth. Now I was inclined to believe him. Once he had fully recovered from his fall Walter would run rings around us. Of that I was certain.

119

I look back on that afternoon as one of the most satisfying and peaceful – even one of the happiest – of my life. While we barely spoke more than a few words, I felt at one with my companion. The act of building, of supporting a length of wood while the other hammered nails, was communication enough. As we worked I felt rested, and silently I hoped the other members of the working party would stay away, allowing Walter and me to get on and finish as much as we could. In that way I was guilty of wanting to claim the hut for myself, just as, many years before, I had wanted to protect Foliage Hill from outsiders, keeping it secret to myself. I wonder if Walter felt the same way. If he did, he never admitted to it. Given what I now know, I suspect he no longer allowed himself to have such expectations – he was far less greedy and selfish than anyone I have met since.

As the sun began to sink behind the mountains, the sky opened up and the clouds that had pressed down on us during the day disappeared. Below in the valley shadows lengthened, transforming the grey-reddish scree slope into blue-black. I watched the light fade and then from far away I caught sight of a bright flash of light. I worked out it was coming from the village – the last of the sun reflecting off the large window – or perhaps the roof – of the Hermitage, bouncing back towards us. In less than two minutes the light disappeared. Turning to Walter I was about to suggest once more that we call it a day when I saw him crouch down, his attention fixed on something he had spotted among the rocks. I walked over to see and there, growing out of a crack in a large boulder, was a small spindly plant I did not recognise. Even in the half light I could see its dark fleshy leaves and the round white petals of its flowers. I glanced at Walter who said, 'It's some kind of parahebe. I don't know its proper name.' He touched the plant with his fingertip. 'Not many plants grow at this altitude. It's a miracle anything can survive, really.' Neither of us spoke again. After several minutes of quiet contemplation we stood up and together walked back to our cave.

I had hoped that the feeling of camaraderie – intimacy –
I had felt the day before while working alongside Walter would continue, and that we might pick up where we had left off. However, all
my attempts to make conversation as we ate our breakfast the following
morning came to nothing. He appeared preoccupied, lost in thought. In
desperation I raised the subject of the hut, asking what he had in mind.
'Framework,' he responded. I nodded and mentioned that the weather
seemed to be holding up and that with luck we should get in a full day.
'We'll see about that,' was Walter's curt reply.

I knew then that there was no point continuing. I didn't know why he
was so withdrawn but I decided to leave him in peace. I pulled on my
parka and scrambled outside, walking the short distance to the hut site,
whistling loudly in the hope of showing Walter that it made no difference
to me whether he joined me or not.

I picked up where I had left off and by the time Walter arrived on the
scene, tugging at his collar, I was fully occupied searching out a piece of
framework. I was glad when Walter opted to work on a different section.
Though the distance between us was less than fifteen feet it felt as if a

crevasse had opened up between us and I was damned if I would be the first to attempt a crossing. I had tried to be friendly over breakfast and now it was up to Walter to come to me. It was frustrating when I realised after only twenty minutes that I needed his help to hold a length of timber while I nailed it into place. I decided not to ask him, intending that he would see me struggle and come across and offer his assistance. I am not sure now why it was so important to me that I not ask him. When he failed to notice my plight I struggled on but, unable to support the length of four by two with one hand and use the hammer in the other, I soon found myself cursing loudly. Not only had I failed, but I had managed to give my thumb a fair old whack in the process and I stood shaking my hand, eyeing Walter angrily as I tried to pretend it didn't hurt.

Despite myself, it was almost with a sense of triumph that I suddenly announced, 'The weather is clearing. I expect the others will return today.' I didn't want them to, and I intended my words to provoke the same disappointment in Walter. He didn't reply. Frustrated, I added, 'We should probably prepare a big meal. They'll be exhausted by the time they arrive – especially if they've carried up a sheet of iron to replace the one you lost down the mountain.' My last remark left me feeling suddenly ashamed. Walter's lack of interest had forced me into a corner but I should not have gone so far – especially as my remark appeared to hurt only myself.

I prayed that Athol and the others would not come back. The very thought of their rowdy party returning to my peaceful camp was distressing. I didn't want the quietness of my surroundings to be shattered by the sound of voices and laughter. In the space of a day I had retreated from the group and I was aware of wanting to guard my space, to keep others at bay. They – my companions – no longer belonged here. I couldn't understand why Walter didn't appear to feel the same way.

We worked all morning, stopping to drink from a billy of snow-melt and refuelling on a handful of scroggin sometime towards eleven. By 1.30 I was hungry and worn out. My eyes stung from the glare and my thumb was throbbing painfully. I needed a break.

My mood had lifted slightly over the course of the morning. Hard work was good for me; it was satisfying to see the framework go up and know I was building something that would last for years to come. I had made a silent peace with Walter, edging closer to him as I worked until I was standing by his side, passing him lengths of timber, holding them in place as he hammered, working around him as I made a start on the roof frame. At one point I caught Walter frowning at a section of framework he had just fastened into place. Approaching him, I heard him mutter about the quality of the wood. He thought there were too many knots in one of the four by twos and before I could stop him he had dismantled the offending section and was cobbling together a replacement from some lengths of timber meant for the roof. As I watched, he suddenly smiled and asked if I was ready for a break, as he could certainly do with a bite to eat.

As we had the day before we sat outside eating quietly, not speaking a great deal. One thing I can say is that we had a good supply of food, the air-drop having included several parcels of fresh meat, vegetables and bread. That day, I believe, we had bacon butties. We were almost done when a gull flew by high above us. I was so surprised I pointed it out to Walter who had, of course, already seen it for himself. The gull paid no attention to us but flew down the valley, disappearing from sight. I said something along the lines of, 'A long way from home.'

Walter smiled and after a short while replied, 'They told me, when I was a young lad, that my mother and younger sister had been carried off by angels.' He took a bite of his sandwich and faced me, mumbling, 'Funny what grown-ups will tell you.' I wanted to jump in and say, 'Yes, you're right!' but before I could speak Walter continued, 'It was the flu. They died during the outbreak. I was a wee chap. My father sent me off to live with my grandparents in a place called Diamond Harbour on Banks Peninsula. My relatives were ancient and I barely knew them. They were very strict and sometimes I would be sent to the coalshed for some misdemeanour or another. Through the open door I would watch out for a flock of pigeons – homing pigeons – which their owner let out for exercise twice a day. One day I set out to locate the pigeons' home and that was how I met a family – a bit like your Dudley's family – who were to take me on.'

Here Walter broke off and I feared he might return to work without finishing his story. I quickly re-filled his mug with tea from the billy and asked him to go on, adding that I had always liked pigeons. This was not true – I had never given pigeons any thought but I was certain Walter's reminiscence would help me to learn more about him. Walter was the human equivalent of one of my mother's jigsaw puzzles and I was eager to get my hands on as many pieces as possible in order to complete a picture of the man.

'The father, Samuel, was a funny old chap. He was mad about pigeons – breeding them, racing them. The day I met him he told me a story about going down to the wharves at Lyttelton to meet Captain Scott – Scott of the Antarctic – to persuade him to take a pigeon with him to the South Pole. He was a mad old bugger, all right. He even made a down jacket for the bird, from pigeon feathers, and, in his logbook he had pencilled in the results of numerous test flights to ensure the bird could still get off the ground. He was mortified when Scott declined to take the bird. He couldn't understand it and held a grudge against the explorer for the rest of his life. But one of the crew members agreed to take the pigeon, promising to release it on the day the first iceberg was spotted.'

Walter sighed and shook his head, laughing quietly to himself. 'The bird was never seen again.' He sipped from his tea and suggested we should get back to work but I wanted to sit a bit longer. I sensed that the real story had just begun and I urged him to speak. 'Samuel had a daughter, a girl around my own age. She told me she had been named after the pigeons. I thought she was joking but then she said, "Win some, lose some."'

I was completely baffled but waited, hoping that Walter would explain. 'Her name was Winsome. Winsome Moore,' he said. 'Gosh, Samuel was a funny one . . . Winsome Moore. The poor girl. She was a toughie, though, a wild one. The kiddies all called her Whinny and made neighing noises behind her back. She didn't care . . .' Walter stood up and began to carry his mug back to the cave. 'She was as crazy as her old man . . .'

124

This appeared to be all the information I could hope for. Nothing in what Walter said provided me with any of the missing pieces of the puzzle. I had wondered if the subject of homing pigeons was leading somewhere – was somehow related to the time he spent in jail, but for the life of me I couldn't make the link. Then I tried to imagine how Winsome or Samuel might fit in. I followed Walter back to the cave, wondering which lead I should follow. I settled on the pigeons, asking if Walter kept birds himself. To my surprise he began to talk about the homing pigeons that had been kept at the Hermitage back in the old days. Then, before I was sure I had fully understood that story, he started on another, telling me that he had a few pigeons once, but after the war he had settled on bees. In detention, he had met a man called Rex Hillary, who taught him the fundamentals of bee-keeping, and Rex had managed to persuade the supervisor to let him keep bees. 'It was the best honey I ever tasted.' He ran his hands over his face and tilted his head, rather like a bird, adding, 'They kept Rex locked away for four years.' Something about the tone of Walter's voice – or perhaps the strangeness of the story – made me laugh. I couldn't help myself but, meeting Walter's eye, I quickly fell silent. It was clear that he found nothing funny in what he had just said.

'I was moved around a lot, from one prison camp to another – a real tour of the North Island . . .' Walter broke off and glanced around. He was ready to go back to work. 'I met a lot of chaps but, apart from the other Methodists, I never got to know them very well. Harry Scott kept in touch . . . and Merv Browne became a good friend.' He caught my eye and held it. 'I was with Merv in Mount Eden. We went on hunger strike together.' He made for the exit of the cave, walking over to the hut site, waiting for me to join him.

I didn't get any more out of him that afternoon. When we did talk it was about the hut we were building, the growing number of tourists visiting places like Mount Cook, how much the place had changed in recent years, and about Athol and Douglas and whether they would return before nightfall. Walter thought it unlikely.

Over the course of the afternoon the wind had swung around to the northwest and was blowing harder than it had over the past two days.

'They won't bother returning while the weather's like this,' Walter said. 'Once this wind blows up, we'll be forced back into the cave for a day or two.'

I wasn't so sure. Like Walter, I had noticed the flying-saucer shaped clouds forming overhead but as the sky had been clearing rather than clouding over, I believed the worst was behind us. Towards dinnertime, however, the wind picked up and spots of rain began to fall. I was just finishing up, rearranging a few heavy boulders on top of some sheets of roofing iron, when something Walter had said earlier came back to me with new force. It was to do with him having been a Methodist. Somewhere in the back of my mind I had a vague memory about one of the teachers who taught at my old school, a youngish man, also a Methodist. I must have been only six or seven when there was some scandal concerning this teacher. I couldn't recall all the details but I did remember something that took place almost a year to the day after my brothers had been killed. My mother and I passed this teacher on the street and to my amazement she accused him of being yellow. I had had no idea what she was talking about – he looked no more yellow than the next man in the street – but, before I could satisfy myself completely on that matter, I was yanked by the hand and dragged away. I asked my mother what the matter was. 'Nothing. Nothing at all,' she snapped. The incident was over so quickly that, despite being bewildered by my mother's remark and her expression, I forgot about it almost immediately.

The teacher left town shortly afterwards. Once again I had no idea why – but was not particularly interested. I do recall my mother saying something to the effect that the school board had done the right thing, that men like that shouldn't be allowed to poison the minds of children. I also had a faint memory of my father responding that war solved nothing, that men weren't put on this earth to kill one another – but my mother would have none of it.

Walter was right about the weather. By the time we settled down for dinner a full-blown storm was raging outside. Every now and then a fine puff of snow would spray through the cave entrance and Walter commented that the spindrift put him in mind of a dragon. It was as if there were a large beast lurking outside our cave, snorting steam through the opening. Dragon or no dragon, the spindrift diminished as the evening wore on and the cave entrance, as before, began to fill in.

I was very unhappy about the storm. Having made good progress on the hut I wanted to finish it. I was fooling myself but I also wanted to get it built before our companions returned. I imagined a scene in which Walter and I were lounging in front of the completed shelter enjoying a cup of tea as the others staggered into camp. I wanted to see the look of amazement on Athol and Douglas's faces and hear their grudging appreciation of what we had accomplished. That was my dream, but there was little chance of it coming true. My only consolation was that we were alone, at least. The weather would prevent the rest of the team from returning and the cave, without them, felt spacious and comfortable – albeit slightly more chilly.

I was imagining what it would be like to be cut off from the world for a long period of time. I tried to think of all the things I would miss but I thought that as long as I had books, paper and ink and something to look at – a beautiful view – I would probably be all right. I had nothing against other people, but I was happy in my solitude. Having reached my conclusion, I had to concede that such isolation would have to be voluntary. I wasn't sure I could cope with having it imposed on me. That would entail a great loss of freedom, even if the end result, the fact of being alone, was the same.

Walter could have offered a useful perspective on my meandering day-dreams but I could see he was busy with thoughts of his own and so did not interrupt him. He had spoken little since our return but, having spent more time in his company, I was growing used to his silence. I knew, now, that Walter would speak when he had something to say and there was no point in trying to force the matter. Even in his silence I found him pleasant company. I was just congratulating myself on being such an accommodating cave-mate when Walter glanced my way and said, 'You don't see many ginger-haired people these days.' I must have stiffened, bracing myself for what must surely follow – more comparisons to bird feathers, fur, or perhaps soft furnishings. It was a disappointing moment. 'Before our marriage, my wife-to-be, Elspeth, shared lodgings with two women. One was called June and the other, a ginger-haired woman with very fair eyelashes like yours, was named Rita.' He fell silent and I have to admit that my first thought was that it was odd he had noticed my eyelashes, let alone commented on them. Still, I was pleased to have got off so lightly. He hadn't likened my hair to straw or a clump of bracken, for example. But where was Walter going with his story about Elspeth, June and Rita?

'I didn't know it then,' he suddenly spoke up, 'but Rita would later become a good friend. I couldn't have coped without her.' He stopped abruptly and sat for several seconds rubbing his hand across his chin, lost in thought. When he spoke again he seemed to pick up a long way from where he had begun. He was back to Elspeth. 'Elspeth was a very timid girl when I met her. Her father, George, was very domineering, very vocal – a violent man – who was feared by both Elspeth and her mother, before the latter died. He had fought in the war and when he came back he took to the bottle. His home was the RSA – or so it seemed. He didn't take to me, naturally enough. I had my own way of thinking on certain matters and I was pretty obstinate back then. Fortunately I wasn't introduced to him until a good nine months after I had started seeing Elspeth – by which time we were very much in love. Elspeth's father lived in Blenheim, you see, and I had met Elspeth in Nelson.' He smiled at some private memory. 'As I said, Elspeth was lodging in a boarding house when we met. I knew one of her friends, June, through the Methodist Bible Class. Elspeth herself wasn't religious, but we used to bump into each other every now and then. June made sure we kept bumping into each other.'

I was beginning to drift off. Walter appeared content to ramble on about life in Nelson, about several fellow members of his Bible Class – people I had never heard of, unsurprisingly – before returning to the three girls: Elspeth, June and the ginger-haired Rita. I had given up hope of Elspeth being in any way interesting. In my mind she was timid and dowdy, with mousey-coloured hair, and she was bookish too. I could also picture her friend June – blonde, bossy, and destined to become a nurse and life-long member of the church. Even Rita barely aroused my interest. No doubt she went on to sell frocks and gloves in some department store. For a brief moment an image of her holding up a sheer stocking slipped into my mind but, feeling myself redden, I quickly locked the image away and prodded Walter to continue.

'After we married,' Walter said, 'we moved south to Rangiora. It seemed like a good idea as we wanted to put a bit of distance between her father and me. He was very much against our marriage. I think he had intended Elspeth to remain unmarried so that she could take care of him in his old age.'

Feeling drowsy, I suddenly offered to make a fresh pot of tea. I needed something to do, something to keep me awake. As I pumped the Primus, I wondered if it would be rude of me to try and hurry Walter along somehow. Just as I was plucking up courage to give him a nudge, he suddenly changed subjects, asking if I had come across a New Zealand writer called Charles Brasch.

My ears pricked up. I knew that name. He was one of the poets whose work was included in the collection I had bought in Christchurch. It was now one of my favourite books, and I had brought it. I passed Walter his mug of tea and rummaged through my belongings, taking it out and opening it at the page featuring Brasch's 'The Silent Land'. In my best reading voice I began: 'The mountains are empty. No hermits have hallowed the caves . . .' Given our present living situation I couldn't help snickering and had to stop my reading. Trying to stifle my laughter I scanned through the poem to the line '. . . the Oreads will haunt the fields near the snowline . . .' I began to laugh once more. When I first read the poem I had to look up the word 'oread' in the dictionary. I knew now that it related to mythology – it referred to nymphs who were believed to live in the mountains – and this image as it related to Walter and me very nearly reduced me to tears of laughter. It was in this silly, desensitised condition that I joked, 'Was Brasch another of your cell-mates? Along with the bee-keeper, the drama teacher and the librarian? It must have been quite a gathering . . .' I caught sight of Walter's expression and the words faded on my lips.

129

Quiet now, all trace of laughter gone, I lowered my eyes and concentrated on the page in front of me, reading the poem aloud, before passing the book to Walter. He took it with a frown and ran his hand over the page, his lips moving slightly as he read the poem to himself. I didn't expect my companion to say anything. Having outlined a little of his life story and introduced the subject of Brasch, I imagined he would retreat back into his own private world, leaving me to figure out for myself where his story might have gone had I not so rudely interrupted him. My complete lack of sensitivity was unforgivable and I was annoyed with myself. My untouched tea was lukewarm and the skim-milk powder had not dissolved so clots of dry milk filled my mouth with every sip. The taste and texture transported me back to my childhood, when our school milk was always warm and lumpy, blocking the straws through which we sucked.

I owed my friend an apology but I was also feeling put out. Yes, I had teased Walter about his cell-mates but I had meant no harm by my remarks. Wim might have done the same thing in a similar situation. And anyway, it was only because our living conditions seemed so incongruous in relation to Brasch's poem that I laughed so long and so heartily.

I was making excuses for myself but I honestly believe that had I been at home, settled down in my room, worn out after a long day's work in the shop, I would have seen Brasch's work through entirely different eyes. I would have appreciated his skill and his imagery. I had never exactly warmed to his work, but I sensed that beyond all the references to Oreads, unicorns, hermits and the like there was an anchor – an everyday, common voice – expressed through his verse. It was as though he wished to place himself somewhere, within the landscape – perhaps – more specifically, within this southern landscape. At times he seemed to feel pummelled by his surroundings; he, as much as anyone, needed to find peace. Mine was no great analysis but, given my youth and lack of formal education, it was the best I could do.

'I first met Brasch through the drama teacher,' said Walter, stressing the words 'drama teacher' for my benefit as he handed the book back to me. 'I was visiting Rodney Kennedy not long after I got out, when Brasch turned up.' I kept quiet, fearing that if I opened my mouth I would put my foot back into it. 'Shortly after the war Brasch started up a journal – a literary journal, *Landfall*. From time to time he sends me a copy.' He paused, cleared his throat and added, 'Harry – the librarian as you call him – has also sent a few copies. He's had a few pieces published in it.'

I shook my head. I hadn't heard of *Landfall*. I wasn't even sure I knew what went into a literary journal. I was aware of pulling a face, one that indicated I found Walter's information interesting but not so startling that I felt a need to ask more. In that vein, I flicked absently through the book of verse, and reaching the acknowledgement page, I read the word *Landfall*. It seemed strange to put it mildly, that Walter, of all people, should know some of its contributors – and that he had met two of them in jail. 'I'm sure,' Walter said, 'that if you ever felt so inclined, you could show Brasch some of your work. Even if he doesn't accept it he would probably offer you some good advice.'

My work wasn't at a stage where I could consider showing it to a real poet or editor. It had been embarrassing enough when Wim had caught me jotting a few words into my exercise book and had persuaded me to read some of my poems aloud to the others. I can recall even now the glances exchanged between Douglas and Athol as I read my best poem, 'The Road to Tekapo'. Walter had not been present at the time – he must have been outside. Still, I felt flattered by his suggestion that I submit my work to Charles Brasch. It was the first time in my life that anyone had given me any real encouragement.

'Should I tell Brasch that you told me to write in?' I asked, barely able to conceal my glee. 'Would it help if I mentioned your name?'

Walter slowly turned away, back to the cave entrance, quietly watching the drifts of snow build up. A moment later he turned back to me and, smiling ever so slightly, said, 'I can't say – I have no experience in these matters. It's really up to you.'

The storm grew in strength. Unable to work the following morning, I decided to apply myself to my poetry and complete a few verses I had begun during the past week or so. In light of what Walter had said, I thought it might be a good idea to get five or six poems up to scratch. Any editor worth his salt would be able to assess my talent from that number. I decided to concentrate on a series of lyric poems I had been working on. These were not as long as some of the other poems in my notebook and they were held together by a common thread: the Mackenzie Basin. I knew that some of Brasch's own poems dealt with the landscape of the South Island and I felt I might have more chance of gaining his attention if I submitted poems that were similar in subject to his own.

After some time I had achieved little besides moving a few words around the page before crossing them out entirely. I looked up from my exercise book and decided to engage Walter again on the subject of Brasch himself. I coughed to make sure he was listening and then said, 'The thing I don't like about Brasch is that he always seems unsure of himself, unsettled somehow. Just when you think he's going to write about mountains, he switches to the sea. You can't help feeling that something – or someone – is pushing him around, this way and that.'

Walter looked at me and calmly replied that he had no idea which poem I was talking about. He said he knew Brasch's work quite well but I would need to be more specific. He paused, waiting for me to say something, and then added that he had been on several tramping trips with Brasch and that in his experience Brasch was a keen observer of his surroundings. He took a great deal of pleasure in the outdoors. He was the type of man, Walter said, who could sleep rough.

I wanted to keep the conversation going and so hastily flicked through my book of New Zealand verse trying to find a poem to support my earlier statement. I scanned the pages again but couldn't find the passage I had in mind. I could recall images of the sea, bush and mountains all in the one poem but the poem in question eluded me. So I said, somewhat grumpily, that Brasch took a bit of getting used to. His work didn't jump off the page.

In hindsight, I think Walter knew far more than he was letting on about Brasch. If I had been in his position I would not have managed to stay so quiet: I'd have wanted to display my knowledge. But he allowed me to babble on about Brasch's perceived shortcomings before finally stopping me with a rather odd question: 'Have you ever climbed a mountain?'

I shook my head, then added that I felt that I was in the mountains now, if that counted. Walter said, 'But you've never stood on top of a mountain?'

'No,' I replied, shaking my head. I was about to say that I had every intention of climbing one or two mountains while I was here – which was a lie – when Walter interrupted saying, 'Well, you should.'

So much for the conversation about poetry. Frustrated, I said, 'Do you think climbing a mountain is going to make it easier for me to understand Brasch's poetry? Is that it?'

Walter shrugged and I could have shaken him. I barely stopped myself suggesting snidely that I should probably go outside into the storm and sleep with the hills 'like a lover' – to see if Walter picked up the Brasch reference. Instead, I bit my tongue and went back to my books – flitting now between my own poetry, Brasch's and that of a poet I truly admired, James K. Baxter.

Once I had had my fill of poetry and mountains, I put all my books down and began to think about food. What did I most feel like eating? I settled on roast beef with Yorkshire pudding, thick, dark gravy and roast spuds and peas, which made me wonder what my parents were up to. I imagined my mother working away on one of her jigsaw puzzles, and my father in his shop, experimenting with the seasonings in his sausages or perhaps tinkering with my motorbike, fine-tuning the engine in anticipation of my return.

My parents, as I imagined them, seemed a long way away, and I began to feel homesick. I missed them, and I also missed other little things that I'd never really thought about before. I discovered to my surprise that I was quite attached to my everyday domestic world. Chores that had irritated me – the deliveries I had been required to make to the local hotel, the maternity hospital and some of my father's elderly customers – touched me now, reminding me how many things were absent from this snow-bound life. I remembered being given a paper bag containing newly dug potatoes by old Bob Green. I had barely stopped long enough to thank him and had even rather ungraciously mentioned that we had a vegetable garden of our own, so we weren't short of spuds. But, as I had continued making deliveries the temperature inside the van had increased and the smell of potatoes and warm earth filled the cab, transporting me back to the happy time I had first been entrusted with the job of fetching vegetables from my father's patch.

Still thinking of Fairlie, I recalled how, only a week before coming to Mount Cook, I had wandered across the road to Dudley's house and bumped into his daughter, Geraldine, who was lounging in the back garden reading a book. Dressed in a one-piece swimming costume, her face shaded by the brim of an enormous straw hat, she had called out to me, asking if I had heard the latest news – that her brother Ted had got engaged, that he was going to marry his 'frumpy librarian' at last. As I spluttered my surprise and congratulations, it dawned on me that I had never been out with a girl. Despite being very nearly twenty I hadn't given any thought to finding a match, and yet here was Ted, only a few years older, ready to tie the knot. I was relieved when Geraldine piped up, 'I wouldn't think of getting married until I'm at least twenty-three. I want to see the world before I settle down.' I must have nodded rather more enthusiastically than I imagined, because she laughed and said, 'You'll never get married, though. You're not the sort. I can tell.' Her comment didn't really make much of an impression on me. I was used to hearing her speak her mind and had come to regard her as little more than an annoying surrogate sister. Still, I found her frankness attractive. It made me feel close to her, as though everything was out in the open – where it should be. She had spark – a trait that was not common among the other girls and women I knew.

I was surprised by the rawness of my emotion as I began to dwell on these inconsequential events from my past. I am certain that had I been outside working, none of these memories would have preyed on my mind. But, because we were once again snowed in, with little to distract us, these thoughts – and others like them – conspired against me, increasing my loneliness and the distance between me and the people I knew well.

Cut off from my familiar world, I began to think once more about isolation and solitude. Where before, I had allowed myself to believe that living alone wouldn't be so bad, provided I had books and the like, I now felt in great need of human company. It wasn't enough for me to simply share a cave with another human being. I wanted conversation, words to warm me up.

In this melancholic frame of mind I toyed with the idea of encouraging Walter to talk about himself again. I hadn't found his domestic life very interesting but because I missed my own family I decided it might be a welcome distraction. More than that, I still hadn't found out about his time in jail. Like other lads of my age, boys who had grown up in the sheltered community of Fairlie, I had mythologised the sheep rustler McKenzie, and I have to admit to being slightly dazzled by Walter's past. I wanted to find out more about his crime – or crimes, which I suspected might have had something to do with his brutish father-in-law. It was a tricky topic to raise, however. I skirted around the issue before finally leading him back to the subject of his timid wife, Elspeth.

To my surprise, Walter was not only prepared to talk but appeared grateful for the opportunity to do so. It was almost as if he had been waiting for permission to finish his story.

'Just before the start of the war,' he began, 'we were living in Rangiora – not far from Christchurch.'

I nodded. I knew where Rangiora was. I hadn't been there but I had seen it on a map. Another small farming town, I thought to myself. I could imagine it quite easily. The fact that I had a pretty reasonable mental picture didn't prevent Walter from describing, brick by brick, his house and the street on which it was located. He mentioned the oak trees in the garden, the paddocks that bordered his section and even the view from his back door of the foothills, which in winter were dusted with snow and in summer could be obscured by the dust blowing up from the plains during a strong nor'wester. It could be my own house, I said, and I meant it. My own quiet street, my own quiet life.

Changing tack, Walter described his working day. He told me he had trained as an electrician, and after moving to Rangiora he had set up on his own. Most of his customers contacted him through the local electrical goods shop where Elspeth worked part time. 'The manager was a good, honest man. He was reaching retirement age and Elspeth and I hoped to buy the business from him eventually. We were happy back then. Elspeth, who had always been quite shy, came into her own during those first few years. She really flourished. Customers liked her.'

I was pleased for Elspeth. I knew from the butcher's shop how difficult certain people could be. There had been a few awkward occasions when I had been bailed up by some woman intent on having a go at me over the quality of our meat. There are always people who expect fillet at blade steak prices.

Walter continued. 'In the evenings I attended Bible Class meetings alone or went for walks with Elspeth around the block. Very rarely we went to the cinema. I wasn't that keen on the pictures. Like a lot of people I saw *All Quiet on the Western Front* back in the early thirties. It made a big impression on me but most films don't. Few are worth the price of admission. They are silly and I get restless sitting down for too long. I don't like the smell of cigarette smoke, and the cinemas reek of it. Going to the pictures makes me feel as if I am being slowly gassed. Elspeth liked them, though. I'd take her into Christchurch for a matinée. We'd start with a film and then go to Fails Café for dinner. She liked that.' He paused then asked me if I had ever seen *All Quiet on the Western Front*. I said that I hadn't. He said, 'Of course not – you're far too young. It was before your time.'

Switching topics, he told me again that he had kept a few pigeons but had never been serious about competing. The birds had reminded him of Samuel and his daughter Winsome and the days he had spent as a child in Diamond Harbour.

I nodded, silently organising his life into marriage, work, church and pigeons. It wasn't nearly as exciting as I'd hoped. I wondered if he would ever get around to his crime. That's what I was waiting for.

'With the start of the war, business slowed down . . .' Walter's voice trailed away and I wondered if he had noticed my mind wandering because suddenly he cleared his throat and said, 'Things didn't become really difficult until I was sent away.'

I swallowed hard. This was more like it. Trying to conceal my excitement, I said quietly, 'You haven't said what you did.' I didn't want to seem too eager. I had had a fairly conservative upbringing and, like most people in my town, I saw myself as being firmly on the side of the law. I respected the law and I respected authority. That much had been drilled into me during cadet training at school. And, despite my soft spot for James McKenzie, I believed that people who stepped outside the law should be punished.

Walter contemplated my face for a few seconds. I could see he was weighing up his words, that he was considering where to start; more than that, I think he was trying to gauge the effect his words might have. Then it suddenly hit me that Walter was no cartoon villain but very much flesh and blood, a friend of sorts – and a man who was about to take a huge risk in revealing himself to me. He was looking at me, wondering if he could trust me with that information. I realised the enormity of what was about to take place and I very nearly begged him not to go on. I wasn't sure I wanted to know after all.

'I was a conscientious objector. When I was called up, I wrote back saying I would not report as directed, nor would I agree to undergo a medical examination. I also made the decision not to go before an Appeal Board. As far as I was concerned, no one had a right to judge the sincerity of my conscience.'

He paused and held my eye. I don't know what he expected but I was so shocked I couldn't think of anything to say.

'I was given an indefinite sentence and sent away for the duration of the war. That was late 1941. I wasn't released until May 1946.'

His voice was flat. He had spoken with little emotion, slowly stating the facts as if to a reporter taking notes. He must have noticed the confusion on my face because he suddenly frowned and in a voice that seemed to belong to that of a kindly teacher dealing with a stupid pupil, added, 'I could not kill another human being, nor could I support the war in any way. No dispute can ever be solved through acts of violence. That's what I believed then – and it's what I still believe.'

I wanted to leave the cave to find a quiet place by myself. I needed to think. But I was stuck in a cave with a man who had sat back and allowed my brothers – and others like them – to fight and die in a war against fascism, while doing nothing himself. Walter had spent four years in safety! He might have been locked up but at least he knew that at the end of the war he would still be alive. When the war ended he had returned to his old life and continued on, none the worse for wear. What freedom had he lost? What was his sentence when compared with the suffering of my mother, who fourteen years on was still mourning the loss of her sons?

I took a deep breath. The silence inside the cave was oppressive. I could hear my rapid breathing – see the evidence of it every time I exhaled. Beside me, drops of melted ice plunked into a billy next to my sleeping bag. I watched as each drip formed, a small nipple of water that lengthened and stretched before falling, splashing into the container below. I counted the seconds between the drops, waiting for the next drip to appear, and the next . . .

I couldn't bring myself to look at Walter.

My brothers. A precise image of them came into my head. They were sitting at the kitchen table, watching me blow out candles on a cake. It must have been shortly before they left for war. My last birthday spent in their company. That's right – they sang 'Happy Birthday' to me, and Ralph told me I was a bit of a scallywag but not too bad for a wee chap. My father *and* mother laughed. 'Don't tease him,' my mother said, tugging at a strand of hair that had fallen out of place, she'd been laughing so hard. 'It's all right,' said Edward, before turning to me. 'You can take a bit of fun, can't you?' We sat together – the whole family – me at the head of the table, my brothers either side. Did I even see them again after that?

Walter had heard me speak about them, my brothers. He knew about the sinking of the *Neptune*, it was a well-known story. He had even recalled the details. He knew that only one of the seven hundred and sixty-three men on board had survived. And yet, while others fought to protect us – men like my brothers – Walter had done nothing.

It took all my willpower not to lash out at him. I clasped my hands firmly between my knees, palm to palm, clamping them together. I started to rock slowly, swaying back and forth, my lips working away at the sour taste of betrayal in my mouth. Still, I could not meet Walter's eye. I wished with all my heart that he had been a bank robber or a sheep rustler. At least I could try to understand those crimes.

I didn't even notice that he had started talking again; I was too busy with my own thoughts. There was nothing he could say that would have made any difference to me but it annoyed me, all the same, that there was no note of apology in his voice. He wasn't even asking for forgiveness. He had a nerve, all right.

He spoke slowly, as if expecting me to stop him. It was tempting to do just that but I didn't. Only half listening to Walter, my mind wandered to my mother's grief, my father's pain, Walter's betrayal of my friendship. I recalled the acorns I used to collect for my brothers. The row of trees planted for the men lost in the war.

Walter's smiling face fixed in my brain as I imagined him kitted out in costume, taking part in some theatrical comedy directed by his prison-mate, Rodney Kennedy. I saw him deep in discussion with the other man, Harry Scott, talking about books, and their various philosophies, the sacrifices they had made – their lost years. I pictured Walter standing outside, beneath a clear blue sky, collecting honey from his friend Rex Hillary's hives, and I imagined the air filled with the peaceful drone of hundreds of bees as they swarmed harmlessly around his hat.

Walter kept talking – about his sentence, the conditions of his im-prisonment and then his wife. As he began to describe the reactions of the Rangiora community towards her once it became widely known that he was a conscientious objector I had a vision of her, the timid Elspeth, and I thought to myself: I expect she did have a hard time of it. I didn't feel sorry for her; in fact I wanted her to struggle, to face the humiliation of being married to a . . . I couldn't say 'coward'. I longed to call Walter a coward, to spell out the wrong he had done me and my family. But I couldn't. Even in my anger I stopped short of using that word.

If I hadn't worked alongside Walter and held him in such high regard I might not have felt obliged to hear him out. In other circumstances I would have felt duty bound to ask him to stop talking, if only out of loyalty to my mother. As it was I felt guilty of betraying her. I was a grudging audience.

'Elspeth knew I was a member of the Methodist Bible Class when she first met me through June. She had heard me talk about the pacifist Ormond Burton, and although she wasn't a Methodist she accompanied June and me and some others on a trip to Wellington where we heard Burton speak. He was a powerful orator, very charismatic. I never joined the Christian Pacifist Society but hearing him and Barrington speak had a profound effect on me. Burton described his experiences of the First World War and his words cemented my already strong belief that war was wrong.'

At that time I knew very little about the preacher Burton. It wasn't until years later, during the anti-Vietnam war protests when his name cropped up again that it meant anything to me. I heard him speaking then and although, like many, I opposed the war, I dismissed him as a religious crank.

All of a sudden Walter appeared reluctant to continue with his story. I waited impatiently. By this time I was torn by a desire to cut him short and express my contempt, and my curiosity about his past. I wanted to hear what happened next but only so I could confront him, and tell him in no uncertain terms how misguided he had been. No one had *wanted* to go to war, but everyone agreed it was necessary, that Hitler had to be stopped. Everyone knew that. I was very sure of myself on that count. What's more, Walter's wartime experience was directly implicated in the breakdown of my own family. Walter and my family were inextricably linked.

My voice cold – or so I hoped – I directed him to go on and to my great surprise he laughed. The sound of his laughter unsettled me. I suppose it had never occurred to me that it was Walter – and not me – who commanded our conversation. Because I believed him to be so squarely in the wrong, I made the mistake of thinking that he was on the back foot – if not exactly apologising for his actions he was at least struggling to justify them. It came as a shock to realise that that was not the case. He had no intention of justifying himself. If anyone was going to be tested it was me, not him. He knew the strength of his conviction, whereas I had never looked deeply into my soul and been forced to account for the sincerity of my beliefs. I was self-righteous, however. And, although he was stubborn, no one could accuse Walter of being self-righteous.

By now it was late morning. If Walter was tired from talking he showed no signs of it. During our brief stand-off he had found a candle stub and was working the wax between his fingers, creating figures which he sculpted with the small blade of his pen-knife. Each time he completed a figure he held it up for inspection before squashing it into a ball and starting again. The whole time he was making his small models he ignored me. It was as if I had ceased to exist. Eventually, unable to contain myself, I snapped, 'Is that something else you learnt in jail?'

Walter glanced up. 'Yes,' he said, and passed the figure to me. Perfect in detail, it was a mountaineer, complete with rope, haversack and ice axe. Despite myself, I remarked that it was very good and then handed it back quickly. Walter squashed the figure flat and began working straightaway on a replacement. He said something about beeswax being more malleable than candle wax and smelling nicer. Not to be outdone, I replied that as a child I had spent hours in my father's butcher's shop carving figures out of dripping. This was an out and out lie but it gave me the confidence I needed to take charge again. Meeting his eye, I asked him to tell me more about his time in jail.

For the next hour he spoke without a break. He talked about the living conditions, the small huts, the high barbed-wire enclosures, the 'screws' who patrolled the camps and the superintendents who ruled them. He described the various inmates, telling me about the Jehovah's Witnesses and how he had found their literal translation of the Bible very hard to take. He frowned as he recalled work parties where the Jehovah's Witnesses had driven everyone mad with their attempts at converting the 'Hoons' – the non-religious inmates – and the others. Other inmates were the loners who appeared to have no religious or political leanings but were simply anti-war; the intellectuals – men like Harry Scott, who thought deeply and read widely and who took part in discussions covering a great many topics: nationalism, peace, war, isolation. The communists who were torn between their individual pacifist leanings and their desire to see fascism destroyed. Simply put, these men regarded war as benefiting the ruling classes at the expense of the workers, the cannon fodder. And then he spoke of his own group, the Methodists, who had spent so much time studying the Bible they could not conceive of war as being a Christian – or a just – means to ending conflict. He spoke of the human cost of war, the necessity for men to find a peaceful means of dealing with their differences, the need for men like him to stand up for what they believed in.

His voice became charged with conviction. I knew he meant every word he said, that he was absolutely sincere. I even could see the sense in much of what he said but I kept returning to two facts. My brothers had died fighting for freedom, and peace had been obtained as a result of that war. War had been successful. When I said as much to Walter he looked at me for a good minute and then in a quiet voice said, 'It's said that fifty-five million people – perhaps even more – died as a result of the war. *Fifty-five million . . .'*

I didn't want to hear any more.

Suddenly, being inside the snow cave made me feel sick, trapped. I felt as if I had been buried alive. Without saying a word to Walter I went to the entrance and began to dig. The relief I felt was immediate. I attacked the snow that had built up in the storm, driving my shovel into it, working in a frenzy to clear a small tunnel to the outside. I couldn't bear to spend another minute breathing the stale air. I honestly felt as if time were running out, that if I didn't escape the cave I might suffocate.

I have no idea what Walter was doing while I dug. Whether he sat and watched, or made wax figurines, or read – I have no idea. I wanted to get away from him. That was the main thing. I don't know how long it took but, as before, I was suddenly aware of a slight cool breath against my face and then I was through.

The wind, though strong, did not immediately push me off my feet. My exit from the cave must have coincided with a slight lull because for a minute or so I remember standing, thinking, This isn't so bad. Then all of a sudden a gust hit me square in the face, blasting me with fine, icy particles that froze my cheeks and stung my eyes. As I raised my hand to wipe the snow away I was struck again, and this time I was shunted backwards, as though I were a small child playing in the waves at the edge of the surf. Spindrift swirled around me and my frustration and rage increased: I felt a terrible urge to return to the cave and fill in the escape route I had made. The thought that I would be left in the storm didn't occur to me; I simply wanted to prevent Walter from following me outside. I could not bear the thought of standing next to him, shoulder to shoulder, feeling his body close to mine. I didn't want him anywhere near me – I didn't want to be tainted. If I hadn't had to lean on my shovel for support, I might have succumbed to my desire to fill in the hole and trap him inside. I'm not sure. I hope not.

The snow that filled the air was so thick that it cut out the light. It was still early afternoon but I felt as if I were looking at the world through cheesecloth. I had no sense of distance or depth. It was as though I had been drawn upon a sheet of white paper. I found it difficult to balance because every time I took a step I had the distinct impression of falling off the edge of the page. I've experienced a similar feeling when descending stairs in a darkened house. I anticipated a last step only to discover that I'd already reached the floor.

I took a few hesitant steps and discovered that the ground was not where I expected it to be. I'd failed to discern a slight rise and I fell forward, lunging out with my shovel as if it were a cane, or a crutch. I actually felt dizzy, as though suffering from vertigo, and I had to concentrate on standing still. But even that didn't fix my problem – not entirely. The ground continued to move; snow whipped across its surface, obscuring my boots, my legs, my torso. I experienced a phantom movement – it was as if I were still walking even though I was simply rocking on the spot. The sensation scared me. I was afraid of disappearing entirely.

I don't know what real mountaineers do when they find themselves in such a situation, but what I did next strikes me now as both bizarre and banal. I had a pee. I had been storing it up for hours and my need to urinate was suddenly urgent. As I fumbled with my trouser fastenings, my body shunted one way and the other by the wind, I had to command my bladder to hold on – sure I would wet myself. The sense of release upon finally urinating was terrific but even more incredible was the way my urine, a golden yellow colour and carried in all directions by the wind, appeared to disappear into the void. That yellow stream spraying away from me – as well as splashing onto my trousers – was the only thing that gave any definition, any dimension to my flattened world. Had a bolt of lightning issued forth from my fingertips, the impact would have been the same.

When I turned around and faced the wind I felt unbalanced again, the problem exacerbated by the noise, a thrumming in my ears. There was no pattern, no rhythm to the sound made by the wind blowing against my hood. As someone who had always been attracted to unusual words, unfamiliar sounds – an interest that dates back to my childhood when I first encountered that impossible-to-spell word onomatopoeia – I allowed myself to stand still for a moment, unravelling the noise. Gunfire.

The word stuck in my throat and I retreated to the cave entrance where I hunkered down out of the wind, trying to think what to do next.

I didn't want to go back inside. I hoped that if I stayed out a little longer, Walter might have the good grace to fall asleep. Determined to avoid him, I lingered in the cave entrance, shivering uncontrollably, cursing my bad luck. If only I had left with the others – I could have been sitting in front of a fire at the Hermitage. Eventually I had to go in. I braced myself and crawled back through the tunnel.

Walter heard me, of course, and looked up. He watched silently as I walked towards him. I stopped in front of the sleeping platform and stood shivering, wondering what to do. I hadn't realised quite how cold I was but now that I was inside, out of the wind, my teeth began to chatter and I couldn't stop them. My only thought was to get warm. Spotting a half-full billy of tea, I asked if I could have some. Walter nodded. 'It should still be warm, I just made it.' I thanked him, but made no attempt to start a conversation.

For several minutes I held the mug between my hands, absorbing its heat through my palms, feeling myself grow calmer as the hot liquid warmed me. I paid little attention when Walter left the cave and I was on to my second cup by the time he returned, brushing snow from his jumper, his hair standing upright from the crown of his head. Glancing at him as he climbed stiffly back into his sleeping bag I noticed how tired he looked. In the space of one day he had aged; his face, lined and haggard, was that of an old man. I didn't care about him but I asked in a matter-of-fact tone if he was all right. He nodded. Despite myself I felt relieved.

Now, of course, I can see that speaking about his past was painful for him. I didn't know that then – at least not straight away. I didn't speak to him again but climbed into my own sleeping bag and pulled the cord tight around my head. I lay there in the half light, not daring to move as I tried desperately to fall asleep.

Far from sleeping, I was aware of my brain going over everything Walter had told me. It did this systematically and although I tried to direct my thoughts elsewhere they kept returning to the subject of his story. Every time a particularly vivid image entered my mind my eyes opened and my eyelashes made a swoosh against the cloth of my sleeping bag. I had taken in far more of what he told me than I had thought. I must have been paying close attention to his arguments because they re-entered my brain easily, in their entirety, and each time I tried to dismiss them with arguments of my own they interjected, taking up from where he had left off, patiently stating their case.

Angered by this inner dialogue and wanting to put a stop to it, I loosened my sleeping bag and sat up. I could see, out of the corner of my eye, that Walter was reading. He showed no sign of being aware of me. Feeling restless, I grumbled that I was hungry. Walter simply nodded and continued with his book. I got up and lit the stove and was in the process of frying bacon when I heard him speak. He asked if it was all right if he finished telling me about his wife.

Whatever he had to say would make no difference to me and so, without looking up from my cooking, I gave a shrug and mumbled, 'Up to you. I don't care.'

It was all the encouragement he needed.

I already knew that Walter had trained as an electrician and worked in tandem with the owner of the electrical goods shop where Elspeth was employed. I could understand that it had been a good arrangement and I didn't think I needed to hear much more about it. But Walter had his own way of telling things and, as I didn't particularly want to eat my meal in silence, I allowed him to continue.

'One morning before breakfast two policemen arrived at our front door,' Walter began, pausing to check that I was listening.

'I knew one of the constables through Bible Class. We attended meetings together but now he was leading me by the arm to a police car. He couldn't meet my eye. He said, 'Sorry about this, Walter.' To put him at his ease I said, 'It's a lousy job all right.' When he heard my remark the other policeman laughed and said, 'It's not so lousy that you can't go home to your wife at the end of the day.' It was a cruel remark and I felt its sting. It really hit me then, that I wouldn't be coming back. I wouldn't see Elspeth or my home for a long time.

I was sent straight away to the North Island. Others were sent up to Balmoral, near Hanmer, but not me. I was sent north. As soon as I found out what was going on I wrote to Elspeth, telling her not to worry, but in my heart I felt sick. There was little chance of her being able to visit me – not with so much distance, and the sea, between us. She had no money to spare and with petrol rationing it was impossible to travel far. In any case she could never have managed such a trip on her own, not in her condition.'

I didn't know what he meant but I didn't have to wait long for an explanation. 'We were expecting a child. Elspeth wasn't showing when I was arrested so no one knew. In fact I'd only just found out about it myself. It wasn't a good time to be starting a family but there wasn't much we could do about it. I wish we'd had more time, though. If only I'd been able to arrange something for her, somewhere for her to go . . .'

He stopped abruptly. Several seconds must have slipped by and then, looking past me, he continued. 'Her boss kept her on but the situation was hardly ideal. Customers who had been happy enough to be served by Elspeth in the past now made a show of asking for Mehrtens, the owner. I heard about this in the letters Elspeth wrote. She put a brave face on it but it was impossible not to see what was happening. "Mr and Mrs Marsh came in today looking for a fridge," she wrote. "Another customer followed them in, a few steps behind. It was a man wanting a heater. I apologised to him, explaining that I would serve Mr and Mrs Marsh first, but before I got the words out Mrs Marsh piped up, telling me not to bother, that she wouldn't dream of letting herself be served by the likes of me, that she would wait for Mr Mehrtens himself to become free . . . I hate to say this Walter," the letter continued, "but this is becoming an all too frequent occurrence these days and I fear Mr Mehrtens may have to let me go, before he loses all his customers."'

Walter hesitated and fell silent. While he had been speaking I'd managed to finish my food and put the billy on for a fresh brew. I kept my gaze fixed firmly on the blue flames and as I watched I found myself brooding, *That's not right. It wasn't her fault.*

I passed a mug of tea to Walter, who took it from me silently and sat drinking, lost in thought. After a minute more he said, 'Elspeth decided the best thing to do was resign. She would have had to leave in any case, because of the baby, but she thought that it would be better to go straightaway, while she was still on friendly terms with Mr Mehrtens. He was sad to see her go. He had liked us and he felt sorry for Elspeth. Had business been better he might have persuaded her to stay on but he needed the customers. He couldn't afford to lose them.'

I must have nodded or shown some sign of understanding Mr Mehrtens' situation because I caught sight of Walter surveying me and felt guilty. He was lumping me in with those customers – the ones who had judged Elspeth because her husband happened to be a conchie. I didn't see myself that way and I wanted to defend myself against Walter's unspoken disapproval but I lacked the courage to do so. I sat quietly, sipping from my mug, waiting for him to continue.

'It was hard to find out what was going on with Elspeth. Our letters were censored and it was difficult to stay in touch and keep up with news from the outside world. And of course neither one of us wanted to write anything that might cause the other to worry. Anyway it would have been impossible for me to send a letter describing camp life accurately. I could only hint at the futility of the work we were doing, clearing scrub and planting trees. I was stuck in the middle of the North Island, smack bang in pumice country. Nothing grew except manuka and fern. No sooner was a plot of land cleared than the bush returned. Pines didn't stand a chance – the rabbits got the saplings before they ever got established. We slaved on the land but it was a complete waste of time. That was the worst thing – wasting day after day doing a job that would amount to nothing.' He frowned. 'There were two things that really upset us: the absolute futility of the work and the injustice of being handed an indeterminate sentence. We had no idea how long we would be locked up. It was very hard to stay positive.'

Walter fell silent and I feared that he might have had enough talking for one day. I wanted to hear more about Elspeth. I wanted to find out how her story ended.

With a little prompting he took up the tale again. Elspeth was now visibly pregnant and no one wanted to hire her. She was forced to rent out the house and go home to Blenheim, to her father. 'By this stage,'

149

Walter said, 'Elspeth's mother had been dead a year or two and her father, George, had been living on his own. From what she said in one of her letters the house was filthy. It made me shudder to think of her stuck out there, but whenever I wrote begging her to move away she replied that things weren't so bad, that she could survive.' Walter exhaled slowly and, catching my eye, asked if there was any more tea in the billy. As I refilled his cup he went on. 'I knew she wasn't telling the whole truth. She was around seven months pregnant and had no way of supporting herself. The rent from our house, combined with what little savings we had, barely covered the mortgage and eventually we would lose the house to the bank. She had no option but to stay put. She was trapped and there was nothing I could do. I felt completely helpless. I contacted the church in Blenheim but that didn't amount to much. Whenever anyone went around to the house George would send them packing. He had it in for any member of the Bible Class movement, largely because they were opposed to war and he also hated other pacifist organisations: the Quakers, the Peace Pledge Union – especially the communists. They were all shirkers in his eyes. As for me, he said that if we ever crossed paths again he would have me up against a wall as soon as look at me. He told anyone who would listen that his daughter had married a coward. As far as he was concerned I'd be better off dead, but, failing that, I ought to spend the rest of the war and then another seven years on top of that locked away. He wasn't alone in thinking that. Half the RSA blokes felt the same way about us.

'Knowing how much he hated me, I had a fair idea of how he would be treating Elspeth. On the few occasions I had been to his house I had taken issue with him over his habit of addressing Elspeth as "the ninny". He loved putting her down, and his enjoyment was all the greater if any of his mates happened to be there, sharing a drink. I remember the time one of his friends had stood up to fetch a beer and George had signalled him to sit, saying, "You stay there – the ninny will get it . . ." It was a poisonous atmosphere and, locked away, I spent a great deal of my time feeling anxious about my wife, praying that she would find the strength to leave.

In the end I became so worried about Elspeth I applied for compassionate leave. I explained that my wife was expecting a child and that I had to help her find somewhere to live. I put my case as best I could but I was laughed down. Why, they wanted to know, should they let me go home to look after my wife and child when I had refused to do anything to "protect" the wives and children of all the other men in the country?'

Walter looked up, his eyes blazing at the memory of that discussion. I could see how it must have weighed on him. His expression conveyed a mixture of rage and helplessness, and then, thrown in on top of that was an air of guilt. Walter had referred earlier to losing his faith and I wondered if this had been the turning point. It seemed to me that if he hadn't lost his faith in God at that point, he at least must have lost his faith in man. I felt sorry for him and was about to suggest he take a break from his story when I heard him mumble, 'It's good to talk about these things.' His remark caught me by surprise. It didn't strike me that the conversation was doing him much good – he looked worn out from the effort. If anything, I would have said he was coming down with some kind of illness, so grey was his face. He must have noticed my look of concern because he added, 'You can only keep things bottled up so long.' Though I was still angry with Walter, I could appreciate the truth in that remark. I recalled all the times I had tried not to think about my real mother; I had a fair idea of what it was like to keep thoughts pushed to the back of your head. It ached.

'For reasons I could never fully understand, the camp supervisor had taken an immediate dislike to me. He wasn't keen on any of us – we were regarded as cowards and stirrers – but he tended to single me out, make an example of me whenever there was trouble brewing. But he offered to make a deal. He implied that if I gave up all my pacifist nonsense and agreed to join up, he would see to it that I could have ten days' leave to sort out my wife before reporting for duty. That was the only time I ever saw him smile.'

He paused and rearranged a small bundle of clothing behind his back, making himself more comfortable. 'I decided to go on strike. I couldn't see any way around the situation so I refused to do any work or to co-operate in any way. The screws didn't like that kind of trouble – there was always a chance it would get out of hand, especially if others joined in. I was naïve, but I thought I might be able to frighten the screws into reconsidering my application. Instead I found myself bundled up into the back of a truck and ferried from Strathmore to Hautu. Once there, I was sent down to the Dummy, where I was to be locked up in solitary for a month. That was the worst time. I couldn't get any letters out and none of Elspeth's letters were allowed through.

'I had been there almost three weeks when one of the screws brought me a message. That morning Elspeth had fallen ill and been taken to hospital. Details were very sketchy but I gathered that she had gone into early labour, and then in hospital had begun to bleed heavily. It was her father who had called the doctor and then the supervisor at Strathmore, who passed on the message to the superintendent at Hautu. I asked to be allowed out, but again I was denied leave.

'In response to my request the supervisor asked if I was a doctor. When I said no he asked how I planned to help my wife. Did I possess healing powers, for example? I could see that I stood no more chance with this supervisor than I had with the last one, but I had to keep trying, hoping to wear him down. Early the following morning, just before six, I was shaken awake by one of the screws and told to get up. As I crossed the compound in the pre-dawn gloom he turned to me and smirked, muttering out of the corner of his mouth, "Looks like you'll be going home after all." When I heard those words my first response was one of tremendous relief. At last I could go and take care of Elspeth, get her proper medical treatment, find her a new home. I was overjoyed. Even if it was to be only for one or two days – that was all I needed.

'As I was ushered into the supervisor's hut he got up from behind his desk and walked towards me. He greeted me by name. He had never used my name before. It had always been Shorty! or, on good days, Field! His face was grave as he said, 'Mr. Field . . .' I guessed instantly what had happened.

I was given four days to organise my wife's funeral. It took all of two days just to get down to Blenheim. I went straight to the hospital and was taken into the matron's office and told to sit and wait. When she came in she didn't acknowledge me – she was all a bustle, very busy, distracted. She gave me a quick glance and then marched across to her desk, rustled through some papers, sighed with exasperation and then picked up the note the nurse had left when she ushered me in. Only then did she look at me, her features suddenly gentle as she shook her head sadly from side to side. She offered her condolences and murmured one or two more sympathetic remarks. Then she asked quietly, what I intended to do with the baby. It was as if the chair had been kicked out from beneath me. I gasped. "What baby?" The matron looked up and when she saw my face she looked embarrassed and said gently, "Your daughter."'

Listening to Walter, I think I must have gasped too because he glanced up and explained that his wife had died in childbirth. By some miracle the baby had been saved. She was very small, and not very well. He was warned she might not survive. She was all right where she was in hospital at the moment – but something would have to be done when she was stronger. She needed a home.

'It was too much for me to think about,' said Walter. 'I had less than two days of leave left. No one at the camp had told me I had a child. I had a funeral to arrange. The worst of it was that I couldn't get it out of my mind that if only I had made a deal with the supervisor at Strathmore, I could have saved my wife.'

'But you weren't to know that at the time. You were . . .' Surprised to hear myself defend him, I stopped talking and stared uncomfortably at the wall opposite.

Walter shook his head. It would take more than my feeble outburst to assuage his guilt. Very briefly he told me that his daughter, Rose, was taken in by Elspeth's friend, the red-haired Rita. Rita was married by that time, had two boys of her own and lived in Nelson. She was happy to care for Rose; she had always wanted a girl. Walter stumbled over the story, almost sobbing when he described having to say goodbye to his baby at the hospital before returning to camp. Despite myself, I could see that the whole world had been against him. He'd gone back to Hautu and had gone on hunger strike again. He had no intention of dying, he said, but he felt sick with grief and anger and wanted to draw public attention to what was going on in the camps. 'They thought they could get rid of us, keep us hidden from view,' he muttered. For his troubles he was sent up to Mount Eden and spent the rest of his sentence in jail. He continued his hunger strike for 43 days. Others, striking for different reasons, lasted longer, he said. 'In the end it became a personal battle where I was concerned,' said Walter. 'It was personal.'

Rose was four years old by the time he was released, in 1946. She had been told that he was her father and yet regarded him as a stranger and with suspicion. He didn't want to drag her away from her new family – the only family she knew. 'I visit once a year now and she calls me "Uncle Walter".

It had grown dark inside the cave; the glow from the candle I had lit flickered dully against the cave wall. While Walter was speaking he'd picked up a piece of wax, modelling it in his fingers. He held it up now for me to see but all I could make out was a small human shape, its features lost in shadow.

the poet

The editor of *Landfall*, Charles Brasch, sent a brief but polite note rejecting all my poems. He did say that one – a poem entitled 'The Hut Builder' – showed potential. If I was prepared to work on it he would be happy to look at it again and in the meantime he wished me well. He enclosed the latest issue of *Landfall* and suggested I might like to take out a subscription. Once again, before signing off, he thanked me for my submission.

Up until that stage in my life – it must have been around 1956 or '57 and I was twenty-two or twenty-three years old – few letters came my way and I don't believe I had ever received one addressed only to me. Even at Christmas the mail was delivered in envelopes marked 'The Black Family'. For me to take delivery of a thick manila envelope, therefore, was cause for comment. I think my mother may have called my father inside from the back of the shop to take part in the opening ceremony. I clearly remember both of them standing over me as I read the brief note, before reaching into the envelope to retrieve my unwanted poems and the journal itself.

I wasn't sure at first whether my father's exclamation of disbelief was

157

directed towards Brasch for rejecting my work or me for submitting my poems in the first place. I have an image of him standing beside me rubbing his hands against his apron as he muttered, 'Goodness me,' over and over again until, exasperated, I asked him to stop. Even then he managed one more before glancing across to my mother and saying, 'What do you make of it? Our son, a potential *poet*. Goodness me.'

Had I not felt such overwhelming disappointment I might have found it within myself to laugh. Instead, I lowered my eyes and read the first lines of Brasch's letter again, hoping that this time I would find some unqualified remark of encouragement, one that didn't propose a great deal more effort with no promise of success. Far from helping, my father's unconditional pride in the fact that I showed 'potential' weighed me down. My secret was out, and I knew I would not be allowed to rest until that potential had been fulfilled and one of my poems published. Closing my eyes, I could picture the poem cut from its page in the journal and mounted on the wall beside the image of me standing atop the Middle Peak of Mount Cook.

Finally, a week later and after a great deal of prompting, I reluctantly opened up the folder in which I kept all my poems and let my father take a look. He stood transfixed, his expression a mixture of puzzlement and wonder as he hesitated over whether or not to touch the loose sheets. He marvelled at the sheer volume of words I had written and asked why I hadn't sent all my poems to Brasch. With so many poems at my fingertips, why had I restricted myself to only six? I mumbled that six seemed like a good number but he was not satisfied. 'If a customer doesn't know how many sausages she wants,' he said, 'I don't tell her she can only buy six. Where's the sense in that?'

I shrugged and he went on. 'Edmund Hillary – your chum – how would he ever have managed to reach the top of Everest if he'd been too scared to put one foot in front of the other?' I nodded. He was right, in a strange sort of way. 'Now,' said my father, 'you go and make a start on that carcass while I wash my hands and have a look at these.'

I did what he asked but I felt uncomfortable. Some of the poems in the folder were unworked – little more than thoughts roughly sketched onto the page. Others were very personal. They hinted at the unease I had felt throughout my childhood, my troubled relationship with my parents, the complexity of my emotions. My father might be hurt to discover all the things I had kept so deeply hidden, buried within myself as I tried, successfully I thought, to lead a 'normal' life.

As the day went on I would hear a sound behind me and glance up, expecting my parents to march in, their confused and dejected expressions silently accusing me of betrayal, or worse – cruelty. It was my father's response more than my mother's that I feared. My mother was beyond hurt. Throughout much of my life she had remained so locked in by grief that I didn't think she had enough of an emotional core left to feel further hurt or disappointment. She was past caring. But my father had done everything in his power to support my mother and present a brave face to the world. He was much more fragile than her. He, I knew, would be devastated by some of the things I had put down on paper. He wouldn't have seen them coming.

I recall I was trimming fat when my father came into the shop, a piece of paper gripped between his fingers. My hands began to tremble slightly as he approached. I searched his face for some inkling but then to my immense relief I saw that the poem he held was written in ink. Only a few of my pieces were done in ink. Most – including all my 'personal' poems – were scribbled in pencil. I suspect, now, that my father had skipped through these pencil poems, thinking they didn't look finished. As a man who took great pride in a job done properly he had often taken me to task over the presentation of our products. 'There's an art in all of this,' he would say, prodding at a tray of cutlets. 'You haven't trimmed these nicely.' I would nod, annoyed that I would have to re-do what I thought was a perfectly acceptable job. At these times my father always watched, telling any customers present that I still had a lot to learn. If we were alone he would try and make me see my mistake. Using an example of two women walking down the street, he told me that one woman's skirt had come unstitched at the hem and was hanging unevenly, whereas the other woman had a perfectly ironed, beautifully hemmed skirt. Which, he asked, was the more attractive? Once, in an impatient mood, I replied

159

that I'd like to see their faces before I answered that question. 'It's not about faces!' barked my father. 'It's about presentation. No one cares about faces . . . as long as she's smiling.' That particular day I recall I was sent outside to hunt down some sprigs of parsley or rosemary. 'When presentation isn't up to scratch, revert to camouflage,' said my father.

Now I eyed him as he stood near the chopping block, the poem held tightly in his hand. I could see that the ink had smudged in one or two places, presumably from his damp fingers. Despite being a fervent hand-washer, he wasn't much good when it came to drying them. I used to think he believed that having damp hands proved they had been washed, whereas dry hands could be hiding any number of sins. Whatever the reason, I was sorry that the ink had run. The poem was a finished, corrected copy and now I'd have to go make another. In a voice that was remarkably steady and full of gravitas, my father began to read aloud from the page in front of him, not pausing until he reached the end and looked up, his expression thoughtful.

I did not tell him that the poem was actually two pages long and that he only had the first page. There were many times throughout my life when I failed to take my father seriously, but this was not one of them. 'You know, Boden,' he said, placing the sheet of paper on the chopping block and prodding it with his finger, 'I think you have real talent.'

It's difficult, even now, to describe the effect his words had on me. Never had I heard – from either of my parents – even a hint that I might be something beyond their normal field of vision. It wasn't a question of being either loved or unloved, but rather of being seen – or invisible. For much of my life I had been so thoroughly absorbed into my parents' life that they hadn't given a second thought to who I was as a separate being. There were times when they must have wondered about me. My retreat to Dudley's house, my night-time wanderings – even my more recent trip up Mount Cook – must have given them cause to think I was different, at least. But I don't think they ever dwelled on the subject. Why would they? I was their son.

I picked up the untitled poem and read through it silently, trying to reconstruct the missing stanzas from memory as I came to the end of the page. As I read, my father restated his view that I had real talent and for a minute I felt a vague disappointment, imagining how much better it would have been if it were Charles Brasch saying it. Still, I read the poem through once more and had to admit that even as a half-poem it wasn't too bad. In fact the shorter version – without the climax and long denouement of the second page – was better than the first. Why hadn't I sent this one to *Landfall*?

The poem chosen by my father, which would eventually go by the name 'Three Days at Least', had been written shortly after that summer at Mount Cook. I had never told Walter's story to my father and so he wasn't to know that the poem was about him. It was, for want of a better word, an elegy.

The storm that Walter and I had been sitting out had passed and we had awoken to the muffled sound of a voice calling from outside. Groggy from sleep, it had taken me a few seconds to remember where I was. For a split-second I thought I was back at home, lying in my own bed, and I reached out automatically for the light on my bedside table before realising I was still in the cave.

As I looked around I saw Walter take up the snow shovel and begin digging, clearing the entrance for the new arrival. Instead of going to help him I drew up my knees and sat huddled inside the warmth of my sleeping bag, wondering what I should say to him, whether I should acknowledge our conversation from the night before or simply let it lie. After some minutes agonising over the decision I decided on the latter course of action, so I took over digging while he got the Primus going.

I had been digging only a short while when my shovel struck another and I caught sight of Len's face staring down at me. A second later he edged his hand towards me, saying 'Dr Livingstone, I presume?' He smiled and then urged us to get a move on as the plane with our second air-drop was due at any moment.

It was one of those occasions when life feels like a mad rush – and then nothing happens. We struggled outside to prepare the target area for the incoming aeroplane – a Dakota this time – and then sat for over an hour and a half waiting for it to appear. During our wait we were filled in on the details of the past few days. Though only at the Hermitage for a short time, Athol and Douglas had succeeded in rescheduling the second air-drop. Then Hugh and Maurice headed back to civilisation while Athol, Douglas, Len and Wim started back for our camp. They were weighed down by heavy loads, including several window panes, so their progress up the valley was slow and they had decided to break their journey at Gardiner Hut until the weather cleared. They were in radio contact with the village and managed to confirm the air-drop for this morning during a forecast break in the weather.

I listened in silence, trying to keep focused on what Douglas was saying but I found the speed with which he talked and the sheer amount of information he was imparting overwhelming. There was no need for so much noise. Here I was outside, in the fresh air, surrounded by high mountains and a near-cloudless sky, being subjected to a blow-by-blow description of Douglas's few days away. It was difficult, to say the least. I felt my general level of hostility towards Walter increase to include Douglas. Not just him personally, but also all this unwanted *activity* he had brought with him. I just wanted to be left alone, in peace.

I noticed, too, that as Douglas spoke he occasionally tilted his head slightly, jerking it in the direction of Walter. I saw that he was trying to say something through the corner of his mouth but I played dumb – which annoyed him. It made me feel better, however.

Later, as we were clearing the dropped bundles from the snowfield, he took me by the elbow and asked conspiratorially what I had discovered about 'the criminal'? 'Nothing,' I said.

Douglas didn't seem terribly bothered. 'I called the police down at Tekapo,' he muttered, his eyes latched on to Walter's back, watching him struggle with a parachute that refused to deflate. 'He's not wanted for anything.'

I showed no reaction.

'Reckon he was just having you on,' Douglas continued, patting me on the back. 'Probably just . . .' He broke off as Walter passed within earshot and then he patted me on the back once more and dashed away, calling back over his shoulder, 'Don't suppose you ever recovered that crowbar?' He knew full well that I hadn't.

It took a long time to complete 'Three Days at Least', the poem that took seed in my head that day. I don't think I was ever completely satisfied with it, but in many ways it marked a major change in the way I wrote. It was this poem more than any other written during the same period that made me slow down and consider, word by word, sound by sound, how I might create an atmosphere, or tone, encapsulating my state of mind. I wasn't so much trying to say something outright as explore something within me and give it form.

The poem's title – which I did not settle on until after it had been accepted for publication – was given to me by mountain guide Harry Ayres. His arrival at our camp, in the company of Edmund Hillary, was so unexpected that even as I shook hands with the two men I could not believe they were really there.

All day Walter and I had been working in near silence. I had done my best to keep out of his way but we were together inside the hut lining the walls when we heard a man's voice calling, 'Got those bunks ready yet, Walter?' We went outside and joined Athol and the others while the new arrivals put down their packs and pushed up their snow goggles. As Hillary's face was revealed I think Douglas actually gasped. He most certainly did as Hillary stepped towards Walter and shook him by the hand, saying, 'Good to see you again. How are you?' Harry Ayres stood back a little – seemed more interested in the hut than any of us – but then he too shook Walter warmly by the hand. It fell to Walter to introduce the rest of us to our visitors. To my immense embarrassment, I was so flustered that I performed a slight bow as I took Hillary's hand.

From Ayres we learnt that the two men had just climbed a mountain in the region, Mount Magellan, and they had decided to come and see what was going on up our way – and maybe take a look at Cook while here.

As Hillary and Ayres chatted to Walter I noticed the easy way Walter asked after various members of Hillary's family, and in particular his brother Rex. Only when he mentioned bees did I make the connection between the Rex Hillary Walter had mentioned previously and the man standing in front of me. I didn't say anything but I well recall the dramatic impact this realisation had on me. This man, Edmund Hillary – a man who represented everything that was great about our country, a hero admired by everyone – had a brother who had been imprisoned for refusing to go to war. It was hard to believe. Two brothers: the hero and the shirker. I was equally disconcerted by the thoughts that started to force their way into my head.

Not long before, I had registered for compulsory military training – it was something all men my age did. At the time, I had no strong feelings one way or the other about whether it was the right thing to do. As it was, I failed the medical examination on account of a minor problem. I was troubled by this result and felt slightly ashamed – as though having flat feet somehow made me less of a man. Had I not been excluded, however, I am quite certain that the whole process would have had little lasting effect on me, or my view of the world. If my number had been called up in the ballot, I might have viewed military service as a slight inconvenience – or maybe it would have seemed an adventure. The memory of that episode now made me so uncomfortable that I was actually relieved when Athol ordered me to go and put on a brew.

I don't think I spoke more than ten words for the rest of the afternoon. When Hillary took up a hammer and began to work alongside me I had a sudden bout of nerves, a kind of stage fright, such as I had experienced at school when playing the porter in *Macbeth*. Unable to string together more than a few words myself, I eavesdropped on his conversation with Walter but tended to sidle away whenever the discussion touched on Hillary's family – and Rex in particular.

I was far more comfortable around Harry Ayres. He worked hard but said little and I was happy to hear snippets of information relating to his recent climbs and his life in general. I was taken by his modesty, and also by his apparent thoughtfulness. More than Hillary, I decided, Ayres belonged in the mountains. I put this to Harry himself many years later, when we were better acquainted and he was living in Christchurch, employed as the gardener at Mona Vale. I was not overly surprised when he changed the subject and drew my eye to a clump of deep blue irises growing at the edge of the river. Even so, I believe he had a sense of his own worth, of his place in the history of mountaineering. Later, when it was reported he committed suicide by drowning, I realised I shouldn't have been so surprised. I was shocked, though. We all were.

Unbeknown to me at the time, it was at Walter's suggestion that Harry take me with him to climb Cook. I am certain, now, that I owe him my thanks. Harry no doubt would have preferred to take Walter. Both Harry and Hillary had climbed with him before, first during the rescue of Ruth Adams from La Perouse, and then later, early in the fifties, on a number of routes in the region. But Walter was not feeling well. Seeing him work, I had all but forgotten about his fall into the crevasse but towards evening it was clear that he was in pain. He carried himself stiffly, one arm held against his chest as he walked around the building site, nodding with satisfaction at the almost completed hut.

As I prepared supper, frying up a huge feed of sausages that had been sent up to the Hermitage by my father and then carried in by Wim, I noticed that Walter was sitting by himself quietly dozing as Athol and Douglas questioned Hillary at length about his trip up Everest. From time to time I glanced across to Walter but if he saw me he showed no sign of it.

I was almost ready to serve the meal when I heard Walter ask Harry to step outside for a moment, as he had something to discuss.

As Harry followed Walter out I saw Douglas frown. He had not said anything but it was clear that he was put out by Hillary and Harry's friendship with Walter. Earlier in the day he had complained that Walter had made no effort to befriend any of us but that the moment Hillary and Harry appeared he had gone all out to be sociable. 'He obviously thinks he's better than us,' Douglas had muttered as he stood scowling at a painted sign reading 'No Dogs Allowed' which Wim had nailed to the door of the new hut. Before I could reply, he added, 'And you're not much better, to tell the truth. Fooling yourself into believing that a butcher can be a poet.' As he spoke he tried to ease up one corner of the thin

165

metal sign – hoping, I suspect, to rip it from the door. 'Do you honestly think,' he continued, glowering at the entrance, 'that just anyone can write poetry? I mean, what life experiences do you have to draw on? To my way of thinking, it's a bit like expecting a secretary to write a decent novel.' He rubbed at the lettering with his gloved fingers, then shook his head in annoyance and stomped away.

Because I had been on the receiving end of Douglas's sharp tongue it gave me a cold satisfaction that Hillary and Harry spent more time talking to Walter than to the rest of us. Douglas could go to hell.

Harry and Walter returned just as I was dishing up the dinner. Then during the meal Harry suddenly asked me if it was true that I had never climbed a mountain. The question caught me off guard and I glanced at Walter, wondering what he had been saying behind my back. I knew I was the only one of the group who was not a mountaineer but I was loath to give the impression that I had done no climbing at all. Athol was constantly on about all the peaks he had climbed and very eager to draw Harry and Hillary into a discussion comparing snow conditions, routes and ascent times. He had brought the discussion around to the men's recent first ascent of Mount Magellan and remarked that he had been thinking of giving it a go himself – he had just been waiting for the right time and the right team. He made it sound as if Hillary and Ayres had been unsporting and had stolen the mountain from him.

My only 'peak' was Foliage Hill – the knob that had taken me ten minutes to climb. There was nothing for it but to come clean in the most dignified way I could. After a moment's awkward silence I mentioned my early discovery of the Mackenzie Basin. I'm not sure what I hoped to achieve by describing one of the flattest pieces of land in the area, but no sooner were the words out of my mouth than Harry cleared his throat and, glancing across at Hillary, invited me to join them the next day on a climb of Cook.

Can a heart simultaneously leap and sink? Even now I am not sure how I felt when that invitation was made. Was my first reaction, 'I am going mountaineering with Edmund Hillary; I can't believe it?' Or did I think, 'There's no way I can refuse – my father would never understand.'

There's a chance I thought, 'Why me?' I hope, looking back, that I felt thrilled. I would like to believe that my heart was thumping with excitement. I would like to think that I had no reservations, and that I leapt at the chance; that the possibility I might not make it to the top never even entered my mind. I hope I did not simply conclude that I had no choice but to go.

It was dark when we left the camp next morning. Light from our torches created a fragmented path that we followed, one behind the other. Hillary put Harry at the front, with me in the middle between the two of them. I was groggy from lack of sleep. As I stepped carefully into the shallow prints left by Harry's boots I dipped in and out of the conversation that was playing between my two companions, the words bouncing back and forth above my head. I almost had the impression that they had forgotten about me entirely. I heard Harry mumble something about the perfect conditions. It was the second or third time he had mentioned the weather and the snow. The first time had been shortly after our alarm went off and he slipped out of the cave to look. Part of me had hoped the report would not be good, and that I would be allowed to slip back into sleep. I was just stretching out my legs, enjoying the warmth of my sleeping bag, when Harry returned to deliver his verdict in dry tones: 'Wind's from the east; three days at least.'

The rhyme stayed with me as I laced my boots, struggled with a pair of crampons and shouldered my pack, and now, as I walked behind Harry, the words created a restful background sound, helping me along one steady step at a time. *Wind's from the east. Three days at least.* The words still in my head, I took in enough of the climbers' conversation to realise that Harry had climbed Cook less than a month before, that this was his second trip up the mountain that year and that he expected the climb to be straightforward. His authority gave me confidence and I began to believe that I really was in the company of the 'greatest climber of our age', as I had heard Wim refer to Harry the day before. I began to relax, enjoying the waltz-like three-step – my ice-axe, right foot, left foot – as we sidled across the snow slope.

I had only once walked in crampons before and I was impressed by the difference they made on the ice. Although I occasionally miscalculated the increased length of my boot and tripped over my toes, each step felt solid by comparison to the step-slip of boots alone. The sound of the sharp points slicing through the frozen surface was pleasing, bringing to mind the sensation of biting into a new season's apple. Even the snow itself, its texture and colour, became apple-like in my mind and I spent a happy twenty minutes or so imagining myself as some tiny creature, an ant maybe, traversing up a peeled Granny Smith, arriving at the summit to find a single tree-like stem under which to sit and rest.

In this dreamy state it took me a while to notice that Hillary was asking Harry about an accident that had taken place on Cook the day of Harry's most recent ascent. I had not been paying enough attention to catch the names of the men involved but it was clear that three of them had met their death somewhere on the mountain. From what I could gather, Harry had been resting on the summit when he had heard voices calling back and forth, sometimes loud, sometimes muffled, far below him. It was not until he returned to the hut and made radio contact with the Hermitage later that evening that he learned about the accident and realised that the voices belonged to members of the search party. I was surprised by how easily the words 'met his death' edged into my thoughts, knocking my homely apple image from its branch. Firmly lodged in my head, the phrase now began to niggle away at me. In my mind I saw myself slip and imagined the speed I would travel, first sliding and then tumbling over the snow, bouncing like a tyre rolling down a slope before hitting a rock and soaring up into the sky, then falling again, landing with a thud, bleeding and broken at the bottom. *Met his death, Granny Smith, Three days at least, Wind's from the east.* Words jumbled in my brain, keeping pace with me as I fixed my eyes on Harry's boots, snatching up each of his snowprints the moment they became free.

We had not yet gone far and I decided I could suggest turning back if I spoke up soon. It would be easy to feign illness – a stomach bug – and retreat to safety. I was certain my climbing companions would not miss me; they would most likely be happy to be rid of the burden. I was on the verge of opening my mouth, when, from behind me, I heard

Hillary ask, 'How's it going there? Enjoying yourself?' It was the perfect opportunity to mention my upset stomach, my sore shoulder or whatever other ailment was available to me. Instead, I answered, 'I'm fine. It's not as hard as I thought.'

I heard Hillary respond that things would 'liven up a little' once we got further up and I heard myself reply with a confident, 'Fine. Good.'

With the ice shelf above us the terrain steepened and Harry began to cut steps into the snow using the adze of his ice-axe. At times the axe dislodged sizeable blocks of snow, creating a complete step with one blow, but more often than not the surface splintered, sending fragments of ice flying into the sky, showering us in frozen dust. As I stood still, waiting to step forward, I kept my eyes on the shadowy bulk of Harry's back, its darkness creating the impression of a deep hole, while around it, halo like, shards of ice glistened in the torchlight and sparkled, diamond gold.

As Harry worked I began to feel the cold of inactivity. It was shivery, standing still while he cut his steps or placed an anchor for a belay, and I bounced gently on my feet trying to get the circulation going. The straps from my crampons were pulled tight across my feet and I could feel my toes beginning to grow numb – not enough to warrant loosening the straps but enough to make me try hard to wiggle my toes, scrunching them up inside my heavy wool socks. Meanwhile Harry grumbled about being too hot. Steam formed around his neck like a collar and he appeared somewhat ghost-like, a match for Coleridge's Ancient Mariner. Every now and then Hillary would urge Harry on, jokingly instructing him to make a good show of it, to which Harry would retort with some remark about his pay not being high enough to warrant so much work. The good-natured banter took my mind off the steepness of the slope we were standing on. I imagined Walter back at work on the hut, fixing the last of the cables to the shelter, ensuring that it would not blow away in the first major storm. Around us the air was still, and I noticed that even though I had been working quite comfortably at 8000 feet over the past few weeks I was now short of breath and panting.

'It will start getting a bit lighter soon.' As he spoke Harry paused and gestured with his axe towards the sky which, though an inky blue and

169

starlit, was seeped through with a paler greenish tinge towards the east. For a moment I simply took pleasure in looking at the sky, measuring out the stars and recalling something my father had said about the night skies above Egypt during the war. He had occasionally talked about the beauty of the desert night. Despite the cold, the sky had wrapped itself around the men and made them feel enclosed, protected. The stars, he said, were the brightest he had ever seen and had filled him with a sense of wonder. But it was not until he was returning home and had looked up one night to see the Southern Cross high above the ocean that he had felt at peace. 'That was my homecoming,' he told me. 'The sight of the Southern Cross.'

The climbing was steeper now, and as we climbed higher the snow became harder, broken up by large areas of hard ice. My crampons, which up to this point had cut into the surface, began to skitter every now and again in an alarming manner, forcing me to concentrate more fully on how I placed my feet. Once my foot slipped from under me and I fell to my knees, my hands gripping my ice-axe in fear as I tried to regain my footing. The fact that I was tied on to a rope did little to alleviate my anxiety. Harry was unimpressed. 'You don't go on your knees unless you're praying,' he scolded. 'And there's no point praying – that won't help you.' He was half joking but I made a concerted effort to be even more careful. Part of my worry stemmed from the knowledge that if I slipped I might knock Hillary off his feet too. For the most part he was not directly below me but I could imagine the headlines. 'Bumbling Butcher Sends Himalayan Hero Hurtling.' That – and the shame I would cause my father – was enough to scare me half to death. I don't know about going down on my knees but I do have a vague memory of praying.

It was only when Harry drew my attention to the sunrise that I was able to put an end to the headlines that circulated through my brain. We had reached Porter's Col and were shortly to begin following an icy ridge towards the Middle Peak of Cook. We had been travelling for over four hours and, at Hillary's suggestion, we stopped for a short break.

Sitting in a scoop in the lee of the ridge we sipped from our bottles, quietly taking in the view. Straight across the valley La Perouse rose up

170

in front of us, a flattened dome like an old-fashioned beehive. In the clear morning air, scale and distance were distorted, and the features of the mountain appeared simultaneously monumental and detailed, as if magnified under a lens. At times I wasn't sure if I was looking at a real mountain or simply a table-top-sized model of one. Hillary and Harry began to talk quietly and I became aware of the faint smell of tobacco as smoke from Harry's cigarette puffed over my head.

The first rays of sun touched the peaks and ridges and the sky was suddenly drenched in salmon pink. As far as the eye could see, the tops were bathed in warm skin tones whereas on the snow slopes and cliff faces beneath us everything was slate-black. It was as if two separate worlds existed: our world of light, and at our feet a world of shadow and mystery. How can I explain the effect of climbing up out of darkness and into the light? It filled me with the joy of life. I was glad I was not alone. My companions, although speaking little and giving no outward sign of being moved by their surroundings, must nevertheless have had a similar reaction. I couldn't believe that anyone – not even a man who had climbed the highest mountain in the world – could ever grow blasé about being, simply, in the mountains.

Given my excitement, I was restless to be off and stood up before the others, willing them to hurry but my childish attempt came to nothing. Harry sat peacefully, ignoring my shuffling as he drew on his cigarette, inhaling deeply and then blowing out a steady stream of blue smoke. Hillary picked raisins from a small bag of scroggin, pushing to one side any monkey-nuts and remarking absentmindedly that he wished he could get a cup of tea.

Eventually, Harry's cigarette stub flicked to one side, we recommenced our journey, following the ridgeline which, in places, was steep and icy. As I trailed behind Harry, grateful for the rope between us, I thought of nothing apart from putting one foot in front of the other, climbing one step at a time. I was aware of the cool breeze against my face, the glare of the ice, the sound of my breath, but my mind was remarkably calm, clear of thought. If anything, I was in a kind of trance, and when Harry paused to rearrange the straps of his pack I practically bumped into him. I was vaguely startled when I looked up. The act of climbing had disconnected me so completely from my surroundings that I could barely believe how high we had come. The sensation of height was intensified when I glanced over my shoulder and was amazed to see the Low Peak of Cook beneath us. Mount Sefton, the massive, heavy-set sentinel I had sat looking up at from my seat on Foliage Hill, now appeared at eye level, but no less of a mountain for that.

As we continued up towards the Middle Peak I began to experience problems with my crampons. The fault was not in my crampons as such, but rather in my lack of skill in using them. The ridge was increasingly steep and icy in places and on several occasions I had to kick my boot into the ice, taking my full weight on the front points of my crampons. This development unnerved me. It was one thing to have one's feet planted squarely on the ground, but to be clawing one's way up a steep mountain was terrifying. I became so tense that the peacefulness of the previous few hours left me and I found myself talking aloud, telling myself to focus, to remain calm, to pay attention. Although belayed on a real rope by Harry, the words I intoned to myself became the safety rope onto which I clung, hoping not to fall.

And then, suddenly, we were standing on the Middle Peak.

I heard Harry joke, 'You can look now,' and it was true, I could. But there was so much to see. There was just so much to see. I did a complete turn, trying to take in everything at once, and then I was shaking hands with Harry and Hillary, pumping their arms up and down, burbling my thanks as they surveyed me in bemused silence. 'Look at it!' I gushed, making a sweeping motion with my outstretched hand. 'Who would have thought? You can see for miles!' I turned around in a full circle. 'You can see the entire country.' Although far from true, I did not feel that my last remark was an exaggeration. It truly seemed as if the whole country was laid out below me, as if I had risen above the land and was hovering in a place that might as well have been called 'Above and Beyond'.

Afraid of missing something – some important landmark – I scanned the valleys, settling on the glaciers of the Tasman and the Hooker and following them down, marking each transition – from green-white ice, to moraine, to blue-grey river. In time even the river became a shimmering lake and then, far away, beyond the yellow-brown plains, my eyes searched out a paler blue haze – the east coast and the sea itself. The Pacific Ocean. I turned away, lowered my eyes to the snow at my feet and then faced southwest, and there, close by, below the dark, bush-clad hills was the Tasman Sea, a long ribbon of surf defining the coast.

Despite – or perhaps because of – my great elevation, I was conscious of standing on a ribbon of land defined either side by a vast, limitless ocean. I was so small by comparison – a speck poised on this marginal strip of land. And, apart from my fellow climbers and a few companions back at the hut, no one in the world knew where I was. The fact that I could see so much – and could even make out roughly where my house should be – while being invisible to anyone looking my way, was both thrilling and frightening. Except in the minds of a few people, I really didn't exist.

A pale puff of smoke floated past me and I breathed deeply, filling my lungs with tobacco, a smell I found reassuringly human. I could hear Harry and Hillary talking quietly behind me but I didn't join in. I stood with my arms folded across my chest and soon I was barely conscious of thinking at all. An immense calm enveloped me. Everything that had happened in my life, everything that might be important in the future ceased to matter. I looked down at the hut far below and I thought I could make out the figures of my companions, black dots against the white snow. For several minutes I watched them and then I raised my eyes to the high, sun-sparkling peaks, and deep within my heart I felt a great surge of gratitude. To be standing on this mountain, on this narrow strip of land, was my good fortune. And if I couldn't preserve this day, I could at least honour it. Quietly, I gave thanks.

'Three Days at Least' was the first of my poems to be published in *Landfall*. Even now, more than forty-five years after its first publication, I continue to make excuses for it. It doesn't matter that it was to become one of the most famous poems in recent New Zealand literature, that every fifth-former throughout the 1970s and '80s was required to study it, dissecting it line by line for School Certificate English. It doesn't even matter that in a recent anthology of *Best New Zealand Poems,* selected by an editorial board of 'notable' New Zealand writers, it was named the third most widely read poem after Glover's 'The Magpies' and Tuwhare's 'Rain', just beating Baxter's 'High Country Weather'. Now, when I glance at 'Three Days at Least', my attention is drawn to the title and I am struck once more by disappointment. I should have drummed up something better.

If I stand back a little, however, I can credit the poem with bringing me to the attention of my future partner, Stella.

We met during a very sad period in my life. It was 1989 and my father had recently died, leaving me alone for the first time in my life. I found it very hard to adjust to his absence. It seems an odd thing for a grown man to say but my father was – and I think always had been – my very best friend. Though both of us were nothing other than ordinary people, our friendship was special. We asked nothing of each other and yet somehow we not only fulfilled but exceeded each other's emotional needs. Ridiculous as it may sound, we became each other's loyal companion. We were each other's dog.

It was not so much the things he said that I mourned but the sound of his voice. It was not the memory of the things he did that I tried to retain so much as a sense of his physical presence – the way he stood, or walked, or simply moved around me whenever we shared a space, at home or at work. I missed the slight weight of his body against mine as he shuffled past me when I held the shop door open for him in the morning. I missed the touch of his skin as, for one brief moment, I brushed his hand when I took his hat and hung it on the hook in the corner of the shop where he sat each day, watching me work. I missed the sound of his spoon tinkling against his mug as he stirred his sugar into his tea each morning at ten, and I missed the soft grunts he made in his sleep whenever he dozed in his chair after lunch.

He used to call out my name whenever I failed to respond to the sound of a customer entering the premises. 'Boden? Are you there?' Occasionally I would come in from the back and catch him chatting to the customer, gesturing towards the photo of Hillary and me standing on Mount Cook, which was still hanging behind the counter. 'That's my son, up there with that famous climber – you know the one? What's his name? The man who climbed Mount Everest.' He would glance up at me and smile, and then his face would cloud over and I had the impression he was trying to recall the old game he used to play, the one where he convinced the customers to try 'Ed's bangers'. It made me sad that he couldn't remember, though it never seemed to bother him.

After he died I thought that if I installed a radio, removed his chair and took down the hook for his hat I would adapt more quickly to his absence. I reasoned that if I didn't see the objects that reminded me of him, I wouldn't miss him so much. It was a tactic that had helped us through my mother's death more than twenty years before. But the butcher's shop itself reminded me of my father. Every knife, cleaver, chopping block and meat tray reminded me of him. The freezing air of the coolstore made me think of him. The smell of the meat, the warmth of its flesh, the crack of its bones, the stickiness of its blood, all conspired to bring him back to me. Even though I had been working in the shop for most of my life and was finally as skilled a butcher as he was, I found myself now, more than ever before, needing his advice. I still longed for his approval, to hear him murmur, 'You'll make a fine butcher yet.'

I wanted to preserve the things he had touched or used. For weeks I could not bring myself to sharpen his favourite knife. Each time I set out to hone it my eyes would linger on the marks on its blade, put there by him, and I could not continue. When, annoyed at my own sentimentality, I did finally decide to sharpen it, I felt such abject loss and regret that I could not use it again. I ended up oiling it, wrapping it in a piece of felt and placing it in the dresser drawer.

One evening, several months after my father's death, I found myself unable to stop crying. What had set me off was so absurd, so inconsequential that despite my grief I felt humiliated – almost ashamed. I had been wiping out the vanity unit in the bathroom when I had come across my father's electric razor. Without thinking I had flicked it open and seeing that it needed cleaning, had blown the shavings into the sink. For one stunned minute I looked at what I had done and then, unconsciously at first, I began pinching up his dust-like bristles and held them in my palm, willing them *to life*. Even as I cried out for my father's face to materialise, I knew that what I was doing would have made him uncomfortable, sick in his heart, had he been around to witness it. Despite the grief he had felt over the loss of my older brothers, Nathaniel had always managed to retain his self-control and dignity. He had accepted my mother's inability to do the same but had never been comfortable with her disengagement from life. I think it was only because he loved her, and because she was a woman and a mother, that he was able to continue supporting her. It would have upset him to think that I, a man, was like her in that respect. That would amount to failure.

So, fearful that I was about to make a mockery of all the things my father had taught me, and scared for my future, I decided that my only option was to write myself out of my current predicament. There was, of course, another, less worthy reason for this decision.

For years I had felt uneasy about my supposed standing as a New Zealand poet. Despite having a small collection to my name, as well as several pieces published in journals, anthologies and the like, I had never truly felt entitled to call myself a poet. Whenever I looked in the mirror I saw a butcher. And, with my father's death, it suddenly dawned on me that everyone else regarded me as a butcher too. My acceptance in the small Mid-Canterbury community had depended upon my being a butcher first, a poet second. I had hidden behind my 'ordinariness', the unquestionable acceptability of my profession, and had never once stepped beyond the safety of the counter to assert my difference. Simply put, I had not been true to myself.

Deep down I had always been aware of my cowardice. If I have one true regret it is that I am inclined to give in to fear. I had learned that about myself the moment I turned to descend from the Middle Peak of Mount Cook all those years ago. I remember very clearly my first few steps down from the peak. Where on the way up I had been facing into the mountain, suddenly I was now stepping out into thin air. There was nothing in front of me to 'latch on to'. I recall that I used that very phrase to describe my fear when Harry asked how I was bearing up. He had me belayed on a rope, so even if I had slipped I could not have fallen more than a few feet, but I could still feel my heart thump and my hands and feet grow cold. Harry, I remember, gave me a sympathetic look and offered some reassuring remark, something that implied it would do no good for his reputation if I died, and then he had instructed me to take it slowly, one step at a time, and I could stop once I reached ten. And that was how he got me down the mountain: ten steps at a time. He never took his eyes off me. In the end I don't know which gave me a greater sense of security – the rope or the fact that he was watching me, every step of the way. If he ever lost patience he didn't show it.

When we finally reached gentler ground both Harry and to a lesser extent Hillary appeared to take real pleasure in my relief. I was euphoric.

Nothing could have enticed me back up the mountain but I was beside myself with joy. It was a feeling I was to experience again, many years later, as love. I believe that had I not been so terrified, so assailed by fear, I would never have known what it was to truly appreciate life.

As we neared the hut I caught sight of Walter. My immediate instinct was to wave or call out, but I didn't. I watched him work, lugging some lengths of timber towards a stack of wood that had been piled on the snow, and I had to contain the urge to run across and tell him all about the climb and the view from the summit. Instead, I continued walking towards the cave, accepting congratulations from Wim and the others as I took off my pack and loosened my laces.

I understood later that night, when we were standing around a large bonfire, warming ourselves before its flames, that it was perfectly acceptable to admit my fear when descending the mountain, but I suspect that was only because I had reached the summit. I realised then that for most men fear could be forgiven in the face of success, but never failure. People needed heroes, after all. Yet, as the evening wore on I became melancholic. I wasn't sure if *I* believed in heroes. I wasn't even sure if I approved of them or, for that matter, society's collective need for them. But maybe I didn't reach that conclusion back then. It might have taken a few more years for me to articulate the feelings of that night. It could be that I was simply tired. Maybe it was enough to stand still and watch the flames of the bonfire. In the days to come, I would learn the significance of that fire, that it was to lead to the eventual name of the hut itself, the 'Farlight'. But, even without knowing that, I was mesmerized by the flames. My body ached when I tilted my head back, and I anticipated how high the flickering, sparking tendrils of fire would travel as I searched the jet-black, still night above in the hope that something – or someone – was out there, watching me.

Far below, at the Hermitage, our fire – the 'far light' – had been spotted by the hotel guests. By chance Stella was among those who stood in front of the great hotel, waiting her turn to use the telescope her astronomer father always carried with him. Stella was – is – over ten years younger than me, so she was seven or eight that night. She was the product of her father's first marriage; her mother died when she was young. By the time Stella's father remarried and started his second family Stella had already left home. She felt happier alone, she said, being independent, not relying on anyone.

Later I suggested to her – somewhat hopefully, romantically – that it was possible that at the precise moment I was standing by the fire praying that someone out there was looking my way, she was. It's possible she saw us through the telescope. Stella just laughed. She had the telescope from her father but was unimpressed by the faint glow, the far light that everyone was so excitedly talking about, and turned the lens towards the shadowy summit of Mount Sefton, making a solemn promise that one day she would return and climb it.

That vow struck me as extraordinary. I had never heard of any child making such a pledge, or commit to such an undertaking. 'I couldn't travel to the stars,' she said by way of explanation, 'but I grew up believing that the further away I was from my father, the greater my chance of being seen.'

Was it that, I wondered, or some childish belief that her mother might be up there somewhere, in heaven perhaps, looking down?

'No,' said Stella, 'my mother wouldn't have liked that. I was told she was a pragmatist – like me.'

I imagined this woman, Stella, a young motherless child, alone with her father at the Hermitage, and my heart lurched. She didn't understand why.

'Do you know what I remember most about that night – the night of the fire?' she asked. I shook my head. 'There were two things,' she said. 'The first was that I had bare feet – I could feel the damp grass, which was warm beneath my toes. The second thing,' and she laughed, 'is that I had a premonition that there would be another fire, a bigger fire, one that would light up the night sky. I imagined that the people who watched would not be able to talk, except in whispers, and that afterwards there would be an immense, complete silence – as if a ship had gone down leaving no survivors.'

I was taken aback. I knew by then that only two years after her premonition the Hermitage had in fact burnt to the ground. I had seen images of the fire in the newspaper and for some time afterwards I had wondered what had become of all the paintings and the brass telescope.

'Tell me about this Walter of yours,' said Stella, changing the subject.

For some reason I didn't feel like answering right away.

After all these years I still find it difficult to talk about Walter without feeling a great deal of regret. Stella doesn't really understand my reluctance. Time and time again I have been impressed by her forthrightness and her ability to get to the point. My partner is not lacking in tact but she can be direct, blunt. I believe it was her independence and her ability to speak her mind that caught my attention when I first met her.

She contacted me out of the blue one day, phoning me at the butchery to explain that she had been commissioned to write a short history of Fairlie and she wanted to talk to me about my life and poetry. She didn't give me an opportunity to consider this request but simply announced that she had a number of questions for me, and that if I were free she would call around that evening. She knew where I lived – the new manager at her motel had told her. After a moment's pause she said, 'Spooky, eh?' I took a moment to think about what she meant, by which time she was already saying, 'The manager doesn't know you personally, and yet he can tell me where your house is.' I was about to respond that it had been much worse in the old days, when everybody had a party-line, but she had moved on again. 'I suppose that's the price of fame.'

She was joking, of course. I knew it but I was vaguely flattered by the remark. I had never considered myself famous – there are plenty from the region who had made an impact nationally, such as the Wigley family who had built up the Mount Cook Tourist Company and airline, or Jack Lovelock, whose status as an 'old boy' at my former school was still referred to in community newsletters. To be honest, I suspected that in Fairlie, at least, my father's reputation as a butcher far exceeded my own as a writer. In fact I was sure that was the case. Customers over the age of sixty still consoled me on the loss of my father, speaking of him in such warm tones that I was truly touched. 'He was a good man,' some of them said. 'They don't make men like him any more. He was a real gentleman.' Why his death had made such an impact perplexed me. Up until that point I had imagined that the women of my farming community were far too down to earth for such sentimentality. And yet, time and time again, I was proven wrong. It was as though his passing had brought an entire era to its close – in our small town, at least.

I made mention of this observation during that first evening with Stella. The interview completed, we had started to chat about more general matters, and during a lull in the conversation I raised the subject of my father's death, and the local response to it. She looked at me as if I were mad and then put it to me rather bluntly that I was the one who was guilty of sentimentality. I was so taken aback that I was unable to respond. 'Do you really expect Fairlie to remain unchanged?' she asked. Annoyed by her tone, I answered coldly, 'No, of course not. That's not what I'm saying. What I am saying is that I would like it to remain . . .' and here I faltered. Stella, of course, noticed my hesitation and said, 'Stuck in the past. Be honest, that's what you really want, isn't it?' She laughed and I shrugged. Her manner irritated me but I thought it would be impolite to contradict her. I had no desire to fight, but even less to be stuck in the past. She had misunderstood completely. I *was* thinking about the future. I wanted to feel that my life, like my father's, had real purpose. I wanted to be like him, to live comfortably with myself and feel proud of who I was.

Stella made a strange bitter laugh and then shocked me by saying, 'Do you honestly believe that in thirty years' time this land of yours – the Mackenzie Basin, for example – will bear even the slightest resemblance to the places you depict in your poems? Your grandchildren will get summer jobs picking grapes from vines planted across the basin. You wait.'

'Grandchildren?' I spluttered.

'Children, grandchildren. What does it matter? It's going to vanish, anyway.'

Never in my life had I heard anyone speak with such vehemence. But at that time I still hadn't heard about Stella's family home, which had been built on the banks of the Clutha by her great-great-grandfather and which had provided shelter for her great-grandparents, her grandparents and her mother. The property was about to be taken away in building the Clutha Dam. In only a few years the house would be underwater, drowned, at the bottom of Lake Dunstan. Nothing would remain.

'I didn't even hear about the dam until it was too late,' she explained, once she had calmed down. 'I spent most of the '80s abroad, working. My father was dead and the house was in my stepmother's name.' Her mouth twisted and she looked down at her hands, which rested on the table beside the tape-recorder. 'I guess she had no option.' She glanced up, caught my eye and muttered, 'That bastard Muldoon.'

Stella's language shocked me. Disconcerted, I wondered aloud why her father hadn't left the house to her, given that it had belonged to her mother and not to his side of the family – not that it mattered now, in

182

view of the outcome. Stella sighed and explained that her father had never felt very strongly about houses. He had grown up in England and his street had been bombed during the war. His own house had been destroyed. 'He used to talk about how devastated his mother was and I had the impression he decided then never to become attached to any place. I suppose once my mother died he became even more convinced of the importance of being self-reliant, of counting on no one, of never looking back. But he was seldom happy.'

'Is that why you became a historian?' I asked. 'Because you wanted to assert yourself, to show you were different from him?'

Stella shrugged. 'Could be. Not sure.' She looked thoughtful. 'It might explain why he was an astronomer, though.'

It seemed natural to continue talking about our families. Both of us had touched on our fathers, after all. But when Stella asked if I was married I felt awkward. Earlier, she'd assumed that I had children – grandchildren even – and I didn't know how to account for my single status. I didn't want to give the impression that I had *never* had a girlfriend, but at the same time I thought it would be slightly vulgar to allude to my previous – failed – romances. Even the word 'romances' seemed misplaced. None of my relationships had been particularly romantic. In recent years the women who had been introduced to me were all of a type: decent, intelligent, but most of all lonely. Without exception they wanted com-panionship, a soul-mate, and for some reason I desired something else. I never articulated my feelings because they embarrassed me, but I didn't want to settle for someone who resembled, in any way, my mother. I wanted to feel a spark, a frisson of excitement, but I realised that no woman who was capable of provoking such a thrill would be interested in me – a middle-aged man living at home with his father.

I didn't tell Stella any of this. Instead I turned the tables on her and asked if she lived alone.

'Yes,' she replied, and then hesitated, mumbling, 'No.'

When I looked puzzled she added, 'I'm moving in with my boyfriend.' She paused, as though surprised herself by what she said. 'We've been going out for a few years and he wants . . .' Her voice trailed off, and for the first time that evening she looked uneasy, unsure of herself. 'He asked me to move in.' The last sentence was spoken quickly and Stella glanced away, avoiding my eye. She sighed. Almost groaned, 'I'd better be off. He's back at the motel . . . waiting.'

She gathered her notes together and then fumbled with the tape-recorder, removing the cassette and placing it in its protective case. She caught my eye and blushed. 'It'll be all right,' she mumbled. I didn't know whether she was referring to the interview or her relationship.

I was relieved when she finally scuttled off, leaving me in peace. Much as I enjoyed her company I felt unsettled by our conversation. I was worried about the impression I had created. Replaying snatches of the interview and later discussion through my mind, I began to fret that I had not established the right tone – that I might have appeared slightly ridiculous, lacking in gravitas. I also found it difficult to reconcile Stella's cropped blonde hair, her tattooed wrist and her threadbare slogan T-shirt with my stereotypical picture of what a historian should look like. When I mentioned this to her during a phone call a day or so later she gave a mocking laugh – as if she had heard it all before – and suggested she could wear a tweed skirt at our next meeting if that would make it any easier. She must have thought she'd got the better of me but when I asked why there was to be a 'next meeting' she fell silent. Despite her obvious discomfort, and my own sense that I was undermining the potential for a happy professional relationship, I pressed on. What more did she need to know?

'Nothing,' she fired back. 'I was just being friendly.'

The line went dead and for one startling moment I felt a stab of remorse. Idiot, I muttered to myself. You idiot.

I didn't hear from Stella again for almost a year. I was so caught up in my own work, trying to cobble together a new collection of poems, that I didn't notice her absence at first. Once or twice I might have wondered how her work was progressing, and I probably hoped she had written a flattering profile of me, but really, I didn't dwell on her. I imagined she would be ensconced in Christchurch, living with her partner, and that

I would probably hear from her one day, before the book went to the printer.

My own hopes of getting a book together were fast failing. I had been sitting on a series of poems for a collection with the working title *Kindred Spirits*. I wasn't entirely happy with the title but it seemed to bind together a fair number of the poems that lay about in various stages of completeness on my desk. They were originally conceived as sonnets but I had recently decided to abandon that form, so I felt tired envisaging how much reworking lay ahead of me. My only satisfaction came from the belief that I had laid the foundation of a strong collection – that the poems sat well together on the page. Six poems, however, refused to co-operate. The first of these should have been straightforward: it was a poem about Sam Marsden, who for many years owned Mount Cook Cordials. Stella had mentioned his name in passing during the interview and I had found myself remembering the multi-coloured van he used to drive around in. I recalled, too, sitting on the back step of Dudley's house, watching a wasp buzz around an almost empty bottle of raspberry that Geraldine had left out overnight. I had never seen a wasp before and I remember calling Dudley and Auntie Hilda out to look. For several minutes we all stood watching, wondering where the new arrival had come from, and then Dudley and Hilda went back inside, and a day or so later Dudley reported that it was a German wasp.

I was at my table one evening, staring blankly at my Sam Marsden poem, when there was a tap at my kitchen window. Moments later Geraldine appeared at my door. Since her divorce and return to Fairlie several years before she had become an occasional visitor, popping over to say hello, never staying long as she had so much to do. She was running a Bed & Breakfast from her home. Without ever putting it into words she had always made it clear that I was never to expect anything from her in a romantic sense. She had somehow managed to convey this message even more strongly since the death of my father. I think she was afraid I might look to her as a convenient replacement and she was having none of it. But she was one of my oldest friends, and provided I never overstepped the mark – which to tell the truth I had never wanted to do – she allowed herself the freedom to call by whenever she was in the mood for company – my company.

On this particular evening she brought something for me to look at. She sat down and pulled a small notebook from her jacket pocket, placing it on the table before me. I recognised the cover immediately. It was Hilda's notebook – the one I had last seen fifty years before when I had been asked to copy my first poem into it.

It was strange to see that poem again, stranger still to see my own child's hand. How carefully I had tried to keep my lines straight on the book's plain white page – I had made the occasional slip and placed a capital letter in the middle of a word. I noticed the rather formal way I had written my name at the bottom of the poem – 'by Boden Black' penned in capital letters and then, below that, my signature and the word 'Poet'. It was easy to get the impression that it was not the poem itself that was important so much as my signature and that one defining word, *Poet*.

'I didn't know you wrote poetry back then,' said Geraldine after she had read through the poem aloud for my benefit. 'You hid it well – but I guess you had to.'

I was surprised by her remark and wondered what she meant.

'Well, the boys in your class would have given you hell if they'd seen you writing poetry.'

I nodded, but I had no memory of being bullied at school, and I think it would be reasonable to say that few boys ever showed the slightest bit of interest in me. I was no good at sport, I was slow and flat-footed, and for some reason that fact alone rendered me invisible to my classmates. During my teenage years I was occasionally asked to help with someone's homework but even then I was never picked on. The idea that boys like me spent their childhoods frightened and alone never rang true with me, but perhaps I was lucky.

Oddly, when I finally saw Stella again, during the evening of her book launch, she made a similar remark, asking if I had been bullied or singled out as a sissy. I found the question offensive. It implied that I couldn't stand up for myself; what's more, it suggested that country boys were by their very nature thuggish oafs who liked nothing better than to lash out at anyone who showed signs of being brainy or arty.

I could tell, as I defended the boys at my school, that Stella didn't believe me. I tried to explain that all the families knew one another, that the mothers of my classmates all bought their meat from my father, that there was no room in the town for bullies to operate. They would have been found out.

She laughed and replied, 'You were probably just lucky. I bet there's some old boy out there who remembers having the shit kicked out of him.'

I must have flinched because Stella grimaced and quickly changed the subject. 'You didn't introduce me to your friend,' she said, pointing behind me. I glanced in the direction of her gesture and replied, 'Oh, that's just Geraldine, my neighbour.' I was taken aback by the sound of my voice – it was almost dismissive. Stella nodded and at that moment I realised that she was alone. 'Your partner couldn't make it tonight?'

For a moment she looked confused and then her lip curled and she shook her head, 'Ex-partner.'

A sensation like a flutter went through me, and despite myself I smiled. Neither of us spoke. The silence deepened, became awkward and then we both talked at once: 'I like the book cover I'm not very easy to live with apparently.'

We laughed uneasily.

'Yes,' said Stella after a few seconds. 'The cover's okay. Better than I thought it would be, given the minuscule budget.'

I nodded but I wasn't paying close attention.

'You don't strike me as being the difficult type . . .'

At that the conversation ground to a halt and we parted – or rather retreated – me to talk with the school principal, while Stella, I noticed, singled out Geraldine, much to my discomfort.

Stella and I have never shared a house but we consider ourselves partners nevertheless. There are aspects of my life that fascinate her. With little memory of her own mother to comfort her, she is captivated by the fact that, on paper at least, I had two mothers. The lives of both my 'mothers' have been subjected to hours of speculation but it is the woman I have always regarded as my real mother, Connie, who arouses the most interest. I can tell, now that I know her well, when Stella is thinking about her. Her expression becomes thoughtful and she often begins picking her cuticles, or the skin around her thumb, a habit she is conscious of but persists with.

The questions Stella asks me are ones I have asked about myself but have never been able to answer. 'Do you think Connie would have been better off if she'd lived in a bigger town, with more distractions? Did she ever seek help – I mean, did she ever get any medical help for being depressed? Did she ever get over her grief?' The question I dread hearing is this one: 'Was she ever happy?'

I believe there were times when she was happy, if only for a day or a week, or a month or two. She was happy when I turned fifteen and we went out as a family for a celebration dinner to the local hotel. I know she was happy because I remember her telling me so. I also recall her remarking, as she unfolded a starched white napkin and placed it across her lap, that it was good to get out and celebrate. When she said it she smiled – a wistful look. My father agreed that we ought to go out more often. He actually said, 'I can afford it, after all. We could even go on another holiday together.' And Connie had nodded, saying, 'I'm lucky to have you.' Then she turned to me and added, 'You too. I'm especially lucky to have you.'

I savoured that remark. I never doubted that she meant it, just as I never questioned the genuine nature of her grief. She didn't cling to her sorrow like a crutch. She just couldn't help herself. It was as if she had been born sad and life just made things worse.

In the early days, when I was still getting used to Stella, I answered all her questions. When I grew tired of talking I'd ask a few of my own. 'What was it like climbing Mount Sefton?' To my disappointment she told me she never climbed the mountain. She had been a child when she'd made the pledge and she couldn't be held to such a crazy idea. When she caught sight of my face she laughed. 'Oh, come on. You don't think I would actually go up a mountain, do you? I'm a historian, for God's sake.'

'I'm sure a lot of historians are mountaineers.'

'Name one,' she said.

'Did you ever climb another mountain?' she asked later that same night, when it became clear that, for the first time since we'd met, she had no intention of going back to her motel. 'No.' I shook my head.

'Did you keep in touch with any of the others?' she asked.

'Not really,' I said, remembering the years following the climb. 'I visited Harry Ayres once in a while and I used to ask him about Walter.'

'What happened to him? Walter, I mean.'

I hesitated. 'He died.'

'You don't have to tell me about it if you don't want to.'

I nodded, but I knew I had no choice.

The night of the bonfire was so calm, so clear that I decided to sleep outside under the stars. To my surprise, Walter joined me. The others, keen to christen the hut, hauled their mattresses into the new shelter and carried on with their party. From where I lay I could hear their voices and laughter and I saw the light through the window of the hut, sometimes bright, at other times dim, depending on the number of candles burning and the length of their flames.

Walter, not far from my side, was silent but I was sure he was awake. For almost an hour I lay still, thinking about the mountain I had climbed, the view from the top, and even though I wanted to share my experience with him I couldn't. It was as if I didn't know *how* to speak to him any more. Although I guessed I had him to thank for getting me on the day's climb, I had no way of breaking through the silence. Now that I knew he had been a conscientious objector, everything had changed between us.

Half awake, I kept my eyes focused on the mountain tops and listened as every now and again some small sound – a rock fall, or some indeterminate creak of ice – broke the silence of the night. As I lay there, not really dozing but barely conscious all the same, my thoughts kept wandering back to Walter. I had the feeling that once we left the camp in

189

the morning I might not see him again. I doubted that he was the kind of man who would go to much trouble to keep in touch. I didn't imagine he would seek me out. For some reason this knowledge made me feel lonely.

Only four of us departed the following morning. Hillary and Harry led the way, with Walter and me following behind. The rest of the group remained at the hut. To look at them, you would think they were staying put because they were hung over, but apparently it was because they had decided to do a spot of climbing before returning to Christchurch.

I was sorry to leave the camp but I was glad to be going home. I was tired, and it was all I could do to follow my companions' footsteps in the snow, grateful to be in the company of skilled route-finders, men who knew where they were going and what they were about.

After many hours of walking we arrived at Hooker Hut. With less than three hours to go, the consensus was that we should keep going to Mount Cook village. I was happy to go along with this plan, imagining a hot meal and a bath at the Hermitage. However, Walter and Harry left us at Hooker Hut to return via the Copland Pass to the West Coast. Despite the lateness of the day they also planned to keep going, fearing the weather might close in and prevent their crossing should they stay overnight at the hut. Knowing they were in a hurry, I became flustered and barely managed to mumble my thanks to Harry. When it came time to shake Walter's hand I hesitated. To make matters worse, he unexpectedly passed me a small book of verse, saying he thought I should have it. I opened it at its title page and saw an inscription, 'To Walter, with kind regards, Harry Scott.' Underneath, in pencil, Walter had added, 'To Boden, Poet and Friend – Walter'. I flinched and quickly closed the book, trapping the words inside.

Even then, I had a real sense that he was offering me one of his most valued possessions and I was torn by a desire to keep the book while, at the same time, not wanting to accept it *from him*. Part of me felt as if it were being offered a bribe in exchange for my friendship. I didn't think I should let Walter off that easily.

I might have handed it back, had not Hillary stepped in at that very moment to shake Walter's hand while calling out to Harry to 'give some

190

more thought to the Antarctic problem'. Then all three men turned and started walking.

Like a lone sheep that doesn't know which way to go once the flock has been divided, I dithered and then hurried after Hillary, the book clutched in my hand. I didn't have time to stop and put it in my pack, nor did I try easing it into one of the large pockets in my parka. I held on to it, gripping it tightly, feeling the edges of its narrow spine dig into my palm. Poet *and friend*.

I still had Walter's book the day I learned of his death – and that of his old friend, Harry Scott – in separate accidents in February 1960.

All I know about Harry Scott's death is that he was killed while climbing Mount Cook. His companion, a man by the name of Jim Glasgow, died with him. Walter knew both men. He had climbed alongside Jim during the rescue of Ruth Adams from La Perouse, and of course he knew Harry Scott from their time together in detention. Details were a little sketchy but it seemed that Walter was at Franz Josef when he heard news of his friends' accident. Wanting to assist in locating their bodies he set out from home, intending to cross the Copland Pass and meet up with Harry Ayres and the other members of the search party. He never made it. A day or two later his body was found near the snowline above Hooker Hut. He showed no signs of having fallen or being injured. Neither did it appear that he had died from exposure.

As I had been telling this story I watched Stella, noticing when her mind strayed, when she became restless, but now she sat up and I was certain I had her full attention.

'Had he got lost, do you think?'

I shook my head. No.

'You make it sound like he just dropped down dead . . .' Stella continued. She saw my expression and added, 'Is that what happened?'

'Yes.'

We sat quietly for a moment but I could see that Stella was not satisfied. I anticipated her next question and told her that the cause of death was thought to have been a faulty heart. I couldn't recall the exact name of the condition, but it was connected to some childhood illness – rheumatic fever, most likely. It was a miracle, apparently, that he had managed to live as long as he had.

I felt the silence between us deepen and I knew that when Stella spoke she would ask the one question I have often asked myself – and never been able to answer.

'Do you think he knew? About his heart, I mean.'

I shrugged.

'Because if he knew he had a heart condition he would never have passed the medical examination for the army. He wouldn't have been sent to detention. He might still have a wife and daughter.'

I don't know.

I will never know.

It was the mid-1990s, around the time that mountaineer Rob Hall died on Mount Everest, when it suddenly hit me that I was growing old. I can remember quite clearly what led me to this realisation. It had nothing to do with the state of my health, or the fact that during one of her weekend visits Stella had rather cruelly remarked on my difficulty in maintaining an erection. I felt young – or at least no older than I had felt twenty years before. What brought me face to face with my advancing years was a gift Stella presented to me one day, for no apparent reason. It was a computer and printer – her desktop, to be precise. She had noticed that I always wrote by hand – on scraps of paper, on pages torn from old exercise books and, when I remembered, in a notebook I had bought, at great expense for the sole purpose of composing poetry, although I rarely did as I was loath to fill its beautiful cream-coloured blank pages with my scrawling script. Stella had decided to introduce me to modern technology. It helped that she had just bought a laptop and so no longer needed her old PC.

For what seemed an eternity I sat at the table, Stella by my side, while she explained the mechanics of creating a new folder, a file, saving and backing up onto a disc. She used words I had never heard before: toolbars, icons, scroll-bars, clicks and double-clicks and then, just when I thought my head would explode, she did something so alarming I felt my blood run cold. One second we were looking at the screen, my latest poem before us, and the next second the third stanza vanished, to reappear a moment later tacked onto the bottom of the first. Stella then duplicated the first part of the poem, saying, 'There you go. Just remember those keystrokes: Control A, Control X, Control C and Control V.' Patting me reassuringly on the shoulder she added, 'Let's see you get it back the way it was.'

She stood up and left the room and I sat there, staring at the screen and then slowly, letter by letter, I back-spaced my way through the duplicated section, deleting it letter by letter, and was just about halfway through rewriting the third stanza in its correct position when everything suddenly became so jumbled in my brain that I froze.

I looked around for Stella but she was nowhere to be seen and so, in a fit of temper, I closed the window, tapping 'no' in response to the question about saving changes because I could no longer recall her instructions – and, moreover, I no longer cared. After a minute or so, during which time I sat scowling at the screen, Stella reappeared and, without saying a word, reopened the file I had just closed. To my astonishment the poem flashed up in its original format. I was so mystified that I barely registered her voice when she said, 'See, I told you it wouldn't take long to get the hang of it.'

I gaped from the screen to Stella and then slumped back in my chair, running my hands over my head. 'My poor brain,' I moaned. 'I'm too old for this.'

I eventually managed to come to terms with my computer but those first few lessons left me feeling vulnerable and dull. A nagging thought lodged in my brain. What if I really was getting old? Should I start thinking about my future? Make some plans?

For months at a time I was able to push these questions to the back of my head but every so often, usually in the evening, when I was alone, they would resurface and pester me, demanding attention.

Despite my best intentions, eighteen months passed before I finally placed advertisements in three South Island newspapers seeking a part-time assistant to help in the shop. I expected the advertisement would attract older applicants – semi-retired butchers, for example, who wanted to move to the country and spend more time fishing or gardening but the one reply I received was from a twenty-six-year-old named Benjamin (Beano) Wax. Beano had only been resident in New Zealand for nine months. He was British and his accent, when I spoke to him on the phone, placed him in the north – Coronation Street was my guess.

He arrived for his interview the following week, knocking on the shop door a little before eight in the morning, as we had arranged. His hair stood up from his head in an uneven bristle and his shirt and trousers appeared to have been tugged on over a pair of pyjamas, but he had the most angelic smile I had ever seen and his manner was so polite, so charming, that I was disarmed completely and invited him in.

We stood chatting by the counter for a minute or two and then, to my surprise, he caught sight of the faded photograph of me on Mount Cook and asked, 'Where's that, then?'

'Mount Cook,' I responded, watching him carefully.

Beano cocked his head, 'That you?'

I nodded.

'Impressive, that is.' He turned from the photo to me and grinned. 'You look a bit like a mountaineer.'

Flattered, I took down the photo and passed it to him. I could barely keep myself from smirking as I imagined his response at discovering the identity of my climbing companion.

'What route did you take?'

Flustered, I said, 'The easiest.'

Beano laughed. 'Nice one.'

He placed the photograph carefully on the counter and looked about. 'You always worked alone?'

I shook my head. 'No, this was my father's shop.' I picked up the photograph once more and appeared to study it. Casually, I put it back on the counter but with the image turned towards Beano. I even tapped the glass, my finger pointing towards Hillary's head.

'It's nice,' Beano said. 'Old-fashioned. Better than any of the places I've worked before.'

He had handed me a curriculum vitae but he also gave me a quick verbal run-down of his career. 'I've got good references,' he added. 'I like working.'

I nodded once more and asked why he wanted to work in Fairlie. It was hardly the centre of the world.

He laughed and explained that he liked the outdoors. He had come to New Zealand for the climbing – not mountain climbing, he hastened to add, though he wanted to try his hand at that too – but rock-climbing. There were a few decent crags in the area – Mount Horrible in particular – and one of his mates had told him there were good routes on Mount Misery and Cloudy Peak – mountains whose names I vaguely recognised but felt no desire to explore despite Beano's insistence that they were all local and that I should check them out.

'It'll be perfect, this,' he said, smiling broadly as he walked around, running his hands over the blocks, picking up one or two knives, testing their blades against his finger.

'Your mate looks a bit knackered,' he suddenly said, glancing back at the photo as he came back around the counter.

'How can you tell? He's wearing goggles.'

He took the photograph in his hands and made a low tutting noise. 'You can see it in the way he's standing. I expect it's the altitude – what is it? Twelve thousand feet?' He shook his head gently and then carefully placed the photograph back on its hook. 'Well, what do you think?'

I gave him a fortnight's trial but I could tell straight away that he knew his trade. He was surprisingly light on his feet and he often hummed while he worked, but the best thing was that he smiled. Even when he complained – about the cold, which he seemed to be particularly sensitive to, or his ramshackle accommodation – he managed to sound little more than bemused. He laughed out loud when I eventually gave in and told him who the other man in the photograph was.

He also liked my poetry.

I had been working on my collection, *Kindred Spirits*, for so long that I began to think of it as both a burden and a joke. I didn't have the energy to transfer any of the completed – or near completed – handwritten poems to my computer and so they remained in a folder on the cabinet next to my bed. From time to time I would glance at one or other of the poems and sigh, from frustration or guilt. Very occasionally I redis-covered a poem that sent a small shock coursing through my body as I scanned it. Whenever that happened I took the poem in to work and read it aloud to Beano, searching his expression for an indication of its merit. I learnt after a while that whenever he cocked his head to the left he would respond positively, but that if he looked straight ahead, his mouth fixed in a smile, he was less enthusiastic. Either way he always listened carefully, waiting until he was sure I had finished before passing judgement. 'You should send that in,' he'd say if I had written something he liked. Once or twice he'd go further and add, 'That's the bollocks, that is.' Initially, his use of 'bollocks' confused me. Apparently, depending on whether or not the definite article was used, it could be either a compliment or a criticism. To my relief he never described any of my poems as straight out 'bollocks'.

Beano's enthusiasm for my poetry began to rub off on me after a while. He looked forward to the 'weekly reading', as he called it, and in order to keep up with demand I began to spend more time at my computer, creating new work. These poems gave me the sense that I was working well and achieving something, but I was also aware that none of these recent pieces belonged in my *Kindred Spirits* collection. I had to stop spending so much time on this new work and knuckle down and get the collection completed once and for all.

It was late one afternoon, the day after the 1998 general election, when I was immersed for the hundredth time in rearranging *Kindred Spirits* into some semblance of order, when the phone rang. Irritated and relieved at the interruption, I picked up the receiver, anticipating either Geraldine or Stella's voice – they were the only people who regularly phoned me. Hearing a woman's voice I didn't at first register that it wasn't either of my friends and answered grumpily, 'Yes, what do you want?' My tone must have thrown the caller off because there was a long pause and then, from out of that silence, a quiet voice asked, 'Is that Boden Black?'

'Yes.'

There was another long pause and then softly, haltingly, I heard the woman say, 'I'm sorry, you might not understand anything I'm about to say – but I think you're my brother.'

I did something I have only ever seen actors on television do. I lowered the receiver from my ear and hovered, looking at it. My first thought was not disbelief but confusion. I hadn't thought about my birth mother for a while.

'You are Boden Black, aren't you?'

I could hear her voice in the distance and I was aware that she was speaking very hesitantly, as if, like me, she had no idea what to say next.

Someone else might have asked for her name, or for some proof of familial connection, but I was so taken aback by the woman's presence in my kitchen that I found myself telling her that this was not a good time to call and that I would appreciate it if she would phone back after dinner – in a few hours' time.

It was only after she hung up that I realised what I had done. I had no doubt she was my half-sister, yet I had put her off. I didn't know her number, and if she didn't ring me back I would never find out who I was.

I have little recollection of how I passed the three hours between her first and second calls. I have a vague memory of replacing the phone on the charger and then lifting it up from its cradle once or twice to check that I had not left it in 'talk' mode. I think I walked around the house, pausing at the entrance to my parents' room – now mine – and made a note of how little it had changed since their deaths. The curtains, the wallpaper, the bed, the furniture – it all dated back to the late 1960s. On the wall above the dresser was a framed portrait of a woman, an image that had originally been painted by Renoir but was, in this case, a 5000-piece jigsaw puzzle, glued and mounted. As I looked at the lady's face I felt strangely light-headed and retreated back to the kitchen where I sat down, puzzling over one word the woman had used. Brother. Not half-brother but *brother*.

'It's Kim Morton again,' said the woman when I answered the phone a few hours later. 'I'm sorry if I called at a bad time before.'

In the hours since I had last heard her voice I hadn't managed to come up with a plan of what to say. All the questions I might have asked remained out of reach. I was willing to listen, however.

Kim Morton was married. She lived in Wellington with her husband, a landscape architect, and their two teenage children. Morton was her married name. Her family name – my name – was Butler.

Boden Butler. I rolled the words around in my mouth, trying them for size.

'Once or twice I heard my mother wonder aloud about you, referring to you as Winslow. It was her favourite name and it was what she would have called you, had she been allowed to. It's Old English and means something like "from the hill of the friend".'

I responded that it was an unusual name and Kim laughed, saying that Boden wasn't exactly common. She then explained that her mother had been a scholar, a linguist, a woman who loved words. She was the type of person who would spend hours poring over a thesaurus, searching out the perfect word. She . . .

I must have made some kind of sound, one loud enough for Kim to hear, because she suddenly fell silent.

'What was her name?' I eventually asked. I had the feeling Kim had mentioned it several times already but I hadn't taken it in.

'Lily.'

'And she's dead,' I stated. From the way Kim had spoken I was certain she was.

'Yes. They're both dead: Lily and Matthew.' She paused and then added, 'My father – *our father* – was called Matthew.'

For an instant I thought I had misheard but I know now that the problem was not one of hearing but of understanding. I didn't understand.

From the hesitancy in her voice I realised that Kim was also finding our conversation daunting, if not painful. I heard her ask me if I wanted to know more about my parents. She asked if I had heard enough for one night, if I wanted a break, or if I wanted to go on. It seemed to me that we might as well carry on. We had gone so far, there was no point stopping now.

'Are you sure?' asked Kim. 'I can always phone back in the morning – or you could call me.'

It's funny but I'd never given much thought to my father – my birth father. I had never wondered what he might have looked like or who he was. He had never seemed that important – or real. Never for an instant did I think I would ever learn his name. Matthew.

'My mother was born in Milton,' said Kim. She hesitated and corrected herself. 'Our mother was born in Milton and moved to Christchurch when she was around five. Her father was a bank manager, and her mother looked after the house. They were good people, but quite conservative. They attended church every Sunday and it was through church that Mum's parents met Matthew's parents. Mum must have been about nine or ten when she first met Matthew. The two families became very close and when Mum was fourteen she apparently announced to Matthew, who was older than her, that she intended to fall in love with him.'

I must have coughed because Kim paused and asked if I was all right. I have to admit that I found her story a little implausible. I couldn't imagine any girl of fourteen, brought up in a strict family, doing what Lily was said to have done. But I would save my reservations for later.

'Lily was very strong-willed. These days she would probably be labelled a "difficult" child but I don't think she intended to cause trouble. She was very bright and I think she probably found her family life very restrictive. She told me once that she had known as a child that she didn't want to be like her mother. She wanted something more from life, though she didn't know what. Anyway . . .' Kim sighed, 'Lily and Matthew did fall in love and quite soon after she fell pregnant. Matthew loved Lily but he was a young man, a student. He was the only child of a greengrocer but had won several scholarships so there was a huge amount of pressure on him to attend university and – you know, rise up in the world, become a professional. His mother was certainly pushing him in that direction.'

'So there was no question of them getting married?'

'None at all. They were both considered too young and they were also both extremely ambitious. I gather that it became very difficult . . .'

'You mean the shame? The gossip?'

I heard a kind of mumble and when Kim spoke again I could tell she was feeling very uncomfortable.

'Adoption was the only option,' she said, her voice wavering. 'The other thing was – and I hate to say this – but your grandparents promised your mother that she could also go to university if . . .'

'. . . if she got rid of me.'

How could I be understanding, let alone forgiving, of such a situation? My future had been bartered against that of my mother's. I didn't want to hear any more. I felt disgusted. The fact that all this had taken place in the 1930s, and that society would have frowned upon my mother, failed to move me. At that moment all I could see was that I had been discarded.

'When the time came she was sent away to have the baby. I mean, to have you. Once she returned she took up with Matthew again and just before the war they decided to get married. Not long after that, Dad heard that he had been accepted at Oxford and so they moved to England. I was born a year later.'

'And Lily?'

'She put her studies on hold for a few years but eventually completed a doctorate in Old English.'

I believe that Kim had tried to select her words carefully, that she hadn't intended to wound me but, intentionally or not, she managed to do just that. 'You're a poet aren't you?' she suddenly said. 'My parents made friends with some interesting people. Scholars and writers, mostly – some quite famous. There were quite a few New Zealanders among them.'

I felt too sick in my stomach to ask for names.

There was little point in being angry, much less to despair. The events described by Kim had happened long ago and I kept telling myself that her family history had nothing to do with me, that there was no place for me in it. Even so, I was glad of the unspoken pact between us: that neither one of us would ever speculate, aloud, on how things might have been.

For my own sake I had to maintain my distance.

I determined to finish *Kindred Spirits*. To my relief, Beano offered to take over the shop for as long as I needed so I retreated to my house, sitting alone at the kitchen table, intent on getting the collection to a publishable state. This time as I worked I discovered that my desire to prove myself once and for all as a poet was now tinged with a hint of revenge. Childish though it was, I wanted to show 'them' – my other family – that I had made it on my own terms, far away from the privileged world of Oxford. There was, I admit, something cold-blooded about my approach.

Stella noticed the change in me when she next visited, and warned me against becoming bitter. Her advice was not well received. I snapped at her, telling her in no uncertain terms that I was not bitter in the least.

How could I be? All my life I had been shown nothing but love and support; my father had been immensely proud of me. Being bitter in those circumstances would amount to an act of betrayal.

She remained unconvinced.

'Well, I was just thinking that if you'd grown up in a bookish household like your sister . . . if your parents were . . .'

I cut her off. 'You mean Matthew and Lily? *Not* my parents.'

I could see that Stella was beginning to wish she'd remained silent, but she was the kind of person who could never walk away from an argument. 'Whatever . . . I simply think that growing up in a more intellectually stimulating household might have had some benefits . . . not least,' she rushed, anticipating another interruption, 'not least . . . they may have had connections to other writers or publishers and . . .' She paused, glanced at me and added, 'You've always implied that Nathaniel and Connie didn't share your love of words . . .'

Did she expect me to deny it? I couldn't, but all the same I wouldn't hear a word against my parents. 'I had a hell of a lot of freedom,' I countered. 'I wasn't stifled in any way. I reckon that growing up in Fairlie was probably better for me than being in Oxford. I didn't have to deal with the weight of all that stuff.'

'What stuff?'

I sighed. 'You know . . . colonialism. The British class system. That sense of entitlement.'

Stella made a sharp tutting sound and shook her head in frustration. I thought she was going to make some remark about my small-town upbringing but she didn't. She let it go.

The peace was short-lived. It wasn't Stella who disturbed it, however, but Kim. Having found me at last, she was keen to see me and so I eventually gave in to the pressure. I suggested we meet in the neutral territory of Christchurch – a convenient halfway point between Fairlie and Wellington.

I was taken aback by how emotional I felt when I first caught sight of the tall fiftyish woman who raised her hand hesitantly as I approached the reception area of the YMCA hotel.

In the months leading up to this meeting I had heard the entire story of Lily and Matthew's life. I had learnt of Kim's slow but determined attempt to track me down following the death of her father. She had even hired the services of a private detective. I had no idea how one went about finding a lost relative and I was surprised at how much she had uncovered about me in the process. I suppose it was defensiveness, or arrogance, but I imagined I had heard all I needed to know about Lily and Matthew, and that the proposed meeting with Kim was more for her benefit than mine.

In fact, nothing prepared me for the first time I laid eyes on my sister.

I managed to return her wave but then I became rooted to the spot, unable to take a step forward towards her. She had ginger-blonde hair. Her skin was freckled. I had seen photos of her – and she mine – but they were nothing compared with the flesh-and-blood woman walking towards me. My heart lurched and in that instant I recognised myself in her face. It was as if I had been handed a mirror. She even carried herself like me. As she walked across the reception area, I knew, deep in my heart, that she was family.

Her eyes brimming with tears, Kim shook my hand. Her bottom lip quivered as she placed her arms around me and hugged me, repeating my name over and over again until my shoulders began to tremble and I clung to her – for dear life.

How long we remained like that I'm not sure. When we finally took a step back we both laughed self-consciously and I made some remark about her flight, saying that I hoped it hadn't been too rough. And all the time I spoke I couldn't take my eyes off her. I just wanted to look at her, to reassure myself that she was real.

'You look like Mum,' said Kim. 'You have the same colouring, the same mouth.' She kept her gaze fixed on me as she spoke, and when she mentioned my mouth I felt my lips begin to tremble again and was relieved when she put her arms around me once more, saying, 'It's okay. We'll be all right.'

My voice was muffled. 'I don't even know why I'm crying – I should be happy.'

And then I gave in to my tears again, oblivious to everything except the warmth of our embrace and the trembling in my legs, which would not stop.

Eventually Kim took charge and led me across the road to a cafe in the Arts Centre. I was no longer crying but I felt shaky and was happy to follow.

'I hope tea's all right,' she said, returning with a tray of food and drinks. 'I got a cheese scone and a blueberry muffin,' she added, setting the plates out on the table. She smiled in my direction and then sat down opposite me, cutting each bun in half and placing one piece of each on both plates before passing me one, as I imagined she did when out with her husband.

I took a bite of scone but found it hard to chew.

'Feeling better?' Kim asked.

I was embarrassed. 'I didn't expect it to hit me so hard. I thought I'd handle it better.'

Kim told me she had spent most of the night before awake, crying. 'The people in the next room must have wondered what on earth was going on.'

'So you're one step ahead of me,' I said.

I felt stupid about by my earlier outburst.

'Well,' said Kim, 'let's not worry about it. We're here now – that's what matters.'

We spent the day together but after an initial flurry of conversation, during which time Kim repeated nearly everything that had already been said on the phone, we became quiet. It was my fault. I was still feeling uneasy and vulnerable, and was afraid of the intimacy Kim sought. As a result I became circumspect. Questions which she put to me I deflected or responded to in a polite but noncommittal manner. I felt pushed into a corner, the focus of too much attention. Kim was just doing what anyone else would have done in her situation – she was trying to get to know me, to make up for lost time. But I told her little about my childhood. I barely mentioned Stella, and when Kim tried to engage me in a discussion on writing – revealing in the process that her parents had been friends with

Dan Davin in Oxford – I became tight-lipped, determined not to give her even the slightest bit of encouragement.

I didn't fully understand why I was so reluctant to open up, but if pushed I would have to admit I felt scared. I didn't want to be forced to reveal too much too quickly. I needed more time to get used to her, to establish where I fitted in. I was greatly relieved when she finally caught her taxi back to the airport and left me alone.

At home once more, I was sad that I had not given more of myself to Kim. Full of guilt and remorse I arranged for a large bunch of flowers to be delivered to her house with a note thanking her. Even as I dictated it to the florist I knew the message would do more harm than good. Why I couldn't embrace her and her family and welcome them into my life I'm not sure. But I just couldn't. I suspect I was in some way too shocked or grief-stricken. At least, that was Stella's interpretation.

In the weeks that followed Kim and I talked on the phone, often. However, I made excuses not to attend her family Christmas, and as the months went by, we became increasingly distant. Her efforts to keep the relationship alive were matched by apathy and resistance from me. I sent her a card on her birthday but that was all.

The day I posted the birthday card I also sent *Kindred Spirits* to one of the university presses and was thrilled when it was accepted. It was my hope that this new collection would at last banish my only successful poem, 'Three Days at Least', to the past, allowing me to move forward, to deliver work that I was more or less proud of.

The book's positive critical reception was flattering. It was heralded as a 'long-awaited' collection, one that showcased a writer 'at the height of his powers'. Several of the poems were described as 'dazzling', 'tender and elegiac', and 'tough and uncompromising'.

Beano's response was even more gratifying. He took the copy I gave him and held it in his hands, saying, 'Ta very much. I'll treasure that.' Somewhat gingerly he opened it at the title page and smiled. 'Look at that – you've even signed it.' He read the handwritten dedication aloud, and when I pointed out that I had also mentioned him in the acknowledgements he pretended to frown, complaining, 'I'll have to buy another copy to send to my mum, now. She'll be right chuffed.'

He looked up and grinned, 'She'll put you in her bedroom – alongside all her other poets.'

When he saw my puzzled look, he said, 'She reads a lot of poetry.'

He glanced back at the book and continued, 'She even took a few evening classes on the subject a while back – after my dad ran off. She's a bit of a hopeless romantic, my mum. I can just see her squeezing you in between Auden and . . .' He shrugged and then laughed, 'Leonard Cohen.'

Business was brisk at the butchery. Women who had long ago taken their custom to the supermarket now returned to the shop, congratulating me on the success of my book, which they had seen on display in the cafe gift shop and the library. Speculation concerning the subjects of the poems became widespread. A woman I had barely spoken to since school claimed that one of the poems – the one that had been singled out and published in the *Listener* – was about her. She recognised herself as the girl dressed in nothing but a light cotton shift, standing on stage, washing blood from her hands while 'in the wings, two soldiers stood transfixed . . .'

I didn't mind being on the receiving end of so much attention – even though Beano teased me about it constantly – but I wished my father had been around, for his pleasure would have been genuine, whereas mine was tainted by the uneasy feeling that nothing had really changed. I was still a butcher, a local – someone who had been around for ever, but a bit of a 'strange one'.

I was pleased when Stella invited me to join her for the first three days of a trip around the South Island as part of a research project concerning the history of aerated water and lemonade. She'd touched on the subject while writing her history of Fairlie and was embarking on a journey that would take her through Temuka and Waimate and down to Dunedin before heading back up the West Coast, where she hoped to make contact with some old-timer who knew the story behind the Digger Kiwi brand.

I was reluctant to ask Beano to cover for me for the whole trip but I decided I could manage three days. On the trip I was reminded of just how much I enjoyed Stella's company. She was one of only a few people I had ever met who became more interesting the better I got to know them. I hadn't fully appreciated just how knowledgeable she was. The more I was with her the clearer it became that she was a person who was at ease with herself. Everything she needed by way of acknowledgement or acceptance, came from within. When I asked what it was she liked about me she joked, 'Well, you don't talk much and you travel light.' Realising that I was still waiting she added, 'Plus you've just written a love poem for me so I have to stick with you – I don't have any choice.'

The 'love poem' was hardly that. I'd scrawled it onto a paper serviette while waiting for a pie to be heated at the Savoy Tearooms in Waimate. It was little more than doggerel, a silly rhyme, and it occurred to me, after Stella drew attention to it, that perhaps she had been disappointed, that she really would have liked to been the object of a proper love poem. I hadn't ever thought of her as a romantic – I thought she was far too modern and independent – but I began to think that I might have hurt her feelings by giving the appearance of taking our relationship too lightly. It slowly dawned on me that all the fuss over Kim and my book might have made Stella feel left out. There was the slightest chance that she might have wanted to feel linked to me. For the first time since meeting Stella, I found myself worrying that she might leave me.

When we parted at the bus stop in Dunedin I became quite gloomy. The day itself was sunny, with not a breath of wind to disturb the mirrored surface of the sea as the bus followed the coast north, but I began to fret that I had really blown things with Stella. The feeling remained with me throughout the day, intensifying late that evening when I passed the closed shop and let myself in to my eerily quiet, empty house.

Only rarely have I received an envelope in the mail that has caused me to stop, mid-way down my garden path, to open it. Usually I shuffle through what little post I get before discarding most of it unopened into the wood basket beside the fireplace. I very much doubt that I have missed anything of importance. Most envelopes give away their contents: a discount offer from the local hardware store or restaurant, a form letter from a real estate agent, and once a year a thick wad of Christmas cards from an association of foot and mouth painters. I suspect that the cards that my mother filled out so long ago may also have come from the same organisation. Certainly the images, with their snow-covered winter landscapes, bare trees and red robins look very familiar.

The envelope that stopped me in my tracks one morning in 2002 aroused my interest because of its large size and the quality of its white paper. It was entirely free of logos and featured only my name and address and that of a return post office box number. Tearing it open I discovered a letter commissioning me to write a poem for a museum that was to be officially opened at Mount Cook in the winter of 2003, marking fifty years since the establishment of the national park. Attached was a contract and a brochure containing colour photos of Mount Cook and an artist's impression of the tourist centre. A 'mission statement' encapsulated, in rather ambiguous and lacklustre terms, the 'vision' behind the centre.

The contract was extremely detailed. But why me? I read the letter for a second time and got the feeling that it could have been a form letter that had been personalised. Referring to me as 'one of this nation's leading creative talents' it went on to say, 'We would be delighted if you would join with us to celebrate . . .' Tacked on to the end of the paragraph was a request that I 'compose a poem highlighting the very essence of Aoraki/ Mount Cook in terms of its natural and human heritage'.

My immediate response was mild irritation. I still had no idea why I had been singled out for the task. I suspected that several names had been put forward and that someone who had some faint recollection of 'Three Days at Least' or had read a recent review of *Kindred Spirits* decided I might be worth a try. The fact that I lived in Fairlie – and so was a local – probably helped. In my mind's eye I could see a group of marketing and promotional types sitting around an oval table in some office in Wellington, listlessly ticking off items from a 'to do' list, working their way through the essentials until they came to the performers and, last of all, the poet.

When Stella visited again I told her about the commission before outlining the reasons why I planned to turn it down, fully expecting her to agree. We were sitting in the back garden and as I grumbled away she sat quietly, sipping a glass of wine. When I had reached the end of my long list of complaints she turned to face me and narrowed her eyes. 'I honestly don't understand what your problem is,' she said.

'It seems like a lot of trouble, that's all,' I countered.

Stella rolled her eyes.

'What else were you going to do? It's not as if you've had any better offers recently.'

I shrugged. Stella, I knew, rarely turned down work. There had been times when she had been less than enthusiastic about a particular project but, as she so often said, they all paid the bills. My objection to being forced to 'write on demand' failed to gain sympathy. Stella shook her head and called me pathetic.

In the end it wasn't Stella who forced my hand but Kim. For a long time she had been hinting that she would like to bring her husband and family down to visit. She planned a kind of South Island road trip – it was something she had wanted to do for as long as she could remember. She wanted to come and stay with me in order to experience first hand all the places I had described in my poems. My skill in evoking the countryside was such that she could not only visualise the locations but *smell* them too.

The prospect of having her around was not one I embraced, but I couldn't turn her away cold-heartedly. Even I balked at that. Instead I put myself at her mercy and asked her to delay her trip on account of my recent acceptance of a major commission, one that would take up all my free time for the foreseeable future. In order to give the impression that I was as disappointed as she was, I added that it would be wonderful if she could come down for the opening of the Centre itself, in 2003.

Stella wasn't impressed. She was irritated by the fuss I had made over the commission, and now also by my off-hand treatment of Kim. A kind of stand-off followed that left me feeling downcast and on edge. It reminded me of the unhappy – but thankfully short-lived – period that had followed our aerated-water tour of the south, when I had penned that ridiculous love poem. I was worried that now, like then, I might have upset Stella.

I decided it wouldn't hurt to close the shop for a week and give Beano time off to go rock-climbing. For weeks he had been wanting to go to Golden Bay, to try out some routes on a cliff near Takaka. I arranged to rent a small cottage at Lake Ohau from one of my regular customers. She had made the offer several times before but this was the first time I had taken her up on it. I wanted to spend time with Stella. I hoped that a few days alone in the hills would bring us together. I feared that it was my last chance.

Working alongside Stella at Ohau was a bitter-sweet experience. I had only ever worked with men before and I was surprised at how different it was to labour away in the presence of a woman. True, the nature of our work, being sedentary, was entirely different from what I had done before, but it was the sensation of 'stillness' that impressed me more than anything. Even when Stella asked as innocent a question as 'How is it going?' I was taken aback by how different it was coming from her rather than from my father or Dudley. Stella, I understood, was asking how *I* was doing, whereas my father had been asking how *my work* was going.

I was still working hard on my poem but there were times when I simply could not bear to sit still any longer. Whenever I grew restless I would stand and walk to the window and gaze out at the lake, taking in the view of the massive, limpet-shaped Ben Ohau across the water. It was not so much the mountain as the bulldozer track leading towards its summit that held my attention. This long straight line scored into the hillside was so at odds with the rounded skylines and eroded gullies that I saw it as an incision made by a surgeon. To see a natural landmark cut up and deformed thus had a depressing effect on me. When I wandered outside for fresh air I was confronted by even more signs of desecration. Our modest bach was surrounded on all sides by building sites, and half-finished holiday homes in a new subdivision. The sound of polythene flapping in the wind gave our location a desolate air.

Returning to the cottage, I invariably gave in to the desire to open a bottle of wine. Glass in hand, I would re-focus my attention on my work, finding solace in the laying down of words on a page, sounding them out and immersing myself in a search for perfection – a journey that could go on forever, never bringing me to my destination.

I realised that writing poetry had protected me from loneliness. But I realised, too, that there was a vast difference between loneliness and emptiness, and that although poetry had shielded me against the former, only Stella was capable of safeguarding me from the latter.

I tried to articulate my feelings to Stella but she misunderstood. She eyed me suspiciously, as though fearful I was about to do something rash – like propose or ask her to move in. After a short while she remarked that it might be a good idea if I got a dog. Sensing my objection she added, 'You could feed it on scraps and bones – it wouldn't cost you anything for food.'

I went back to my work but my thoughts were still on Stella. I couldn't decide whether her independence masked a vulnerability or whether she really was that tough. It seemed to me that there was a good chance she would harden as she grew older, and that what stuck me now as 'spirit' might one day manifest itself as dissatisfaction or resentment.

Only the previous day I had been lost in work when Stella sighed loudly and exclaimed, 'I am so sick of all this stuff!' She gestured impatiently towards the papers in front of her.

I was thinking about a response, but she hadn't finished. 'It's all so ordinary,' she said, drawing out the word 'ordinary' into four syllables. 'I get so tired of writing about people who do sweet f-all with their lives . . .'

I was completely taken aback. I opened my mouth to say something but she cut me short. 'All I ever do is small-town stuff.'

'But I thought that was the point of history these days. You want to examine the lives of ordinary people, don't you?'

'Yes, of course – but just once in a while I'd like to do something "big".'

I knew part of Stella's frustration resulted from the fact that she had been unsuccessful in getting funding to write a biography of a former New Zealand diplomat, a woman named Jean McKenzie who had worked in Paris during the 1940s and '50s. Stella was profoundly interested in McKenzie and had been bitterly disappointed by her failure to gain support for her project. Still, I was surprised by the level of her anger and her dismissal of the people and lives she researched. I was a little put out, too, to think that I might be lumped in with rest of the small-town nobodies she complained about. Up until that point I had always believed she not only liked me but respected me. Perhaps she did – but I couldn't count on it.

As it turned out, it didn't really matter. Two months after her outburst – and the very day I sent off my commissioned Mount Cook poem – Stella left the country, heading to Canada and England to undertake research for a New Zealand period film about the life of that most famous of small-town boys, Ernest Rutherford.

Left at home, I began to worry that she might not come back. Feeling particularly anxious one day I asked Beano if he thought I was old and dull. As usual he smiled and then shrugged. 'If you're worried about it why don't you come rock-climbing with me this weekend?' he said. 'We could go to Mount Horrible – that would shake you up a bit.' I toyed with the idea – even though I wasn't sure how it answered my question. I decided against it in the end. I imagined myself becoming stuck halfway up a rock face, unable to go on and too scared to go down. I decided the wisest thing to do was stay at home, where at least I was safe. Besides, I didn't want to embarrass Beano in front of his friends. That hardly seemed fair after all he had done for me.

Not long afterwards I was walking around my neighbourhood late one evening when I was overtaken by an acute sense of boredom. Few of the places I had loved as a child existed any more. The fields where I had collected mushrooms were gone, as were the open spaces where I had stood looking out towards the Two Thumb Range. I had the impression that as the town had grown in size it had diminished in spirit.

The more I became aware of the changes, the more claustrophobic I felt. At this late stage in life I suddenly discovered something that the town's restless teenagers had known for generations. Just like them, I risked being trapped. I needed to get out and broaden my horizons. Moving away was in my genes, after all.

A day or so later I determined to make a break with my home town. I contacted a real estate agent to discuss selling my home, and the following week I drove to Timaru where I traded in my old van for a campervan. That afternoon I experienced the joy I had felt so many years before when I took possession of my old Matchless motorbike and rode through Fairlie for the first time.

I suspect that I was attempting to recapture that earlier sense of freedom and spontaneity when I pulled up in front of Geraldine's house and offered to take her for a ride in my new toy. It was foolish of me to think that she would leap at the chance but I was pleased when, after only a small amount of persuasion, she grudgingly reached for her jacket and followed me out to the van. She climbed into the passenger seat and glanced around at the bed and fixtures in the back, then she lost no time in asking if I was having a mid-life crisis. I replied that I didn't think so, and she said it was just as well, because buying a campervan was something German tourists and old people did. There was an association of campervan pensioners, she went on, who travelled the country in convoy. They had special places where they could park, safe in the knowledge that they were part of a group, a kind of mobile rest home. From her bitter tone I guessed that she was having her own worries. Trade at her Bed & Breakfast was slow and I knew she blamed campervans for the downturn. Not that she would come out and say it. Like Stella, she had a tendency to become abrupt whenever she was anxious. She had known me since childhood – I was her oldest friend – and it was not unusual for her to vent her frustrations on me. As we drove out of town I braced myself for what might follow. I didn't have long to wait.

'It's funny that you found love so late in life.'

I glanced across at Geraldine but read nothing in her expression.

'I don't know if it's love,' I replied cautiously.

'You'd better not tell Stella that,' Geraldine responded. 'She'd be mortified.'

I had the uneasy feeling I was about to be drawn into a conversation I didn't want to have. In a feeble attempt to stave off the inevitable I switched on the CD player, hoping to distract her with Bach's cantatas.

'You know she loves you, don't you?' There was a note of accusation in Geraldine's voice. I wasn't sure if she was testing me or merely adding to my confusion.

'You did know?' she added.

Again the prickly tone of voice. Out of the corner of my eye I saw her smile as she hurried on. 'I asked her the last time she was here. I thought if I left it to you to tell me what was going on I'd be . . .' She hesitated, scrutinised my face and then said quietly, 'I told her you felt the same.'

'What?'

I was still absorbing the news that Stella had apparently confessed to being in love with me. Never having heard such a thing from her own lips, I found Geraldine's apparent conviction hard to take seriously.

'Well, you do, don't you?'

What was Geraldine going on about? Did I love Stella? I couldn't think of any reason why I shouldn't love her, if that was the same thing.

Geraldine had left me far behind. Seemingly oblivious to the features of my new van or the scenery through the window she ploughed on. 'You know, you'll never sell your house at the price the agent has suggested. It's way too high.'

'What did Stella really say?' I felt like a schoolboy, scrabbling for scraps of information from a group of cunning girls.

'If you ask me,' said Geraldine, 'you've got no intention to sell up. You want to believe that you're ready to move, but deep down you're resisting change. You'll never leave, not you. Your heart's not in it.'

I knew she was right, and I had already reached the private – but nevertheless humiliating – decision to reconsider selling up, but I was not going to tell her that. Geraldine was playing with me. Everything she said, I realised, was for her benefit, her own satisfaction. It had little to do with me – I was merely a convenient audience.

I closed my ears to her voice and focused on the view. As the road levelled at the top of Burkes Pass I turned down a gravel road to the left, intending to follow the Grays River south until I reached the turn-off to the Mackenzie Pass. Within a few minutes we entered a world that was so brightly coloured it looked as if it belonged to an animated cartoon. All around us, for as far as the eye could see, were clumps of lupins, growing in shades of dusty pink and violet, blue and purple. Against the background of tussock and dark earth the flowers were so intense as to vibrate. Even Geraldine, who I knew had not yet finished with me, broke off from her monologue long enough to glance around, asking me to pull over so she could take a photo on her cellphone and send it to her brother, Ted, who had recently moved to Singapore.

I was happy to oblige, and as Geraldine loitered at the side of the road taking pictures I wandered a short distance away and sat down, taking in the scenery and thinking over what Geraldine had said about Stella. As much as I felt put out by Geraldine's interference in my private affairs, I couldn't help feeling thrilled and flattered by what she had revealed. I would never have assumed that Stella loved me. I had hoped that she liked me – and I was fairly certain that she did, most of the time anyway

– but to discover that I was the object of Stella's love was thrilling. I knew then that I also loved her, but for some reason had never been able to tell her so. I wondered if I had been waiting for her to mention it first but I didn't think so. I am not so egotistical as to demand someone's love before offering my own. Rather, I believed that both Stella and I suffered from shyness, a lack of confidence where emotions were concerned. It was as if we didn't feel entitled to express ourselves emotionally. Though I couldn't be sure about Stella, I had good reason to believe that I was stunted where women were concerned. I had rarely managed to feel at ease around members of the opposite sex. I seemed to swing between watchful on the one hand and extremely guarded on the other. Simply by virtue of knowing me for such a long time, Geraldine was probably one of the few people in the world who knew me for myself: a man who has nothing much to say for himself but who is occasionally driven to communicate that 'nothing' in words on a page. I found myself feeling quite emotional, and when Geraldine had finished with her phone-camera I made a space and invited her to sit down.

After a few minutes of small-talk about my van and my new-found sense of freedom – which to me felt like power – I fell into a reverie, my thoughts drifting across random episodes from my childhood, most related not to people so much as places I loved. One of these episodes was connected to the scene in front of us. I had told Geraldine about my trip to the Mackenzie with her father and brother many times before, but being right now under the influence of the wide-open landscape and succumbing to the warmth of the day, I wanted her to share my happy state. I started to relate the story once more, dwelling on my gratitude towards Dudley, who was in many ways more of a father figure than an uncle. I had barely started, however, when Geraldine interrupted. 'Not that old story again. Can't you talk about something else?'

I fell silent but Geraldine went on. 'You know I could never really understand why you were always at our house when you were a kid.' She broke off long enough to smile at me – as if to show there were no hard feelings. 'I mean, it was odd, wasn't it? You living with us? It wasn't normal. And you were such a strange, needy kid . . .' She held my gaze

217

and again smiled, as if what she was saying had nothing to do with who we were now. She spoke without bitterness, as if she were reporting some distant piece of news. For my own part, I felt shattered. The image of that golden-toned house, the smiling faces of its inhabitants, the real sense of family and well-being I had enjoyed as a child fragmented before my eyes, and in its place was a picture of a sour-faced child – Geraldine – and her all but silent sister Frith eyeing me with barely concealed resentment as I followed Dudley from the house, setting out on a new day's adventure.

'It was partly because of you that I left home when I did and married that man.'

Her former husband, Greg, was a sullen bully of a man, similar in nature to his father, Ray, the mechanic who had put the fear of God into me as a child. Greg was a little younger than me and yet my memories of him in our school days were of a boy who was so sure of his strength that he thought nothing of taking on boys twice his age, even though he often came off second best. I had never understood what Geraldine saw in him. The wedding had taken place in a registry office and I wasn't invited. I knew that Dudley was not keen on the match. In the photos taken after the brief ceremony he is gazing into the middle distance, a tight-lipped smile on his face, while Hilda, at his side, appears to have her eyes closed as if in prayer. The marriage, eventful though it was, was not happy. Ten years after moving to Wollongong, Geraldine returned alone. The benefits of being married to a successful businessman, with the added perks of worldwide travel, meant little compared with the relief of gaining freedom from a tense and uncommunicative – though never physically violent – husband.

'I only married him because he was nothing like you and therefore nothing like the man my parents would have had me marry. I wanted my parents to notice me for a change.' She laughed and again I found her manner unnerving. 'Do you remember how when we were kids I used to make up all those foreign languages and give myself different names – like Margaret, or Penelope, and Hélène?' She grimaced. 'I mean, for God's sake, "Geraldine"!' She spat the name out. 'Do you have any idea what it's like to share your name with a neighbouring town?'

I nodded uncertainly. I had only a vague recollection of Geraldine's exotic names and it had never occurred to me that her name had caused so much distress.

'I tried out all those other names because half the time I didn't want to belong to my own family. I used to pretend I was adopted – like I was some foreign princess, or someone whose parents had been killed in the war.'

She paused and looked at me, her eyes steady. 'I bet you didn't know that, did you?'

No, I didn't, and I had the uneasy feeling that Geraldine hadn't yet reached the real point of her tirade. Despite the beautiful day, I felt cold.

'When I found out that you were adopted I felt sick.'

I half expected her to lunge at me but instead she shook her head, pulling at a piece of grass, and smiled in my direction. 'It's nice here,' she said calmly.

It was all I could do to nod and when, a minute later, she asked if I would one day write a poem for her I nodded again. As if nothing had just happened between us I asked what sort of poem she'd like.

'Don't know. Anything, I guess.' She looked around. 'Maybe something to remind me of this day.' She burst out laughing and, startled, I found myself joining in, laughing and chortling until my raw nerves diminished. Out of sheer affection for my good friend I touched her on the arm and began apologising until she told me to bugger off and stop being soft. All that was in the past, and she didn't mean half of it, and I was all right really – but I'd better write her a poem, and it'd better be good – bloody good.

It took an entire evening to track down Stella in England. Every time I got through to the hotel where I thought she would be I discovered that she had already moved on. Luckily, she had left a trail of forwarding addresses and as I made my way through them I recalled something she had told me: a snippet that related to her father but now seemed equally suited to me. As a child she had always believed that she stood a better chance of catching his attention if she kept her distance. When I realised she was applying a similar tactic to me I felt a pang of sadness, as if I had let her down.

It was difficult to know whether she was pleased to hear from me. At first she appeared irritated at being disturbed but after a few minutes I noticed the tone of her voice soften, and when I finally managed to make her understand that I had phoned for no other reason than to hear the sound of her voice there was a long silence on the end of the line, followed by a chuckle. 'You're not missing me, are you?' she asked.

'Yes,' I freely admitted. 'Quite a lot.'

In view of what Geraldine had told me, I half expected Stella to reply in kind. When she didn't I was disappointed and, despite myself, I prompted her, asking outright if she missed me too.

'I've been so busy,' she replied. 'I really haven't had much time to think about it.'

I waited, embarrassed by my need, now, to push her for a kinder answer.

'I suppose . . .' she said, her voice trailing off.

I let it drop and began to fill her in on my news – my recent outing with Geraldine and the fact that the event manager for the opening ceremony of the Aoraki Museum had been in touch, telling me that my poem had been enthusiastically received by the organising committee. The opening of the centre was to take place in June, on the shortest day of the year, and they wanted me to read my poem. This last detail alarmed me. I had got it into my head that someone else – a politician, a local dignitary or an actor – would read the piece. Public speaking was not my thing, and as I voiced my concerns to Stella I was aware of my heart pounding. The thought of having to stand before a crowd and read something I had written was nervewracking.

'I hope you'll come with me,' I said, wondering at the same time if there might be some way of getting Stella to do the reading for me. 'I know it's probably not your thing but it's a weekend away and if the weather is clear . . .'

'I'd always assumed I was invited,' she said. 'But if you've changed your mind . . .' She broke off and I heard a distant sound, a woman's voice followed by a man's, and then a slamming door.

'Sorry,' Stella continued, sounding as distracted as I felt.

It took me a moment to gather my thoughts. 'I really want you to come.'

Stella was silent, as though her attention was elsewhere. Again I could hear voices in the distance and then Stella spoke. 'Hang on a minute. There's something going on outside my room, in the corridor.'

The receiver was placed down – on a side-table, I guessed. A moment later I heard raised voices. A man shouted, 'Oi, why don't you just mind your own business and piss off?'

I grew more and more concerned, wondering what was happening.

Seconds later I heard Stella shout, 'Stop it!' and then I heard nothing until the man's voice yelled, 'I'll fucking kill you, you slut!' There was a scream and then silence. I found myself yelling down the phone, 'Stella! Stella! Is everything all right?' The silence lengthened and I became even more anxious – what on earth could I do from where I was? Was there some way of getting the local police to contact the police over there?

I paced around the kitchen, feeling increasingly helpless as the minutes passed. 'Stella!' I yelled as loudly as I could. 'What's going on?' Occasionally I thought I heard muffled voices, but I couldn't make out what was being said. I had a sudden image of Stella slumped in the corridor, surrounded by a pool of blood, and my heart began to pound. 'Somebody do something!' I pleaded, and then, as if by a miracle, she came back to the phone, her voice strangely flat. 'Sorry about that.'

I almost cried with relief. 'Are you all right? Are you hurt? I was going to call the police.'

I heard a sharp intake of breath and then Stella said, 'It's okay. Security is taking care of it.'

'What's going on?' I insisted. Even though I knew Stella was safe, I couldn't rid my mind of the image of her blood-soaked body. I wanted to see her – to see that she was unhurt.

'I don't know. Some kind of domestic. They were both so drunk it was hard to tell.' She gave a hollow laugh. 'Jesus, I'll be glad to get out of here. This country is fucking mad.'

Listening to Stella talk made me appreciate just how much I cared about her. I asked if she had had any other frightening episodes but she assured me that everything was fine. There was no need to worry.

'I could always fly over,' I offered. 'I could look after you.'

She laughed but I was deadly serious. I wanted to look after her.

'Tell you what,' she finally said. 'Why don't you come up to Christchurch and meet me off the plane when I get back.'

'I will. I'll be there.'

Stella laughed again, and asked what had got into me. Was I really that worried about her?

When I said, yes, her voice softened. 'Really?'

I didn't want to let her go. So I asked, as casually as I could, if she recalled having had any odd – or significant – conversations with Geraldine.

'Odd?' asked Stella. 'They're always odd.' She hesitated. 'Could you be a bit more specific?'

I was about to back off but, steeling myself, said, 'Well, maybe not odd exactly. But did you ever talk to her about me?'

I was aware of the silence on the other end of the line. I had the feeling that what I had said had struck some kind of a chord with Stella, that she was weighing up the situation carefully.

'What has Geraldine told you?' she eventually answered. 'Has she said something?'

It was my turn to be cautious. I stammered, 'Nothing.'

To my surprise, Stella wouldn't let the subject drop. There was something almost like a note of relief in her voice – as if she was grateful for the opportunity to broach an awkward subject. 'Well, she asked me if I thought you were any good as a poet. She wanted to know if I thought you were a one-hit wonder or someone to be taken seriously.'

This wasn't what I had been expecting, but I couldn't prevent my next question. 'What did you say?'

I waited, not knowing what I would do if Stella said she thought I was a one-hit wonder.

'Wouldn't you like to know?!' she laughed.

The plain fact was that I did want to know. Recently, I'd been feeling out of step with my times. I saw myself as belonging to an older generation of poets, people who maintained a sense of tradition, rather than the newer generation whose work I had discovered in recent anthologies. I had been taken aback by the confidence and style of some young Auckland poets. I found their voices challenging and I began to suspect that I was too backward looking by comparison. Yet I wanted to believe that my work – unadorned and plain though it is – was capable of bearing witness to some fundamental truth. In order to write, I had to believe my work still held its value.

'Do you think I'm any good?' There, I'd said it.

'You're not bad.'

I wanted more.

'Three Days at Least . . .' Stella began.

I stiffened.

'. . . is a great poem. It's a classic. And *Kindred Spirits* was good too. Didn't some reviewer describe it as elegiac and powerful?'

I didn't interrupt.

'But I think your Mount Cook poem is even better – from what I've seen of it. It's very moving, very honest . . . vulnerable.'

I felt a huge wave of gratitude. If there had ever been a time when I should have given voice to my love for Stella, it was then. I should have grabbed hold of that moment. But I was too slow and the moment passed. All that was unsaid remained unsaid.

Stella stifled a yawn. 'I'm tired. Talk soon, eh?'

The unspoken hung between us and then there was a click as Stella placed the phone on its receiver. I could have kicked myself.

I never found out whether the conversation in which Stella confessed her love for me actually took place. I only had Geraldine's word for it. But knowing that Stella thought I was a good poet amounted to the same thing as far as I was concerned. My subsequent decision to dedicate my Mount Cook poem to her was my way of letting her know that I felt the same way about her. So, although it might have been simpler to say 'I love you,' neither of us did. But it was all right. We understood each other.

One evening, about a month before I was due at the opening of the Aoraki Museum, I was telephoned by Kim midway through dinner. For weeks I'd been feeling guilty about not phoning and so, even though I wanted to finish my meal, I let her talk. I wondered if I had forgotten her birthday but, having no memory of when her birthday was, I didn't think I should say anything. I hoped she wasn't ringing because her birthday was today. That would be very awkward.

It turned out that it was *my* birthday. Had I known, I might have done something to celebrate. It was embarrassing to admit that all I had planned was to finish my dinner and then read a book. I hadn't even opened a bottle of wine. In fact there was no wine in the house.

I mentioned that Stella was in Christchurch and not due down until the weekend. I could tell Kim was concerned that I might be lonely. She hinted that I should go across the road to Geraldine's but given how cold it was outside and that Geraldine had paying guests – a Canadian couple – I decided to stay put.

To draw attention away from my birthday I told Kim about the forth-coming ceremony, forgetting that I had once suggested she join me for the opening. The words were barely out of my mouth before she was reaching for her diary, marking down the dates. Who was going to be there? The prime minister? Anyone else famous? That singer, Hayley Westenra? Could just anyone come? She spoke so rapidly I had trouble keeping pace with her thoughts and so it took me a while to realise that she was indeed planning to come down. I heard her ask which would be cheaper, flying into Christchurch and hiring a car, or flying direct to Mount Cook. She sighed. Both, she supposed, would be pretty expensive. I was about to suggest that she not bother – I wouldn't be offended if she couldn't make it – when she said she wouldn't miss it for the world, she was so proud of me. There was a pause then she continued, 'Our parents . . . Matthew and Lily would have been so pleased knowing you had grown up to be a poet. Nothing would have made them prouder.'

She'd told me before that her parents had always loved poetry, that their shelves had been filled with the works of all the great English writers. 'I always felt that I failed them,' said Kim, her voice wobbling slightly. 'I was good with my hands. I was practical . . . I could make things but I wasn't much good when it came to putting things into words. I wasn't much of a trophy.'

As the word 'trophy' settled into my brain I felt a tide of outrage rise up within me. In that moment I saw Kim's childhood unfold. I pictured her standing before her parents, her expectation of parental love and attention diminishing as, time and time again, she realised she had failed to attain the standards set by her mother and father, the scholars, the dazzling young things. This hadn't occurred to me before. Now I saw that Kim's childhood had been miserable, and that her desire to know me fulfilled some deep longing within her, a longing to be *accepted*. Everything she had said and done up to this point – her initial search for me, all her attempts to keep in touch, to include me in her life – so clearly indicated this. Truly, she had wanted a blood-brother, a link to her past, and someone who loved her for who she was.

I suddenly saw that I had not been guilty of ignoring her so much as dismissing her. I hadn't understood how much I mattered to her. The idea had rarely crossed my mind.

'I guess it's going to cost several hundred dollars all up.' She sounded anxious. 'That's a lot for one weekend.' Nothing in the tone of her voice suggested that she was asking for help.

'We'll go halves,' I said. There was a faint sound, a kind of 'oh' from the other end of the phone. I hoped she would accept. I wanted her to come.

To persuade her I began to tell her how beautiful the hills would be at this time of year. When the snow is low, when it's right down on the plains, it's the most beautiful sight in all of New Zealand. The ground twinkles, I said, laughing at how outlandish such a statement must sound to someone who had never seen the place for themselves. As I pictured the scene for myself I became increasingly enthusiastic. I was like a kid again, describing the dazzling mountains, the turquoise waters of Tekapo and Pukaki, and the sky that was so intensely blue – simultaneously pale and deep – that to stand beneath it, looking up, made you feel dizzy. 'It's true,' I said. 'You wait. I'll take you to my favourite place . . . then you'll see.'

I didn't really care how crazy I sounded, just so long as she agreed to come down. That was all I wanted. I was about to tell her more when she interrupted, saying, 'For a minute you reminded me of Charles Brasch, the way you were talking about the mountains. He loved all that stuff.'

I was stunned.

'I told you, didn't I, about how he used to write to my parents when we lived in England? I think he made stuff up in an attempt to lure them back to New Zealand – not that it ever worked.'

I listened, my eyes fixed on my dinner plate, focusing on a partly gnawed lamb chop.

'When I first came to New Zealand,' Kim continued, 'I did a little tour of the country and called by Charles's house in Dunedin. My parents had given me some books to pass on to him, poetry mostly, by obscure Russian and Eastern Europeans, writers I had never heard of. It was stuff that had been translated by some colleague of my father's . . .' Her voice faded, as if she had lost her train of thought.

'Oh that's right . . .' she continued, 'Brasch. I went on a walk with him – on Flagstaff, I think – and he spent the whole time pointing out plants

227

and telling me about some valley near Queenstown called the Hollyford where he'd been tramping with a friend. I had a nice time.'

'I never met him,' I said. I waited a moment, then said, 'You never mentioned him before . . . I would have remembered.'

I heard Kim mumble a faint 'oh' and then the silence between us lengthened and became awkward.

Less than a week later a large courier envelope was delivered to my door. Inside was a mixed bundle consisting of white envelopes and pale blue aerogrammes held together with a tied rubber band. A yellow post-it note was stuck to the top envelope: 'I thought you would like to read these. See you soon, Kim.' The contrast between Kim's scrawl and the neat, almost spidery, upright handwriting on each of the twenty or so letters was what first caught my attention. All of the letters were addressed to Prof. M. Butler and, turning one aerogramme over, I gazed at the sender's name: C. Brasch.

For several minutes I simply held the letters in my hand. I wasn't sure if I did this out of respect for the letter itself – as if it were something sacred, a kind of museum object requiring special handling – or whether it was because the content of each letter was personal, meant for another person, not me. The thought that I was prying took hold in my mind and, despite my curiosity, I could not bring myself to read them.

Every letter had been opened – by Matthew – using either a paper-knife or some other fine blade. As I held the first envelope – a rectangle of cream-coloured cartridge paper – I imagined him sitting in his study, seated behind a leather-topped desk, or perhaps reclining in an armchair by an open fire. In my mind's eye I watched as he, too, turned each letter, weighing its paper in his fingers before opening it, slowly and carefully. I wondered if he looked forward to receiving this correspondence. Did he reply to Brasch straight away – eager to continue the conversation – or did he allow the contents of each letter to settle in his brain, mulling it over in more leisurely fashion? I wondered, too, if he passed the letters on to Lily to read, or whether he kept them to himself. Up to this point I had given Matthew far less thought than I had Lily, but now I saw him opposite me. Even before reading what Brasch had written, I longed to read my birth father's replies. I wished I had been included in the conversation.

Never having met Brasch myself but having received several notes from him – usually attached to a poem he had rejected – I expected his letters, which I finally began to read in no particular order, to have a purpose, to be *about* something rather than the affectionately worded pieces they were. It was clear straight away that Brasch was fond of my father. He mentioned, for example, that the spring bulbs that were just coming up in his Dunedin garden reminded him of an afternoon he had spent in my father's company, on a long walk near Oxford. There were patches of anemones poking up through the long grass and the ground was damp. They had sat and talked long into the cool of the evening, neither one of them wanting to be the first to stand up and leave.

In another letter, posted from London, Brasch referred to a twilight stroll they had made together through the streets of the local neighbourhood. 'I'm sure Lily would have been unimpressed when she discovered you had not been to the library . . .' Brasch wrote. He went on to say, 'I hope to see you back in London before I leave, but I understand how difficult it must be, what with your teaching and family commitments. Maybe I could visit for the day before I depart for New Zealand. There isn't much time left.'

The next letter I picked up, a pale blue aerogramme, was postmarked Dunedin. It appeared, from its tone, to be a quick reply to some topic raised by Matthew in a previous note. 'By all means send the piece,' Brasch wrote, 'but I'm afraid you'll miss the deadline unless you hurry.' He went on to mention several other contributors whose work was to be included in the forthcoming issue. I gathered he was referring to *Landfall*. Among the list of names the one that caught my eye was Harry Scott. Brasch spent more time talking about Scott's contribution than anyone else's. 'As I may have said before,' wrote Brasch, 'he reminds me of you – though not in looks. He is a mountaineer, but not of the British variety.' I am unclear whether this last was intended as a slight jibe towards Matthew, who by this time was probably more at home in an English landscape than a New Zealand one, or if it simply displayed Brasch's admiration for Scott, or even his own love of the hills.

The last letter I read caught my attention for an entirely different reason. In it Brasch described his own work – the difficulties he was having with an as yet unnamed poem. He complained that he could not fully trust his judgement; that he needed to let the poem sit for several weeks and then come back to it. He went on to say that he admired Matthew's ability to be 'objective – even ruthlessly so' where his own work was concerned. 'I wish I was more like you,' he observed, 'able to submit a work as soon as it is written. I could never be that certain . . .'

It was strange for me to encounter this note of uncertainty in Brasch's voice. It hadn't occurred to me that he might be plagued by self-doubt. I was interested, too, by the high regard in which he held Matthew. In several letters Brasch not only sought Matthew's opinion of a writer or a book, but once went on to say, 'If anyone can make sense of it, you can.' He called my father a scholar – an epithet Brasch clearly did not feel entitled to take for himself. His respect for Matthew was clear and despite myself, despite all the years I had tried to keep these 'other' parents – Matthew and Lily – locked in the back room of my mind, I found that I was envious of the relationship between these two men. My 'other' father and Charles Brasch. By rights I should have been included.

boden

Stella and Kim were with me as I sat on Foliage Hill, taking in the scene of the earth works below.

I knew without Stella telling me that I couldn't expect things to remain unchanged. Things did change, whether or not we wanted them to. As Stella put it, it was yet another example of people 'fucking things up' – in this case turning an area of golden tussock, scraggly fern and matagouri into a huge shingle pit, a car park for campervans. I knew she was right but the more she spoke, the greater the gulf between the two of us. For her to take my personal loss – the destruction of a place that had formed an essential part of my life – and turn it into a rage against 'fucking idiots' made me aware of how different we were. Where I sought stillness, Stella wanted to find the people responsible and give them hell. 'They just don't give a shit any more,' she continued. 'It's exactly the same as when they built the Clyde dam and flooded our old home – they're bastards.'

If I could have made Stella be quiet I would have. I willed her to stop talking but she was working herself into a fury: I should boycott the museum, tell them to stick the whole of New Zealand poetry up their arses . . . she would have a go at the prime minister, the minister of conservation, the lot of them. 'It's not good enough!' she ranted. 'They're ruining this place. They're all the bloody same . . . there will be nothing left of it soon. Tourists are taking over the country and we let them do it!'

On the other side of me sat Kim. She also had been too stunned to speak but then caught my eye and asked, 'What's happened?'

I was able to provide a kind of 'before and after' description of the area below us: before there had been a large open area between the hill on which we sat and the larger White Horse Hill across the flats. 'That was a campground,' I said pointing towards the foot of White Horse Hill. 'A few old huts, a rough gravel road; then over there,' I said, pointing a little towards the right-hand end of the hill, 'is the site of the first hotel – it was flooded around 1913, I think. And that's Mount Sefton,' I continued, indicating the mountain directly in front of us, '. . . and the Hooker Valley . . . see? Over there, where that long line of people is walking . . . and the Hooker River. Up there,' I said, pointing in the direction of a cloud-covered peak, 'is Mount Cook.' I hesitated and then said, 'So it's not all changed. The mountains are still there.'

'But the parking area and the toilet block?' asked Kim. 'You didn't know they were here?'

I shook my head.

'I haven't been here before so I don't know what it was like,' said Kim, 'but at least the parking area is off to one side. I mean,' she spoke hesitantly, unsure how her words would be received, 'it's tucked behind the hill so you can't even see it when you're standing in front of the Hermitage, can you? All this area still looks pristine when you look out from the hotel window.' She made a sweeping motion with her hand, indicating the scrub-covered land between us and White Horse Hill.

'It's only when you're down here, by the camping area . . .' Kim's voice ground to a standstill.

I heard Stella snort and mutter something about the dishonesty of keeping things pretty for the paying hotel guests while ruining it for the locals, and my thoughts turned briefly to Beano, who I knew would be arriving with his girlfriend sometime after dark. I imagined him pitching his tent on a patch of rocky ground and, knowing he was coming all this

234

way just to hear me read my poem I felt guilty. I also had the sickening thought that I could have offered him the use of my own campervan.

Stella was still muttering beside me, and although I was also upset about the destruction taking place I wanted to deal with those feelings later. For now I just wanted to – what? Come to terms with the change in the landscape? Until I saw the new car park it hadn't occurred to me that the memories of my youth – the very core of me – were so dependent on one small parcel of land remaining unchanged. It was as though, instead of being able to see my face reflected in a mirror, I had been handed a piece of plain glass. There was nothing in front of me that brought 'me' to mind. I wasn't out there any more; it was an entirely different world, one from which I was absent.

The poem, which I was to read at a dawn ceremony the next day, was in part about this place. I hadn't realised that the area itself would be so altered. I had planned as I read to say, 'Look, there it is! There is the place that was so special I wanted to share it with you . . . Look, it's precious, a gift!' Now the view was of a huge excavation: banks of shingle, rows of campervans, a toilet block. Damn it, it had only been a little over a year since my last visit – how could this have happened? How could I explain my sense of loss? I had never shared this place with anyone – it had been my secret, my life . . . no one else knew just how important it was. Only Walter had had some real idea.

Throughout the rest of the day I was aware of sounding like a tour guide for Kim's benefit. 'I stayed here with my parents when I was a kid,' I said, pointing towards the main entrance of the Hermitage. 'Not this exact hotel, though.' I explained about the fire in the late 1950s. 'We went for a walk over there,' and I pointed in the general direction of Governors Bush. 'There were lots of keas back then . . .' My thoughts drifted back to the first time I had heard the sound, the cry of the kea, and how I had tried to find a rhyme for it. 'It must be queer to be a kea.' I heard my father's voice intoning 'clowns of the sky', and I remembered the man with the long elegant fingers who had quoted Byron.

We stepped back to allow a group of Japanese tourists to pass us on their way into the hotel. After a few minutes we followed, joining

235

the queue at reception, waiting for our turn to check in. As I gave my name the receptionist smiled and, to my surprise, murmured the first line of 'Three Days at Least', before apologising that that was all she remembered. She had studied it at school and had got 76 per cent for School Certificate English, her highest mark ever. That was in 1979, she said. I looked more closely at her face – she appeared far younger – and then thanked her for the 'welcome pack' she handed me. She told me I was expected to attend a quick meeting later that evening, down the hall in the Sebastopol Suite. She'd be there in the morning – she was looking forward to it. One of the downsides of working in a place like this, she said, was the lack of culture.

Over afternoon tea, hours after our late-morning walk up Foliage Hill, I began to feel angry. I glanced across at Stella and had to bite my tongue, and stop myself from blaming her for making me accept the commission in the first place. I poked at the scone on my plate with a knife and complained that it was stale. Immediately Kim offered to swap it with hers, saying, 'I quite like stale scones.' I also heard Stella hiss at me underneath her breath, saying, 'Pull your horns in.'

The problem, I wanted to say, is that I don't *want* to have to face reality – the area around Foliage Hill – at the moment. I turned to Kim and began to explain how, when I am writing a poem, I don't like to read work by other writers. 'I find their voices interfere with my own thoughts,' I said. 'They make it hard for me to concentrate.' What I was trying to explain was that the earthworks and the car park were smothering the piece I was expected to read – and so I no longer believed in my poem any more. Without me believing in it, it carried no weight, it no longer rang true.

'My father,' began Kim, 'found it hard to be around us when he was working on a translation. He'd lock himself away in his study.'

I pictured Matthew in his study, one of Charles Brasch's letters on the desk in front of him.

'Lily used to accuse him of being Victorian. She hated it . . . well, she hated the fact that she was left looking after me when all she wanted was to escape to a study of her own. Not that she had one.'

236

She obviously hadn't understood what I was talking about, but the greater part of me felt sorry for her. Her childhood sounded much worse than my own. 'It's really good that you could come down this weekend,' I said, taking a bite from my scone. Kim was watching me. I smiled and nodded. 'It's okay,' I said. 'Not as bad as I first thought.'

I left Stella sleeping and, without turning on the light, struggled into my clothes, wending my way along several long corridors and down four flights of stairs until I reached the main entrance of the hotel. The receptionist was a young uniformed Japanese man I hadn't seen before, who was bent over a copy of Harry Potter. He heard me pass and looked up, concealing the book as best he could as he bowed his head slightly. 'Good evening,' he murmured as I passed. I had the feeling he was relieved that I was not going to take him away from his book, and I glanced back through the window to see that he resumed reading the moment I left the building.

I guessed that the temperature was below freezing. Already the wind-screens of the cars in the hotel car park were obscured by a thick film of ice, and the grass beneath my shoes made a crunching sound as I headed towards a patch of ground illuminated by an orange-coloured street lamp. Below this light a sign had been newly erected. Small off-cuts of wood still lay on the ground, and two piles of upturned earth beside the posts supporting the sign were lightly covered with frost. The sign pointed towards the new Aoraki Museum, approximately fifteen minutes by foot along a newly constructed nature walk.

As I stepped onto the boardwalk my foot skidded and I fell heavily onto my hip, cutting my palm on some chicken wire as I tried to break my fall. It seemed to me a bad omen. I suddenly wondered if I could ignore the opening, the speeches all the fuss and simply go away somewhere by myself, to a place where nothing was expected of me. Surely no one would miss me. The idea appealed, but I lacked the courage. Besides, I was a grown man and such behaviour – which might have been permissible or even 'cool' in a man forty years my junior – lacked dignity.

I entered a section of scrubby bush and the air suddenly became warmer, less abrasive against my lungs. Complete darkness settled around me, closing in, and it was easy to imagine as I groped my way along the boardwalk that I was not alone – that someone or something was watching me, following me from a distance, just as Dudley's old dog Bruce had done all those years before as I made my nightly walks around Fairlie. To prevent myself from falling off the side of the walkway I half shuffled, pushing my feet ahead of me, taking the path one slow step at a time. Emerging from the dense bush and into the occasional clearing I found that my eyes were so well adjusted to the dark that I was able to progress quite rapidly, taking four or five steps without hesitation. Despite the cold, the smell of the ground filled my senses – a damp, muggy, earthy smell of fern, moss and tussock. Once I lost my balance, reached out and caught hold of a small sapling, most likely a turpentine bush, and when I raised my hand to my face some minutes later the distinctive smell of its bark was contained in my palm and I inhaled deeply.

I had been walking more than a quarter of an hour when I finally saw a light a short way off, almost directly ahead of me. For a minute I imagined myself as the big bad wolf of various children's fairy-tales – some creature of the night lured out from the forest by the glowing lamp in a woodcutter's hut. I was surprised how quickly I had changed roles, going from the person being watched to the ominous presence myself. Perhaps I was flattering myself. I doubt that anyone else in the world had seen me as such.

239

At the edge of the bush I stopped and looked towards the glass-walled museum. Inside, two people moved about. One was a man in his mid-thirties, the other a young woman called Caro whom I had met earlier during the meeting up at the hotel. She had been brought in to design and set up the exhibition and had left the meeting early, apologising that she still had some finishing off to do before the opening. Caro's hair was long, almost to her waist, and dread-locked. She had tied it off her face with a scarf but, even so, when she stooped to move some kind of CD player, a ghetto-blaster, her hair fell forward, obscuring her face and upper body, giving her the appearance of a tall, macramé sculpture.

The man was painting a free-standing wall. As he swept his paint roller over its surface he moved his entire body in rhythm with some music I could not hear. Despite this, his energy, his face looked drawn, as if he had been putting in too many hours.

As I watched, Caro suddenly walked towards the window facing me and slid back the door. In that moment I caught the sound of the man's voice and then her clearer voice, replying, 'I'm pretty sure there's another tin by the hut. I'll get it.' As she stepped out of the door she turned to face the painter and whatever she said made him laugh. She turned back towards me and I could see that she was smiling, that she looked happy, as if she didn't have a care in the world.

Around the museum was a wide deck and as she passed the spot where her friend might have been able to see her without turning his head she tapped on the glass and blew him a kiss. He gave her a sign, the thumbs up, and she pressed her face close to the window and called, 'Just one more hour and then it's you and me, baby, promise!' She laughed loudly, raised her hands high above her head and wiggled her hips in a kind of dance. I could see the young man's mouth move in response, and I guessed he was saying something along the lines of, 'Yeah, yeah.' But he was smiling, his eyes following her as she walked away.

I trailed after Caro, keeping my distance following her around the museum but stopping at a narrow track leading into the bush. A moment later I saw a light go on and then a few minutes after that she reappeared, carrying a tin of paint. She passed by and I heard the sliding door of the museum open and, with it, a sudden burst of music, followed by a deeper quiet as the door once more closed.

Earlier, during the meeting to discuss the opening ceremony, I had turned down the opportunity to familiarise myself with the museum building when it was offered. A number of others were going down to look at the centre but I didn't want to be part of a group tour and so made an excuse not to join them. No one had minded.

Alone now, I followed the track Caro had taken a few minutes before. A piece of timber, another sign, lay propped up against a tree to one side, its supporting posts nearby on the ground. In the gloom I couldn't make out what the sign said but it hardly mattered as I had already started up the track. I reached a fork, one path leading to a small lighted shed – where Caro had found the paint. The second fork, a wider track, continued on up a gentle slope in the direction of what I could just make out was a bank or hummock of some kind.

Within minutes I was standing on this area of raised ground, surrounded by tussock and low scrub. In front of me, defined by the dull glow of a single garden-type light, was a hut. I remained motionless for several moments as my eyes took in all that was visible: its narrow door, the small, square-paned window on one long wall, and the corrugated iron roof that had been folded, cardboard-like, over the top of the hut's walls. I thought I must be mistaken – some trick of the light was making me see things. I looked about me before taking a hesitant step forward. The grass, heavily frosted in the clearing, crunched beneath my feet and the ground itself was much firmer than that on the forest floor. When, with my third or fourth step my shoe broke a twig I jumped and spun around, certain that someone was behind me, shadowing my every move.

A large frozen puddle the size of a pond separated me from the door to the building and sure enough, sprouting out of the centre of the puddle was a sign reading: 'This historic mountain hut, known to mountaineers as "The Far-light", was originally built in 1955. It was replaced in 2001.' Beneath these words was a company logo and the words 'Proud sponsors of the Aoraki Museum'.

241

Even though the sign confirmed that it was my hut, I raised my eyes and began the slow process of mentally reconstructing it, piece by piece. As I edged around the puddle a bright security light suddenly clicked on and I froze, mid-step, waiting for someone to appear and ask what I was doing. No one did, and after a minute I continued, going right up to the door and cupping my hand over its square pane to look inside. From within I could make out the shadowy outline of the long bench that filled the entire length of one wall. Along the walls were the double-tiered bunks, the top bunk so close to the ceiling that it was virtually impossible for anyone to sit up.

The window pane was cold against my face, and when I breathed, its surface grew cloudy with condensation. I stepped back and ran my hand over the door, feeling its paint, brittle and dry, break away under my fingers. As my eyes came to rest on the faded sign reading 'No Dogs Allowed' I felt a lump in my throat and swallowed hard, recalling Wim's satisfaction and Douglas's displeasure when the former had nailed it to the door, joking 'That should keep the scoundrels away!'

I remembered too the day Athol and the others had headed down the valley, leaving Walter and me alone at the camp, where we found ourselves trapped by a storm – the quiet days we spent talking and in my case writing, my thoughts challenged by ideas of injustice and yet awakened to the beauty of the world.

I recalled the feeling of release upon returning to the task of hut-building, how good it had felt to be outdoors, the newly cut timber and wood shavings so fragrant in that sterile world of snow and rock. For minutes on end the only sound was that made by our hammers, and whenever we paused the quiet was so intense, the air so still that I would look around in wonder.

I traced my hands over the walls of the hut, expecting to see the lead-head nails we had used, but of course those original lead-heads were gone, replaced with new ones when the hut was dismantled and moved to this, its new site, far below the glaciers it had once surveyed.

The original brass doorknob was also gone, replaced at some point by a large handle. It wasn't surprising. The round knob had been so difficult to grip and turn. I wondered how long it had been before someone had finally grown so fed up with the old knob that they had sent in the replacement. I imagined the old brass one being discarded; not thrown out but left behind on the narrow window ledge, or adapted during a long storm, perhaps, into a candle-holder. It may even have been carried out by some mountaineer who had thought, 'I could use that at home.'

I pulled down on the handle and to my surprise the door opened, engulfing me in a smell of kerosene, smoke and the fug of old kapok mattresses and sacking. The interior was just as I remembered it: strips of painted tongue-and-groove lined the walls. In the half light it was possible to see that the ceiling above the galvanised bench was discoloured, grimy with soot, whereas above the opposite wall it was still pale, clean. The beds were the same narrow wire-mesh bunks we had constructed and for a second I remembered the first time the hut was slept in: while Walter and I chose to sleep outside, under the clear sky, our friends had crammed into the small dwelling and laughed and talked late into the night.

I was about to step inside the hut when my legs hit something hard and I jerked forward, only just stopping myself from falling by grabbing hold of the door-frame. In the half light I hadn't noticed that a thigh-high sheet of thick Perspex had been fastened across the entrance, stopping visitors from going further. Out of the corner of my eye I could see another sign fastened to a stand, which I guessed requested visitors to remain outside so as not to damage the heritage building. Something like that, anyway.

I could have stepped across the barrier, but there was no need.

Instead, I closed the door and walked back towards the hotel. It was after midnight and the moon was up, filtering through the trees, lighting my way.

In the morning I would return and read my poem.

acknowledgements

First and foremost I wish to thank Bill Manhire and John Thomson. As a result of their caring attention, I rediscovered the pleasure of writing.

I am indebted to the Creative Writing PhD class at the Institute of Modern Letters, Victoria University of Wellington, for their helpful feedback and support throughout the writing of this book.

Grateful thanks to my dear friend Lydia Bradey and my brother Dave Fearnley for describing various routes and the view from the top of Mount Cook. Thanks to Dean Staples for providing the saying 'Winds from the East/Three Days at Least' during the course of one enjoyable evening. Many thanks to mountaineer and hut builder Graham Bishop and butcher Fred Eskrick for their input.

Again, I would like to thank my family – my mother, Wendy, and my husband, Alex – for taking care of business so that I could write. Love, as always, to Harry.

Thanks to Sue Wootton and the owners of Ohau House for their generosity – especially during the latter stages of writing this book.

I am much indebted to Geoff Walker at Penguin, for his friendly encouragement, and Emma Beckett for all her help. I am especially grateful to Rachel Scott – daughter of the mountaineer Harry Scott mentioned in the novel – for agreeing to edit this book.

The poems mentioned in the novel are:

Mary Ursula Bethell, 'By Burke's Pass'

Lord Byron, 'Childe Harold's Pilgrimage', Canto iii. Stanza 85

Charles Brasch, 'The Silent Land'.

Thanks to Alan Roddick for permission to use Brasch's work.

The poems by Bethell and Brasch are from *A Book Of New Zealand Verse*, edited by Allen Curnow (Caxton Press, Christchurch, 1951).

The sections 'quoted' from Charles Brasch's letters are all fictional.

The 'Far-light Hut' does not exist. Having said that, it closely resembles the old Empress Hut, which was built in the early 1950s and located at 8000 feet on the flanks of Mount Cook. Anyone travelling to Mount Cook village can see it in its preserved state outside the DOC visitor centre. They can also see the carpark that has taken the place of the tussock at the foot of Foliage Hill.

EDWIN & MATILDA

Laurence Fearnley

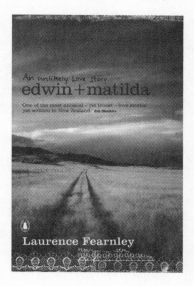

This beautifully written new novel is about finding love in the most unlikely of places. Set in the southern South Island, it describes the unusual bond formed between sixty-two-year-old photographer Edwin and twenty-two-year-old Matilda, as their relationship grows in ways neither could possibly have predicted.

Runner-up for the Montana Award in 2008.

ISLAND
Penelope Todd

An island in a bleak harbour; an isolated quarantine station where a group of nurses works tirelessly to care for sailors and immigrants recovering from the effects of the long sea voyage to the new land.

Kahu swims ashore, searching for a woman. Young nurse Liesel, caught in a passionate triangle, is faced with choices both harrowing and intoxicating. Martha, who oversees the hospital and guides the community, is making a kind of experiment with life.

Some on the island are too sick to live. Others flame with life. The island is cradle and crucible.

ACCESS ROAD
Maurice Gee

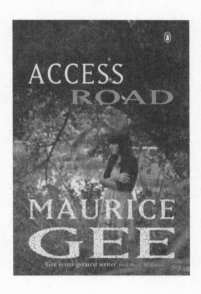

The old family home in Access Road, where Lionel, Roly and Rowan grew up, is crumbling away – but after more than fifty years Lionel and Roly are back. Rowan, too, safe in 'upper crusty' Takapuna, is drawn more and more strongly 'out west'.

The past is dangerously alive. Clyde Buckely, violent as a boy, enigmatic, subterranean as an old man, returns to his childhood territory. What does he want? What crimes does he hide? And how is Lionel involved? Rowan must abandon safety if she is to find out . . .

LOLA
Elizabeth Smither

Lola Dearborn marries into Dearborn & Zander, a family of funeral directors, when she falls for Sam Dearborn at a dance. But when Sam, and her friend Alice Zander, injured in a freak accident, die, Lola devotes the rest of her life to exploration. She takes up residence in an art-deco hotel, she befriends the members of the Sylvester Quartet after gate-crashing a rehearsal. She reflects on the different kinds of love offered by men: Luigi the Italian undertaker who buries a dog with its owner, and Charles the retired surgeon with his disruptive daughter, Brandy.

Lola's themes underpin an exploration of love and death (including pet cemeteries), music and friendship. Set between Australia and New Zealand, it is a story both acute and amusing, knowledgeable and questing – much like Lola herself.